KNOTS

A Justin Barnes Novel

By

Robert Banfelder

BB
~~
BROADWATER BOOKS
Riverhead, New York

Broadwater Books
141 Riverside Drive
Riverhead, NY 11901

The Library of Congress Cataloging-in-Publication Data
is available on file.

ISBN: 978-09859486-4-1

Printed in the United States of America

10 9 8 7 6 5 4 3 2 1

Cover image by Christopher Paparo
www.fishguyphotos.com

Lyrics from the song *Fame* used with permission from Dean Pitchford

For my loving partner Donna Derasmo ~
who truly knows the meaning of the word sacrifice.

AUTHOR'S NOTE

The Reality Movement presented in this work is forged after the actual Raëlian Movement, an existent religion founded in 1974 by Claude Vorilhon.

Likewise, Clonite, Incorporated, introduced herewith, is fashioned after Clonaid, an actual human cloning company having philosophical ties with the Raëlian sect.

This work is steadfastly framed in fact. I have, of course, taken literary license in the construction of this novel. Hence, the events and characters in this work are fictitious, based on extensive research referencing these two institutions.

Robert Banfelder

ACKNOWLEDGEMENTS

Thanks go out to the members of Eastern Flyrodders of Long Island for expanding my knowledge of fly tying and to Christopher Paparo for shooting the cover image. Thank you to Ronald Atkinson for assisting in the book cover.

A special thank you to my son, Jason R. Banfelder, for his technical advice and continued support, as well as to Dr. Luce Skrabanek for her input.

Also, my sincere gratitude is extended to lyricist Dean Pitchford for his permission to use a few lines from *Fame*, which gave a special touch in framing this fictional work. Too, a word of gratitude goes to Mr. Pitchford's music administrator, Karen Schauben, who facilitated the process.

Robert Banfelder
July 2013

ALSO BY ROBERT BANFELDER

Fiction

Trace Evidence

The Author (A Justin Barnes Novel)
"Best Suspense Novel 2007" - NewBookReviews

The Teacher (A Justin Barnes Novel)
"Best Suspense Novel 2006" - NewBookReviews

No Stranger Than I

Nonfiction

The Fishing Smart <u>Anywhere</u> Handbook for Salt Water & Fresh Water

MORE PRAISE FOR KNOTS

"*Knots* is a fascinatingly fast-paced psychological thriller that kept me totally captivated from page one. I would recommend this book to anyone who enjoys intrigue, a host of captivating characters and a plot that takes unforeseen twists and turns, leading to an unexpected, yet discerning conclusion. Banfelder's earlier Justin Barnes novels, *The Author* and *The Teacher*, are must-reads that (unbeknownst to us initially) naturally steer us in the direction of *Knots*. At the same time, unanswered questions from that series are neatly revealed while new ones inconspicuously arise. Is it possible that those answers await us in yet another Justin Barnes novel? Only time will tell. As the author's website discloses, *The Good Samaritans*, the fourth novel in the Justin Barnes series, is on the horizon. I will be looking forward to the author's next psychological thriller to answer my question. And once again, I'll be fighting with my husband, Edward, for equal reading time." - Betty B. Fitch, NC

"An excellent thriller! Mr. Banfelder is quite a master of the suspense. The storyline moved at a good pace and kept me interested from the beginning to the end." - C. Betancourt, NY

"We all have our heroes. Kalvin is no exception, except that his heroes are two serial killers. Thankfully, both of them are deceased, thanks to Justin Barnes, a *ghost* employed by the Suffolk County Police. But Kalvin doesn't remain discouraged for long. Instead he begins his very own career as a serial killer, both to satisfy is developing urges and to impress his heroes: the very same heroes that he knows won't remain dead for long. He's got a plan. Take the ride with Kalvin; if you dare!"
    - Ms. Elva, librarian, NY

"I thoroughly enjoyed reading this book. It captured my interest by the third chapter; after that is was hard to put down. His attention to detail was outstanding. I did have to reread some excerpts to get the full understand of tying knots a certain way and fly-fishing; but it was well worth it. There were times when I just wanted to skip ahead to find out what was going to happen; but all in all I am very glad I did not because waiting for the ending was certainly worth it." - R. Wolf, NY

Chapter 1

May 1st may have ended the last of April's showers, but Kalvin Matheson was still crying into his beer, literally, and had been for most of the morning. The man poured from a longneck bottle of Budweiser at 6 a.m. as he sat listening to 103.9 WRIV, Riverhead, Long Island news. The sadness that engulfed him still centered on the never-ending reports of his two fallen heroes' deaths, although the latter had been shot to death last summer; the summer of 2002. The first man's body was recovered two years earlier, found deep-sixed in one hundred sixty-some feet of water off the coast of the Atlantic, just southeast of Shinnecock Inlet. Both men were gone but not forgotten. The initial accounts of their demise had been sketchy, but Kalvin knew where to lay blame.

Matheson's depression mounted by the moment as he sat there gazing out of the dirty back windowpanes of his home. The yard, in particular, was unsightly. The grass lay bent yet stood practically the height of his neighbor's bordering, manicured, boxwood hedge. Unattended gardens that once bloomed in all their glory, especially the tall purple and pink irises, were already overrun with weeds. Mature male and female hollies stood entwined within a series of thick, strangling vines. Now, merely solitary splotches of splendid color could be seen among the choking, knotted entanglement.

Not only did the dispirited soul lag behind in yard work, but he was painfully aware of a growing list of chores that needed immediate attention regarding the house itself: scraping, sanding, caulking, painting, staining—fixing this and that. Lack of motivation, not time, was his nemeses. Kalvin knew he could no longer blame his melancholy on the two men's cold-blooded murders, for he had been

1

depressed for many months . . . years, actually. In truth, he had been despondent most of his adult life. And when you considered the fact that he never had a childhood . . . well, what could or would anyone make of that? An emotionally and spiritually bankrupt baby boomer would certainly have had to be one's immediate assessment on summing up the situation, the tortured soul ruefully decided.

Alvin's death, a decade ago, had taken its toll, too. Kalvin had not worked since the day of his brother's demise.

"Kalvin and Alvin," he so sadly sighed and sobbed before the old collie sleeping on the floor in the corner of the kitchen. "Alvin and Kalvin," he lamented.

Like a pair of bookends.

Two peas in a pod.

The phone rang, but Kalvin did not answer it. Twenty minutes later, he listened to the doorbell and heard a package drop into the vestibule. FedEx Ground. Doubleday Direct.

"Yeah, like I really have the time and motivation to read a book on saltwater fly-fishing," he said with a sigh. "Maybe in another lifetime."

Matheson knew from the start that he was not nearly as clever as his two unsung heroes, Malcolm Columba and Clarence Emery. The intellectual disparity between the dynamic duo and he could be measured in light-years. Brilliant versus bright. The man was certainly smart enough to realize that and laughed away his tears. Still, Kalvin positively believed that he had something going for him that neither of his two *pals* had possessed in life.

Sanity.

Soundness of mind in a nutshell, he giggled.

Kalvin once heard both men speak at a convention in California. Malcolm Columba had acknowledged him with a smile. Clarence Emery had *actually* spoken to him—even said his name.

"Hi, Kalvin."

It was the happiest and proudest day in his miserable little life. Imagine. Happy and proud. Both proud and happy in a single day. Unbelievable, it seemed. And now they were both gone. Columba and Emery. Brilliant minds. But crazy as they come.

"Not I," Kalvin confirmed aloud before the collie, watching Poochie languidly raise its head from a pair of large paws. "I am as sane as I am sensible."

Kalvin drove a sensible car, wore sensible clothing and shoes, and ate and drank sensibly. His former boss at the insurance company repeatedly told every person in the office, as he had once told Kalvin's brother, Alvin, too, that Kalvin Matheson was the most levelheaded employee he had ever known.

Levelheaded.

Sensible.

Sound.

They were certainly qualities that would put him above suspicion if and when he ever did what he had half a mind to do, now that his two heroes were history.

Levelheaded, sensible and sound, Kalvin ticked off satisfactorily in his mind.

But did he have Columba's and Emery's courage to *act*? Did he have their stamina and drive? Probably not, he pondered.

And so he wept anew.

This time, however, it was more of an exasperated, *I'm just feeling sorry for myself* sob, rather than an expression of sympathy over the loss of his two *pals*. Kalvin deludingly allowed himself to think of the pair as his pals. "And why not? Surely they were. Maybe one day *soon* they will be—once again." Kalvin forced a little smile.

The following morning, Kalvin was all cried out, expressing his condolences (perhaps for the hundredth time), privately, in the form of a silent, somber prayer. He felt sure there had been no formal service or funeral to attend concerning Clarence Emery, wanting, at the time of the heartfelt news, to call Suffolk County authorities for confirmation but was afraid of raising a red flag.

Undoubtedly, as was Columba's dredged-up corpse from the depths of the Atlantic coastline, Emery's body, removed from the floor of a hospital room in Brookhaven, had been slipped and zipped into a body bag then shipped off for burial to an unmarked grave . . . or simply cremated.

But where? Kalvin had wondered.

Where would the state have buried or cremated the unclaimed bodies of two serial killers who, like himself, had no family? Immediate or otherwise. More than likely the authorities had assigned the two masterminds a burial plot—he sincerely hoped—along with a recorded number, just as Pilgrim State Hospital, the psychiatric center in Brentwood, had done with his brother, Alvin.

He would finally make it his business to find out for sure. Clandestinely, of course.

Alvin and Kalvin.

Twins.

Identical.

Even their own mother would have had trouble telling the two children apart at thirty yards if not for their actions and reactions whenever she called them at the top of her voice to the supper table.

Supper.

Their one dependable meal of the day.

Rice and beans.

Beans and rice with catsup for a bit of variety. He cursed her inwardly . . . the two brothers having fought furiously over the small chunk of bacon from the Campbell's can.

Around the holidays, in a time gone by, when business was booming, the local butcher as well as the fishmonger would set aside whatever scraps of meat or fish were on hand, offering up the packages free of charge, from which Kalvin's mother would prepare soup—a rare treat for the family. Both merchants felt sorry for the woman who had lost her husband to a disease of the mind that no one ever spoke about—openly, that is—least of all, the usually loudmouthed relatives. All long dead and favorably forgotten.

Other than the number *246* recorded on Alvin's grave marker, there was no inscription upon the flat 12 x 6-inch weathered sand-colored stone, overgrown with vegetation of the all-invasive weed-bearing kind. With good reason, Kalvin was positive that, soon, not a living soul in all the world would know or even care of its existence. No one but he, that is.

By the following afternoon, Kalvin was consumed with a single question. Did he have the guts and gumption to follow in Malcolm Columba's and Clarence Emery's footsteps, now that both his superheroes were dead? He promised himself to visit Alvin's grave before doing anything foolish.

Chapter 2

The unpaved, single lane road leading into the cemetery was muddy from all the recent rain. Nothing had a chance to dry. Kalvin headed to the northern corner of the property, bordered by a line of sparsely populated pines. Pines and eight thousand five hundred fifty bodies filled the land site, he recalled with utter depression, his expression immediately shifting into sheer anger as the Camry slid sharply to the left, foundering through the spongy, wet earth. He slammed the transmission into low gear and let up on the accelerator, giving the vehicle just enough gas for the wheels to grab. Suddenly, the front end swerved back on track, splashing through the shallow but lengthy mud pocket.

"Oh, the things I do for you, Alvin. In death as well as life."

Kalvin cursed the place and continued toward the designated areas, taking in his bleak surroundings. First, the Catholic section, containing a single dried-up Christmas wreath encircling several wired artificial flowers, placed there by some caring person five months earlier. Next, the Protestant section, calling attention to a small bouquet of withered red roses nestled against a broken headstone. And on to Alvin's section he drove with purpose of mind.

In the far corner of the cemetery stood two dilapidated signs, one beneath the other, leaning out of the perpendicular: **SECTION - A**; then in smaller letters, **JEWISH**, signifying first and foremost, in any visitor's mind, barrenness at best . . . for not a hint of color save the unkempt grass and weed adornment suggested anything more, he seethed, irate at the institution for its utter neglect.

Three sections; three signposts. A total of two remembrances of respect left by loved ones across an entire expanse, Kalvin ruminated. "How very, very sad," he muttered beneath his breath.

Kalvin parked the car and walked over to Alvin's grave, setting down a single daffodil freshly picked from his neighbor's yard when the world was fast asleep; a daffodil; not a dandelion. The latter of which had taken over his yard en masse.

Pilgrim State Hospital, he ruminated: *Thirty acres of mostly unmarked graves over the course of seventy years. Eight thousand five hundred fifty bodies. An average of one hundred twenty-two bodies a year*, Kalvin quickly figured in his head.

Nine hundred *living* patients left occupying space in the southern corner of the prodigious five-hundred-fifty-acre Brentwood facility. Four hundred fifty of those acres were to be put out to bid to developers, including the thirty-acre cemetery site.

"Can you imagine, Alvin? The state of New York is selling these plots to the highest bidder. Bones and all. Pilgrim State is getting out of the cemetery business. They couldn't cure you guys and gals," he affirmed through a giggle. "They couldn't even pave the road or keep the crabgrass cut. So, I guess they figured they might just as well cancel the lot of you in the bargain.

"Well, I'll let you in on a little secret, Alvin. I plan on underwriting one of the biggest life insurance policies of the decade. Underhandedly, of course," he stated through a grin. "I plan on naming it the Alvin and Kalvin Matheson Memorial Award Fund. How's that? But believe me, it's going to take some doing. I'll call it my five-year plan. Alvin, did you know that most well-planned gardens are based on a five-year plan? I bet I can have ours in full bloom by then. I really and truly do.

"Patience, Alvin. Immortality is but a stone's throw away." Kalvin giggled again gaily, heading back to the car to remove a shovel from the trunk of the Camry.

Several yards to the left of his brother's numbered grave marker stood a good-sized rock that had been bothering Kalvin for years. Half of it sat buried solidly in the earth. The sodden ground made it somewhat easier to remove the stubborn stone.

Chapter 3

It was early evening, the beginning of July, when Justin Barnes was summoned before Suffolk County's new commanding officer of homicide in Yaphank, Long Island. Justin believed he had a good idea what was coming. It was a neat assignment while it lasted. But like his estranged female partner had reminded him, nothing lasts forever. Good, bad, or otherwise. Justin had not seen or heard from Jacqueline Rubino since the day he rescued her. *Never ever* would be too soon a time as far as she and her family were concerned, he knew, as Justin had been responsible for putting the woman in harm's way. Justin last visited Jackie in Brookhaven Memorial Hospital, where he shot and killed Clarence Emery earlier, along with the madman's newfound accomplice. It seemed to Justin as though it was during another lifetime when he had deep-sixed Malcolm Columba, Emery's former partner. The two madmen had been accountable for a number of serial murders.

"How have you been, Barnes?" Detective Lieutenant Ethan Powell asked, leaning way forward on a pair of beefy ebony elbows, setting them solidly upon the former commander's desk. It had been seven months to the day since Theodore Groche retired back in January; a year since Justin had done anything constructive as a covert operative for Suffolk County Homicide.

"I've been okay, Lieutenant."

"Good. Good. Keeping busy?"

"Doing the thing I'd been putting off most of my life."

"And that is?"

"Nothin'. Doin' nothin' a'tall. But I'm sure you're well aware of that."

"No. Not really. Been pretty busy cleaning shop," the top cop stated evenly.

"Yeah, I heard. Transferred a few good people out of here, from what I understand."

"Not any good to me if I can't work with them."

"So, I guess that's why I'm here. Right?"

"How do you mean?"

"The old boot in the butt, I figure. That what you wanna say?"

Powell smiled and shook his head. "You've been drawing the same pay just sitting around doing nothing, like you said."

"Yep. You askin' for a giveback?" Justin questioned with a smirk.

Again, the commanding officer shook his head. "You want to start earning some of that money you've been collecting, and continue earning more?" the man said with a straight face.

Justin was nonplused. "You shittin' me?"

"Maybe shit *on* you if you fuck up. But word is you're not a shitbird, or you wouldn't be sitting here right now."

"You got somethin' particular in mind? Or you talkin' sometime down the pike?"

"You interested either way—or not?"

"Interested? Sure. Just like to hear what's up before I commit, is all."

"Then hear this. We got a body at Indian Island Golf Course in Riverhead. Denise Nathan. A waitress at The Clubhouse Restaurant. She was found bludgeoned in the bushes along the Peconic River. Fifty-three-year-old light-skinned black woman. Single and lived alone in Flanders. Back of her head was smashed to smithereens with a large stone. Single blow. Her car's parked back at the restaurant. I say *back* because several employees and her boss saw her leave in it right after her shift. That was eight hours ago. Man walking his dog found the body." The lieutenant handed Justin a crime scene photo of the victim. "Car and the crime scene are as clean as my cat. Still early, though."

"Who's working this?"

"Your two buddies. Archer and York. Insisted that I give you a jingle. That's really why you're here. That and the fact that you really haven't been earning your keep lately," the lieutenant clarified.

"Gotta be something more to it than that, Lieutenant," Justin jawed. "Gotta be more than Brian and Gary having my welfare at heart. Gotta be more than your tryin' to recoup a loss, boss. So why don't you come clean?"

The big man shook his bald head. "Nothing beyond that," he swore. "Except maybe the case detective and his partner are scratching their collective heads and asses as we speak. Couple of things don't ring right."

"Fact that the victim's black couldn't have anything to do with anything either, now could it?"

"Silly of you to even think that, brother. Hey! Where do you think you're going so fast?"

"They stop serving dinner over at Indian Island at nine o'clock sharp."

"Don't you at least want to see the preliminary report? See the rest of the pics? Ask a question or two before you go off half-cocked?"

Justin stopped dead in his tracks, turned around, then smiled. "Just one."

"Which is?"

"Do I still have an expense account?"

Ethan Powell considered the question before he spoke. "Certain members of Team Three, who shall go unnamed, informed me you've put on a few pounds around the middle since last they saw you. And they're absolutely right," he needled.

Justin looked down. "Maybe a few, but I can still see my shoes. Can you?"

"How can I, sitting behind Theo's old desk—both soles collecting dust? Till today, that is."

Justin nodded and headed toward the door.

"You keep me posted. Hear?"

"You sound just like Theo, bossman."

"And so, we'll draw the line right there," the commanding officer growled, not wishing to be compared to his predecessor in any way, shape or form.

Chapter 4

Justin Barnes did not go directly to the crime scene, but rather to The Clubhouse Restaurant at Indian Island off County Road 105 in Riverhead. Up a ramp and through the set of double doors the solid six-foot black figure strode.

A man in his late thirties walked out from the bar area and over to Justin. "Excuse me, but we're closing up early tonight, sir."

"Are you the manager?"

"Owner. Victor Gibson."

Justin looked across the room to a table where a frail old man sat hunched forward. The customer was somewhere in the midst of his evening meal. Against a mirrored wall, a portable oxygen tank wrapped within a black vinyl bag stood on a chair beside him. He was the only customer in the dining area.

"I'll take that table over there in the far corner and won't be a bother to anyone," Justin decided. "Be out of here before he ever finishes his plate, including dessert and coffee—which I feel he should forgo."

Victor Gibson forced a polite smile and simply shook his head. "I'm sorry, but I said we're closing."

Justin withdrew his wallet and flashed a gold badge and ID card. Barnes' thumb covered his title of Consultant. "Police business," he said in a low voice. "Don't want to scare away the crowd," the maverick chaffed with a wink and an impatient smile.

"I just finished talking to the police," Victor said uncomfortably. "At length."

"Huh. Then I guess you're back to square one, Mr. Gibson," Justin said with feigned sympathy. "I just need to sit and take in

Denise Nathan's work environment. Won't bother you unless I have some questions before I leave."

"What kind of questions?"

"Don't know. Haven't even read the report as yet," he added candidly.

"You just want to sit?"

"Sit and observe. Take some notes. Maybe peek around a bit."

"I don't know."

"What don't you know, Mr. Gibson?"

"Your coming in here like this. Strange. You don't want to ask me any questions?"

"Not just yet."

"But the *murder*—" Victor lowered his voice. "The murder happened a quarter mile from here," he said, pointing in an easterly direction past the barroom.

"Ah, but the murderer probably stood in this very room, Mr. Gibson. Maybe even sat at one of these tables—studying his victim closely. Could have had a drink at the bar. I see you have seating inside there, too."

"Smoking section," Victor pointed out.

"Hum." Justin scanned the room. "Nope. Killer probably spent some time watching your waitress, Denise, in *this* room. Guess we can pretty much rule out the guy over there," he kidded, nodding in the direction of the single soul dining on a meat and potato platter. The maverick faced about. "That the kitchen behind the partition?"

Victor nodded.

"Yep. Best seat in the house to watch the staff come and go," Justin declared, gesturing toward the table he had asked for, shifting his eyes back toward the octogenarian. "Think maybe the guy could be a suspect?" he reconsidered jokingly. "Nonsmoker, I'm sure. Emphysema being his problem would be an educated guess, coupled with a heart condition. I suspect he doesn't even know you've lost an employee. Was she any good, Victor? I mean as far as waitresses go," he baited ambiguously, watching the owner's eyes narrow and grow cold. "I'm asking you questions like you wanted, Mr. Gibson. Want to help me out here?"

"You can take that table," Victor Gibson stewed, nodding toward the neutral corner across the room from his customer. "I don't know what you're trying to prove with your unorthodox behavior, Mister Investigator. But satisfy yourself and have a seat."

"Well, if it's any consolation, I've just satisfied myself on two accounts—that both you and Frank Hall, over there, are off the hook," Justin affirmed with a broad grin, displaying a perfect set of pearly white teeth.

"You know him?" Victor questioned with genuine surprise.

"Nah, name is on his oxygen tank bag reflected in that wall mirror. At first I thought it was a set of miniature clubs," Justin jawed in jest.

Victor Gibson seemed impressed with the man's reasoning and power of observation but not the man himself. "I didn't get your *name*. Just your *number*," he said smartly.

"*Touché*," Justin surrendered good-naturedly. "Barnes. Justin Barnes," he offered in the best James Bond-like manner he could muster.

"Jesus! I know who you are. You interviewed that Tom Cousins fellow on those serial murders. Yeah. Serial killer Professor Clarence Emery. Last year. Newspapers called him The Teacher. And there was another guy. Your name was all over the news."

"Keep all that under your hat, Mr. Gibson. All right?"

"I don't have a hat. Marlow has a hat; like the magician. He's my chef. Cooked for the Kennedys. Shriver family, actually. And I'm going to send him out in a hot second to see what you want while you 'sit and observe,' as you said. Rhonda—she's new here. But she can tell you anything you want to know about Denise. She's in the back with Marlow. Pretty broken up. But I'll send her out, too."

"Did the detectives interview Rhonda yet?"

"Not that I know. No. I don't think so. I didn't give them her name. She officially starts Monday. Police asked me for a list of employees. I didn't mention her to them. But she knows—knew—Denise well. Denise had recommended her highly."

Justin nodded. "You're owner/operator. Right?"

"Yes, sir."

"J. Call me J," Justin said, warmly extending his hand.

Victor Gibson took and shook the man's hand firmly. "Okay, J. Sorry we got off on the wrong foot. It's been a day from hell. Denise was the best waitress I ever employed—not enjoyed," he clarified with a sad grin.

Justin nodded understandingly.

Chapter 5

Kalvin Frederick Matheson had not felt so good about himself in years. He was chipper. Alive from the moment he took away Denise Nathan's final breath.

"Wham!" he exclaimed excitedly. But with no one around to share his exultation, he turned momentarily depressed. "No! I'm not going to give in to this melancholy mood of mine. Not this time. No, siree. Let it get the better of me after what *I've* accomplished? I don't think so. Next time, I'll consider having someone along to share the thrill of it all . . . before I *wham-bam* the two of them. Double my pleasure. Double my fun. I'll even chew that silly Doublemint gum," he promised himself deliciously. "But then, of course, it'll only compound the chances of my getting caught. That would *not* be too smart, Kalvin Matheson. Now would it?" Suddenly, he had a bright idea. "Oh, it's a winner, and it will positively work. It's perfect. Why didn't I think of it before . . . before putting myself through all this unnecessary anxiety?"

Kalvin practically ran out the front door. Off he drove a good distance to buy himself a camcorder. Next, he traveled sixty more miles out of his way to buy cord and rope and other materials. Another twenty miles north to purchase two books. A beginner's book on fly tying. Another on knots. All items paid for in cash.

That evening, Kalvin stayed up late and read. He was fascinated with the history of knots, dating back thousands of years. His stomach was in one when he finally put down the tome. Could he possibly continue along the line of what he had a mind to? "*Knot* in a million pages," he punned and applauded loudly. *But maybe . . . . just maybe . . . with a bit of patience and practice . . .*

"Hell," he decided aloud. "I'll leave them clues that'll leave them clueless. Thin but telling."

Kalvin told himself that if he could manage a simple loop and half hitch with tippet material, as he had done in repairing Denise Nathan's decorative pin after he killed her, he could certainly learn some basic knots by the time victim number two appeared in a *new* series of serial crimes.

Why, it might even become my trademark, the killer smiled knowingly. *And why not?*

Why had he even bothered traveling all that distance for those items in particular if he was not to become a serious serial killer? Why did he buy those books? Oh, he would learn the ropes, all right. He would learn all he could about knots and their applications. He would just have to learn to control his rage and not hit anyone as hard as he had hit Denise.

Hit them just hard enough to incapacitate but not to kill them right off the bat. He shivered, putting aside the club Alvin had used to kill game fish many a year ago.

Later, Kalvin would compare *his* pictures to the crime scene photos that the only living male friend he had in the whole wide world would review as a matter of course—provided that the bodies turned up in Suffolk County, which of course they would.

Kalvin shuddered as a blanket of goose bumps chilled and covered the tops of his naked shoulders.

Chapter 6

It was a hot August afternoon, with still no leads in the Denise Nathan case. Homicide was stumped. Justin Barnes sat across from Detective Lieutenant Ethan Powell in the man's well-appointed office.

"A million vehicles go in and out of Indian Island," Justin told his boss. "Golfers and restaurant customers. Fishermen and bird watchers. Joggers and picnickers. Boaters and hikers. We got zip."

"Now tell me something I don't know," Lieutenant Powell droned. "Like maybe the guy could have come in by foot from the park. Maybe you can hit the adjacent campgrounds again, Barnes. Ask around some more."

But Justin shook his head. "Been there, done that. Fucker could have come in by parachute, for all we know," he exaggerated. "First it rained for days on end, followed by a week of ninety plus degree weather to dry things up real good—turning the area into a proverbial dust bowl back there. And *then* we have a murder on our hands."

"C'mon. Are you saying he purposely waited for a dry spell in order to cover his tracks? Tire tracks as well? Because Gary and Brian seem to think it was a random act. Look. Denise Nathan probably tells some guy the relationship's over and that she's seeing someone else. The guy goes berserk, picks up a rock and bashes her brains in."

"More like a boulder, you mean," Justin magnified to make his point. "And picks it up from where? Bottom of that stone's been in the earth forever, forensics says. Dug out recently with a shovel. We searched every square inch bordering Route 105: the woods and marshland behind the pro shop; every fucking field in-between. Then back around and through the entire golf course. The campgrounds to the north. Several times. Again, no depression made by that rock to be found anywhere. And there's nothing uncommon about the trace constituents taken off it either. Mica, quartz and feldspar mostly. Decomposed pine needles being the predominant composition. Could come from almost anywhere, Marcus and Peter tell us."

"So, you're saying the perp dug it up elsewhere—a twenty-pound stone, for crying out loud—carted it into those woods and bashed her skull in." The lieutenant shook his head. "Makes no sense."

"Neither does Brian and Gary's theory that it was a jealous boyfriend gone ballistic."

"How so?"

"Because if that were the case, you don't come up and hit that special someone from behind with just one blow. You'd want to pulverize their puss. Face to face. Punish the person repeatedly for betrayal. And you got to rule out robbery as motive. She had nearly fifty bucks in mostly singles, and her paycheck. Remember, she had a diamond and sapphire tennis bracelet worth plenty. Five grand, from what I'm told."

"Maybe the guy didn't want anything that could be traced. Maybe that's why he didn't take the bracelet and check."

"Yeah, but fifty bucks is still fifty bucks, boss."

"I don't know. Maybe he got spooked." Ethan Powell leaned back in his chair. "So, tell me what you think."

"About what specifically?"

"Gut reaction as to what we're dealing with here. Random act? Love triangle? What? Speak openly."

Justin Barnes locked his eyes on the lieutenant. "I think we got ourselves a *stone*-cold killer out there—" he replied without any trace of humor on his face—"biding his time. I think another body's gonna turn up real soon."

"How did you arrive at that conclusion?"

"Well, for one thing, I'm sitting here before you once again."

The commanding officer studied his charge for a moment before reaching across his desk to a folder and removing several photos. He slid them right-side-up under Justin's nose. "It already has," the detective lieutenant stated evenly. "Only, I don't see any correlation."

Justin took the pics and studied each one carefully. "Garrote."

"No rocks or stones. Clubbed then strangled the man with a

length of knotted rope attached to two solid oak handles." The lieutenant referred to a preliminary lab report. "Twenty-two inch, nine-sixteenths plaited white nylon rope. Inexpensive. Very common. Hardware stores. Discount department stores. Marine centers. You name it. Dowels: one-inch in diameter by four. Three-quarter inch hole. Crudely crafted but effective."

"When was the body found?"

"Ten o'clock this morning. Approximate time of death? Several hours earlier."

"Where?"

"Riverhead. Immediately east of the Moose Lodge. Wooded area. Sixty yards in."

"Less than a mile from Indian Island."

The lieutenant nodded.

"Who's the poor bastard?"

"William Walker. Twenty-eight. Local carpenter. He was doing some work at the lodge. Went for lunch; never came back."

"Who found him?"

"Woman walking her cat."

"Cat?"

"Yep."

"She check out?"

"Hundred percent. Seventy-three-year-old widow. Lives next-door to the lodge, overlooking its marina. Walks her cat three times a day just to the left of that property, along a wooded path back there. She found the body as the trail turned south toward the water. Zena Towers—neither saw nor heard anything."

Chapter 7

It was a quiet autumn evening. The young woman lay bound and gagged on the linoleum floor.

Kalvin sat before a small desk and clamped a number six barbless Mustad hook in the rounded jaws of the fly-tying vise. With a bobbin that held a spool of fine white thread, he made a series of wraps around the shank of the hook, tying in a tiny section of marabou fibers for the tail at the start of the bend.

"Enjoying your visit, Gretchen? I'm tying a Woolly Bugger. It's an easy way to practice my half hitches. You see, I'm learning all about knots. So, if the authorities do connect you to this room, which they won't, all they'll find are feathers and thread and such. Immediately, they'll suspect that a hobbyist resides here," he remarked with a giggle.

The cord ran from the back of Gretchen Bowers' neck, around the wraps of monofilament line securing the woman's wrists at the small of her back, down to a pair of sturdy ankles, crossed and connected to coils of stronger pound test line that held her legs solidly rearward. She tried desperately to free herself as the knotted nylon cord at her throat and the sides of her neck tightened.

"Those are Constrictor Knots or Binding Knots, Gretch. The more you struggle, the tighter they bind. Therefore, my suggestion is that you lie still. You're not going anywhere just yet."

Kalvin cut the thread then tied in a long black feather followed by a length of chenille, circling the latter along the shank and up to the eye of the hook, securing the material before clipping off the excess. Next, he stroked the hackle rearward, separating the fibers at its center so that they shot out in all directions. Finally, he spiraled the feather forward.

"This is called palmering, Gretch. It's what gives the fly its wild and woolly look." Kalvin locked the saddle hackle in place, tying it off with a series of half hitches. "See? Pretty neat, huh? A good pal of mine was an expert flytier. I say *was* because someone shot Clarence Emery down in cold blood. I'm sure you remember reading about him in the papers."

Gretchen's mouth was covered with strips of gray duct tape. She mumbled something as her stomach rumbled noisily.

"I guess you're trying to tell me that you're hungry," Kalvin said with annoyance, consulting his *Beginner's Guide to Fly Tying*. "Damn it! I wound the feather the wrong way. Shiny side is supposed to be facing away from me; dull side toward me is the way it's supposed to be tied. Oh, well. No harm done. I'll just tie another one after this. We have some time. Then maybe we'll think about getting you out of here. All right?"

Gretchen's mind raced ahead both with fear and anger, then back again in complete confusion.

"I know, I know, Gretchen. You're saying to yourself, 'Why did I ever accept a ride from this man?' Well, I'll tell you a secret. You really had no choice. Tell you another. You're going to leave someone a tidy sum of money, and soon. And in turn, that person is going to hand half of it over to me. A little later, all the rest," Kalvin swore confidently. "I bet you didn't think that your Uncle Sal would be collecting so soon as the beneficiary on your life insurance policy. Did you? Good old Uncle Sal. I know, Gretch. Why in God's name did your car have to die back there? you're thinking. Fate, I guess you're figuring, or just plain bad luck," he offered quietly, whip-finishing the head of the fly before adding a drop of head cement with a dubbing needle. "There."

Gretchen's tears rolled down her ashen face like a leaky faucet.

"Actually, things were planned out well in advance. Life insurance and electrical systems are things I know a bit about. Fly tying? Well, that's another matter. But I'm trying, Gretchen. God knows that you know I'm trying. Getting the hang of it so to speak," he said with some satisfaction. "You see, my two heroes knew lots about a lot of things. They were what you would call Renaissance men. Me? I'm what some would call a loser. Dull. Just like the side of this feather. Dull side toward me," he repeated as a reminder. "Yes, the side that should be facing me." Kalvin stared at the bug curiously. "But isn't it interesting to note that I inadvertently faced the *shiny* side toward me. Maybe it wasn't an accident, Gretchen. Maybe it's a sign. A sign that things are changing for me. For the better. There's no question that I'm gaining a certain confidence about myself daily. I can feel it in my bones. No more coming up behind a person and, with a rock or club, bashing their brains in. No, ma'am. Kind of messy, too, when you stop to think about it." Kalvin paused in consideration. "Now I can look a person right in the eyes and tell them that they are going to die by my hand when *I* say and how *I* choose. That doesn't sound like the kind of a man who's a loser, now does it? Sounds more to me like the kind of man who takes charge and isn't afraid of anything."

Kalvin removed the fly from the vise and began tying another.

Gretchen was staring up at Kalvin with dread.

"Yes, I have it all worked out so neatly. The money will never ever be traced back to me. Know why, Gretchen? Because I refuse to take a check!" he announced with uproarious laughter. "Shh," he shushed himself, biting his bottom lip to keep his sides from splitting.

"The problem is that I can't write too many people off and not raise a red flag. So, I've carefully researched who to sign off on—and exactly what I need to do. I want you to know, Gretchen, that I'm not doing this strictly for the money for me alone, although I'll be the first to admit that it is going to come in very handy. You could even say it'll prove to be *my* life insurance policy. Mine and Alvin's, actually. I'm also doing this as a confidence builder. You see, I'm on my way to becoming a confidence man!" he declared through a howl that literally took his breath away. "You don't think that's funny?" he questioned the second he loaded his lungs. "A confidence man, Gretchen. A man who swindles . . . never mind. I can see you're really not in the mood."

Gretchen again strained against the restraints, fiercely trying to free herself . . . until she finally lost circulation and, consequently, all consciousness.

Kalvin screeched. "Did I not tell you? Didn't I? Make me get up and break my concentration. Damn you!"

Chapter 8

The sun was setting as Salvatori Passaro briskly walked the unmanned, unfenced minimum security grounds of Pilgrim State Psychiatric Center, approaching the tree line not far from the Catholic cemetery.

"Over here," Kalvin called, stepping out from behind a tall oak.

"There you are!" Salvatori snapped with irritation. "I thought you said eight o'clock sharp."

"You sound a bit impatient, Sal. As a matter of fact, you sound just like the patient you truly are," Kalvin rode the man while grinning from ear to ear. "But not for long, pal."

"What are you so damn happy about?"

"About a million bucks," he offered calmly.

Salvatori forced a queer smile. "It's done?"

Kalvin nodded. "That's why I insisted that you attend the hospital's annual picnic this afternoon. You had to be away from here and above suspicion if anything went wrong. You should be receiving a check in several weeks if all goes smoothly. Couple months at most. It might even coincide with your release. How does that sound? How does half a million dollars apiece grab you, partner?"

"Right by the nuts," Salvatori said rather distantly before allowing a moment to rejoice, suddenly grabbing hold of his crotch. "*Oogots* to this fuckin' hellhole," he added, looking back over his shoulder in the direction of the psychiatric hospital. "Twenty-one years, my friend."

"Well, now at least you'll have something to show for it."

"What? That's not even twenty-five G's a year. I used to pull that down on one good score."

"Pulled you down the crapper is what it did. Especially when you started using. I hope you're going to be a little bit smarter this time around when you get out, pal."

"Shootin' a little bit of heroin is what saved my ass."

"How do you mean?"

"By convincing the doctors and the judge that that one little psychotic episode—"

"One little episode?"

"Yes . . . was the root of *all* my problems. But now I'm completely cured and have learned a hard and valuable lesson," Salvatori Passaro recited with basset hound eyes, followed by a mischievous wink and a nod.

"Yeah, learned not to shoot up dope or take aim at seven people in a disco, I hope," Kalvin reminded the lanky man.

"It wasn't a disco, pal o' mine. It was a cheap saloon. Besides. Six of the seven bastards survived."

"Lucky for you."

"Lucky for me the one who bought the bullet was black and lusterless," Salvatori snorted.

"If you say so. Just don't forget that we're partners and try to skip out on me."

"Just don't forget that you needed me to work this scam. And you'll need me for others."

"That's why I picked you, Sally," Kalvin assured him.

"Chump change. This is just the beginning, kid."

Kalvin shook his head. "Big mistake. You're already getting greedy. From this point on, we go nice and easy. We'll have enough to keep us going. Later, we'll score a forty maybe fifty thousand dollar policy. You don't want to raise any red flags. Understand?"

"You know I'm going to have expenses. Bribes and other improprieties don't come cheap."

"Then you'll tell me what they are and how much you'll need. Just don't try to rip me off."

Salvatori looked down at Kalvin as though he were an annoying bug. "I could rip your head off your shoulders and take a dump in your neck if I had a mind to."

"You mean during one of your psychotic episodes?" Kalvin challenged calmly, although he was shaking like a leaf on the inside. "I don't think so, partner."

Salvatori surrendered a crooked little smile. "Fact is we really need one another."

"No, Sal. You need me. Guys like you are a half a million a dozen," he kidded.

The tall figure fixed his gaze, staring down oddly at his partner. "I often wonder why you picked me."

"It's very simple, Sal. Because you were nice to my brother."

Sal nodded understandingly and extended his hand. "Partners to the end, Kal?"

Kalvin took and shook Sal's hand confidently. "Till the very end."

Chapter 9

Gretchen Bowers' backbone was so bowed rearward that she thought her spine would crack. Again, the cord that connected her ankles to her wrists and to her neck slowly tightened and closed around her throat.

"Before we leave here, Gretch, I want you to know that your Uncle Sal loved you very much, in his own strange way. He made me promise that you wouldn't suffer. He even had this sad look on his face when I told him the deed was done. I just didn't have the heart to tell him what I really have in store for you. I don't think he'd like it one bit. It would probably drive him crazier than he already is. But he sure as hell has those doctors fooled. Got to give him that. Anyhow, it will all be over for you soon.

"You like music, Gretchen?" Kalvin asked as he placed a pair of headphones over his prisoner's ears. He switched off the external speakers before turning on the stereo and putting up the volume full-blast, spinning the channel dial one way and then the other. "I'll bet neither Clarence Emery nor Malcolm Columba ever thought of this," he said more to himself as he sent erratic sounds back and forth across the band before flicking to FM. "I'll bet you a million bucks you won't last the night before your weak heart gives out and you die of fright sooner than the ligature stops your breathing altogether. Wish to wager? In any event, it's kind of like a footrace to the finish. But we really won't know the winner until the medical examiner performs your autopsy. I've warned you, Gretch. The more you struggle, the tighter it's going to get," Kalvin reminded his captive, although she could not hear a word as the distorted big band sound of Tommy Dorsey filled her eardrums. "Either way, you're the loser," he decided, walking over to the tripod on which sat his new camcorder, capturing her in close-up before a stark white wall.

There, in a semi-quiet corner of the room, Kalvin recorded—from every conceivable angle—what he noted as a remarkable and outrageous outpouring of expression.

Five minutes later, the man stopped the camera, then went over and removed the headphones from his listener, holding the headset a good foot away from his own ear. Kalvin cringed.

"Sorry," he said sincerely.

Tuning in another station until it turned crystal-clear, he slipped the earphones back upon the trembling woman's head, leaving the volume exactly where it was.

"See if hard rock doesn't leave you with a headache. See if it doesn't wreck your precious heart, wretch. Then I have to think seriously about getting you out of here."

A short time later, Gretchen Bowers lay still as her stare.

Her bound body was discovered the following morning near an entrance to a park off Sleepy Lane, in Half Hollow Hills—approximately thirty miles east of Pilgrim State Hospital.

Chapter 10

The eleven-year-old girl watched with fascination as her next-door neighbor gracefully waved a long, black graphite rod in a steady back-and-forth motion through the air while stripping several yards of fly line from the reel—suddenly sending the yellow length along the hedgerow that divided the two properties. Locking the cork handle beneath the hollow of an armpit, Kalvin began retrieving fifty feet or so of line, hand-over-hand, depositing the coils into a shallow plastic container secured at his waist.

"Hi, Kalvin," Vivian Osip called and waved, having waited politely until the man finished taking up the line from the lawn.

"Hiya there, Vivian," he said pleasantly. "What are you up to?"

"Just watching you."

Kalvin shot the girl a glance that made her giggle. "Watching me what?"

"Watching you try and catch fish in the grass." The pretty girl laughed gaily, stretching her arms back and around her jacket, locking her hands in place.

"Really? For a second there, I thought you might be spying on me."

"If I was spying on you, why would I wave and say hello?" she challenged with a big grin.

"Well, maybe you're not a very good spy. Or maybe you are, but just trying to catch me off guard."

"No, Kalvin." The child shook her head emphatically. "If I was a spy, I'd hide in your grass like a snake and watch you—and you wouldn't even know I was there. So there."

Kalvin looked all around him. "Where in the grass?" he asked in feigned confusion.

"Anywhere over there," his little neighbor answered with a titter, sweeping an arm in a wide arc before returning it to the small of her back.

Kalvin scratched his head. "Are you saying that my lawn needs mowing and that's the reason why you could hide like a snake in the grass?"

Vivian nodded her head solemnly. "My mom and dad say so, too."

"Really?"

"Uh-huh."

"What else do they say?"

The little girl looked high in the sky for the answer. "I know. My mom says you're a shut-in."

"A shut-in?"

"Yep."

"What's a shut-in?"

"I'm not sure. I asked my mom, and she said never mind. So I asked Dad, and he didn't know, or pretended not to, because my dad knows everything—or thinks he does," she added with a certain satisfaction. "But I think it's a person who stays home pretty much. It wasn't in my small dictionary, and then I forgot to look it up at school."

Kalvin loved her innocence and directness. "I think you're right, Vivian. But I am getting out more and more."

"I guess. Mom says you lost your job a long time ago and that you must have a lot of money but won't spend it on your house or lawn."

"Did she, now?"

Vivian nodded. "My dad lost his job once when he was working in construction. Well, not exactly lost it because his boss laid him off. That's when Dad and you built our staircase when I was just a little girl."

"I really didn't help him build it, Vivian. All I did was put in that special lighting along the steps."

"Oh. Anyhow, that's when my mom went back to work, and Dad watched me during the day then went to school at night to get his science degree so he could get a good-paying job at the lab and have health benefits. Mom used to be a secretary for a big pharmaceutical company before I was born."

"Is that right?"

"Uh-huh. That's why she says I have to be smart and pay attention in school because one day I may have to go to work."

"She's a very smart mom. Your dad, too."

"Oh, they are. They've both got skills. That's how Mom immediately found a job the first time Dad lost his. She can type sixty words a minute on our old typewriter. Even faster on our new computer."

"That's really something."

The girl nodded. "Do you have any skills, Kalvin?"

Kalvin subtly changed the subject somewhat, along with his application, looping a short blue shooting taper to the end of the line. With a clear leader and a piece of yolk-colored yarn tied to its end, the killer false casted the line twice before shooting it a good sixty feet through the air. "You see that?" he asked, impressed with the distance he gained with the heavier front section of line.

"You mean that yellow worm?"

Kalvin smiled, lifted his rod tip and moved the item slowly atop the high grass. "That's not a worm, Vivian. That's a piece of yarn."

"Yarn? How do you catch fish with just a piece of yarn?" she baited the man on whom she had a crush.

"Well, you don't, exactly. You'd first need a hook tied with yarn and feathers—called a fly."

"You don't have a hook on?"

"No, no hook."

"Why do you fish without a hook?"

"I'm not fishing; I'm practicing."

"Practicing what?"

"Practicing my skills. Look. You see that old tire leaning against the shed?"

Vivian moved in closer and nodded.

"Watch." Kalvin took up the line again then shot the yellow piece of material into the center of the tire.

"Wow! That's pretty good, Kalvin."

Kalvin was tickled pink. "I can cast a line almost twice that distance and hit the bull's-eye every time."

"Really?"

Kalvin nodded.

"Show me."

"Can't."

"How come?"

"Not enough room to backcast. I'd be in the reeds over there."

Vivian nodded her understanding. "Hey, I know where you can practice where there's all the room in the world," she said excitedly, sending her arms in a wide semicircle.

"Where?"

"The Field Club, here in Quogue."

"The what?"

"The golf course." She pointed in the general direction.

"Oh, that's just for the golfers, Vivian. I don't think they'd like it very much if I went up there to practice my fly-casting. Do you?"

"Mom and Dad and their friends play there all the time. I could ask them."

"Your mom and dad don't make the rules, Vivian," he explained patiently. "I'd have to get permission, but—"

"Oh, but they do," Vivian insisted. "Their friends say they make up their own rules *all* the time. That's why nobody likes playing with them."

Kalvin laughed good-naturedly.

"Maybe you can go when nobody's there," she suggested.

"Maybe," Kalvin agreed. "I'll give it some thought. Say, maybe you'd like to come with me sometime. When it gets a little warmer, I mean."

"Oh, I don't mind the cold. Really."

"Think you'd like to learn how to fly-cast?"

Vivian looked back up at the sky, a fingertip supporting her chin. "I'll give it some thought," she answered rather coyly with a big bright smile.

Kalvin smiled warmly. "You do that."

"Daddy and I go fishing sometimes."

"Do you?"

Vivian nodded. "But we don't wave a rod back and forth like that."

"No?"

The girl shook her head. "We just bait the hook and drop it over the side of the boat and wait."

"Ever catch anything?"

"Daddy caught a bluefish once. Only it really wasn't really that blue. More like a silver color. But I guess you could say it had some blue; green, too. I never catch a thing. But I still like to go—cold or not. Kalvin, why do you put your fishing line in where you put your fish?" she asked, pointing to the square plastic container strapped at his waist.

"That's not for fish, Vivian. It's to hold the line so that it doesn't get all tangled up," he explained. "Look." Kalvin stooped and showed her the vertical cones molded throughout the inner base of the bin. "This way, the fly line stays nice and neat and shoots cleanly through the guides—those little wire snakes along the rod," he expanded.

"Seems hard."

"Everything's easy once you know how. You'll see; that is, if you'd really like to learn one day."

"Sure."

"But first you'll have to ask your mom and dad for permission."

"You sure you won't forget?"

"Forget to take a pretty girl like you? Never. Not in a million years."

Vivian blushed and stepped back into her own yard. "Bye, Kalvin" she said without looking back, running happily toward her home.

"Bye, Vivian," Kalvin called after her, following the youngster's giddy flight. The man's steely cold-gray eyes collected and firmly held her image . . . long after she disappeared from view.

Chapter 11

Homicide detective Brian Archer and his partner, Gary York, sat at opposite corners of their commanding officer's desk. Justin Barnes stood between them, staring down before the detective lieutenant as the pensive cop lolled his head while massaging his nape.

"Not much to tie these three together, fellas," Ethan Powell said quietly, rubbing his temples.

"Well, we believe we're dealing with the same perp," Gary stated firmly.

"Who's we? You and your partner? Or the three of you?" the lieutenant fired back with apparent annoyance, the man's patience wearing thin from obvious lack of sleep and hard evidence.

The two detectives glanced up at Justin as the lieutenant pointed to an empty chair.

Justin took a seat in front of the recently appointed head of homicide—a man with barely nine months on the job as Theo Groche's replacement.

"Well, Barnes?"

"The three of us," Justin answered decidedly.

"So, then let's hear it," the lieutenant invited, leaning back and stretching his arms out widely before lacing a set of stubby fingers behind his neck.

Justin glanced at Gary and Brian.

"C'mon, c'mon," the top cop coaxed. "There's a reason why I had you wait outside while these two theorized and hypothesized about this and that. I want to hear if you're all on the same page for the same reasons. So lay it out."

Justin folded in his lips in consideration before speaking. "I figure the guy to be in his mid to late thirties. I'd rule out a minority altogether. White dude. They generally are. Serial killers, that is," he clarified, quickly reclaiming the smile across his face. "Anyhow, I'd put 'im at medium height. Around five-seven or eight. Strong build. Southpaw. Most likely from around here—meaning Riverhead Township. He knows the area rather well. Loner by choice, but can fit in well with others when he has to. Probably never committed a murder before the Nathan woman, but getting more and more confident as he moves from one victim to the next. Fairly knowledgeable when it comes to knots. An emulator rather than a copycat. That's about it, Lieutenant," Justin concluded.

Gary and Brian dropped their eyes from their copartner, fixing them on one another before setting them on the commanding officer.

"You a profiler now, Barnes?" the lieutenant snapped. "You sure you don't know this guy personally?" he jabbed jokingly. "I was asking for a connection, not a psychological analysis based on whim and conjecture. And who's he trying to emulate?" He let the last question hang for a moment. "Well?"

Justin, again, shot a glance at his two associates as he answered. "Malcolm Columba and Clarence Emery," he offered quite seriously.

"Oh, really? And how did you arrive at that?" the lieutenant inquired with derision.

"By those knots our sicko used on the Bowers woman," Justin answered straightaway.

"The knots?"

Justin nodded.

"Care to elaborate?"

"Well, generally speaking, there are certain knots you'd use with fishing line like monofilament, fluorocarbon, and braided lines. Those of small diameter. And there are other knots you'd use with rope or cord or heavy twine. Neither Columba nor Emery was that choosy when it came to restraining their victims. Our new challenger, however, is highly selective—selecting the appropriate knot and material for the job."

"That a fact? Because I don't see any clear distinction like that in these reports," the man stated, picking up then dropping forensics' analyses along with blowups depicting their latest victim found along a roadside.

"That's because someone failed to read between the lines, Lieutenant," the maverick funned.

"Is that supposed to be funny, Barnes?"

"It's just that certain lines lend themselves to certain applications better than others. In this case, cordage vis-à-vis monofilament."

"Vis a who? Speak English, man!"

"Yes, sir. Cord compared to fishing line."

"Go on."

"Well, sir, the knots our killer used are consistent with the knots Columba and Emery used to restrain their victims, but with a twist. Figuratively speaking, that is." Justin pointed to the current file. "May I?"

The lieutenant handed over the folder on Gretchen Bowers.

Justin flipped through several photos, selecting one in particular. "Look. Note the type of knot below the wrists." Justin pulled out the written report. "Bag, Sack or Miller's Knot."

Brian and Gary stood up, staring down at the photos.

The lieutenant sat impassively behind his desk.

"Same knot Columba used," Justin reminded the pair who had worked the case. "Also, check out the knots at Bowers' ankles and compare them to the one around her neck. Same knots Emery used. But only someone knowledgeable about knots would know to use a Strangle or Constrictor Knot here at her throat, while connecting the line with an Albright at her feet, there. Not necessarily the other way around like Emery and Columba had done with their victims."

"And why is that?" the lieutenant pressed, seemingly unimpressed.

"Because a binding knot tied with a greater diameter, as rope, wouldn't hold as well. But materials such as cord or monofilament line bite and bind extremely well. Actually, constrict. With this gauge line, these types of strangle and seizing knots have to be cut in order to be removed in most cases."

Gary and Brian nodded their understanding.

"So, what are you saying, Barnes?" the lieutenant barked. "What's your point exactly?"

"Well, the way I see it, the victim wasn't goin' anywhere—

regardless of either knot the killer used. The point is this guy wants to show us that he's some kind of knot expert—that he knows how to tie the appropriate knot with the proper material."

"Then why do you say he's an emulator of Columba and Emery, and not an originator?" the lieutenant posited. "Why not just some guy who knows a few knots and how to execute them? The knots as well as his victims."

"Too coincidental," Justin Barnes put forth plainly. "Consider all the knots there are, of which there are hundreds if not thousands, coupled with an assortment of material: rope, cord, mono, twine and their type: natural, synthetic—even miracle fibers such as state-of-the-art Kevlar, compounded by a dizzying list of diameters. What you have here are the same knots, cord and mono employed by Columba and Emery. I've already checked their files and matched the knots to this creep's handiwork. Except for how and where they're employed, they're identical."

"Then what you're saying is that he had to have had intimate knowledge of their handiwork."

"Either that or he had access to their files," Justin concluded, dropping the photos upon the desk.

The lieutenant was scratching his head. "Once again, Barnes. Why an emulator as you put it?"

"Our man wants to excel, Lieutenant. He wants to top those two sickos of yesteryear."

Detective Archer, who was initially responsible for bringing Justin on board three years earlier, was nodding in agreement. "I think Justin's on to something, Lieutenant."

Detective York concurred. "I think we might have a hero worshipper on our hands. One who wants to make a name for himself by standing tall in their shoes," he put forth firmly, alluding to The Author (Malcolm Columba) and his protégé (Clarence Emery), The Teacher: two serial murderers who Justin Barnes had killed. The former in cold-blood. The latter in the line of so-called duty. "Nice work, J."

"Whoa! Now hold on just a damn minute," Ethan Powell ordered. "Let's not go off half-cocked. All right? This is merely speculation at this point. We'll certainly take a good look at this. Okay?"

"Lieutenant."

"Yes, Detective York."

"Just a moment ago you wanted to know if the three of us were on the same page—"

"Yes, but with sound reason," Powell interrupted.

"Well, at this point, sir, with all due respect, I think we've turned that page and are heading into the next chapter."

"Oh, you do, do you?"

"Yes, sir."

Brian Archer quickly interjected. "Sir, I think what Gary is saying here—"

"Is that you suddenly got this guy all figured out. Yes? Well, if you three care to know what I think, I'm not a hundred percent sure that one person did all three killings here. This last one, I'm sure you'll agree, is a bit removed from the first two. Like by forty-five miles from Riverhead and practically in another county."

"Maybe to throw us off the beaten track for now," Gary York said matter-of-factly. "The perp probably—"

"What was that, York?"

Once again, Archer started to come to the aid of his partner.

"No, no, no!" the lieutenant exclaimed, waving the case detective off and addressing his partner. "What did you just say to me, York?"

"That the perp probably—"

"Stop right there!" The lieutenant put out his palm. "Your very last word, Detective. Repeat it."

"Probably."

"Thank you. And by the way, your first word was 'maybe'; maybes and probablys don't cut it. When we can agree on something more *definite*, we can all move in a single direction. But for now, we treat these as separate homicides. Two bludgeonings—albeit the Walker victim succumbed to strangulation—which may or may not be connected, and a woman who had her eardrums blasted to bits but died of heart failure. Not blunt trauma or asphyxiation as the result of any Constrictor Knots. Clear?"

"Lieutenant."

"Are we clear?" the lieutenant reiterated.

"Clear," Brian Archer answered up abruptly, speaking mainly

for his colleague and friend.

"Good. We don't need to announce that we *probably* have a serial killer on our hands when we don't know for sure that we do. All right?"

"Right," the case detective deferred. "We don't need to say that."

"Barnes."

"Yes, sir?"

"I don't want to hear anymore about knots as it relates to Columba or Emery until I've had a chance to look into this further. Okay?"

"Yes, sir."

"Archer, I want you to dig up anything and everything on that Nathan woman, going back to the day she was first burped, if you have to. Barnes, I want you on the Walker case. He was a member of the Moose Lodge and their yacht club, as well as a day laborer for them. Continue interviewing his fraternity brothers. Especially those he slept with on his thirty-two footer, named *Just Us.* York, you got the Bowers woman."

But Gary was shaking his head.

"What is it, York?"

"Sir, may I speak frankly?"

The lieutenant leaned far forward in his chair. "Speak."

"Brian and I are partners. We're investigating Nathan and Walker. You *haven't* ruled out the possibility that the murders are connected. We believe all three are tied in. Justin is doing a fine job on the Bowers case. Why jockey us around now?"

"Finished?"

"No, sir."

Brian was holding his breath while sadly shaking his head.

"To put it bluntly, Lieutenant," Gary plodded along, "our investigations take us wherever destiny leads. Hunches. Hard cold fact. Supposition. It's all in the mix. You know that. Brian and I are making headway. Justin is putting things together whereas other members of our team are floundering in the dark. Those knots are something more than theory and conjecture, Lieutenant."

"Detective York."

"We're going to be working at cross purposes. Wasting a lot of valuable time," Gary pressed onward.

"A fresh eye on an aspect of these cases or case, as it remains to be seen, is a waste of time, Detective York?"

"I didn't say that, but it's not the way we work. Even Theo would have at least kept—"

"Detective Lieutenant Theodore Groche is retired, gentlemen," Ethan Powell stated firmly, taking in their ireful faces one by one, starting with York and slowly working a pair of cold, dark eyes in a clockwise fashion past Barnes and Archer, returning and resting an angry glare upon York. "I'm the head of this squad. *I* am your destiny. And *I* will lead and point you where I so choose."

Gary York stood. "Permission to leave, Lieutenant."

"Denied. Sit back down."

Gary sat.

"Just so that we're absolutely clear, gentlemen. Justin Barnes does not have a crystal ball. Justin Barnes is an ancillary member of this team. An adjunct, if you will. Should I dispense with the euphemisms? Justin Barnes is a paid assassin. A killer, plain and simply put. Not unlike the kind you collar when you can. The only difference being in that he has license to liquidate. Not at will, but on command. He does not run an investigation. He may collect information at my behest as I am telling the three of you to do now. I will assimilate that information and form a strategy. You will follow my instructions to the letter, or I'll be putting one in your file. Do you read me loud and clear?"

Gary sneered. "You bet. May I go now?"

"Dismissed." It was the tone of the lieutenant's order that sounded the note of finality.

Gary had knots in his stomach before he hit the hallway, smashing his fist solidly against the concrete wall. "Son of a motherfucking bitch!"

Chapter 12

It was the latter part of a sunny Wednesday afternoon when Harriet Osip returned from her garden club meeting and food shopping. Her husband, Christopher, had finished work early and came through the side entrance, placing his keys and briefcase on the kitchen counter. Vivian came down the winding staircase from her room to greet her parents.

"Hi, Mommy."

"Hi, honey."

"Hi, kiddo. How was school today?" her father asked.

"Fine."

"Ms. Ellison assign any homework?"

"Uh-huh."

"Please don't leave your schoolbag on the stove like that, dear."

"Can I stick it in the oven, Mom? Then I won't have to worry about any homework," Vivian commented matter-of-factly as she picked up the hefty nylon backpack and placed it on the kitchen table next to her father's briefcase.

"Boiled or fried?" Christopher joked, pretending to whisk his daughter's bag toward the oven door.

"You don't boil or fry homework in an oven, Daddy. You broil, bake, or roast it."

"Can't boil or fry your homework in an oven, sweetheart?" he feigned ignorance, helping Harriet put away the perishables.

"You do that on top of the stove in a proper pot or pan."

"And what kind of pot or pan might that be, kiddo?"

"A cooking pot or a skillet, Daddy. Whattaya think?"

"What's a skillet?"

"You know what a skillet is."

"No, I don't."

"Yes, you do."

"Do not."

"Do, too."

"Not."

"It's a frying pan, silly."

"Is it a pan for small fry? Something along the size and likes of you?"

The eleven-year-old could not help but laugh. "You're so silly, Daddy."

"Is it smaller or bigger than a breadbox, kiddo?"

"It's a pan for cooking pancakes and eggs, and you know that."

"Oh, then I guess small fry and kiddos get put into a pot. Right?"

"They do not."

"How about the oven? Shall I stick one of them I know personally in there?"

"You're sick, Daddy."

"Don't talk fresh to your father, Vivian."

"I can when he talks stupid."

"Hey! What did I just say?"

Vivian opened wide the door to the refrigerator and took out a half gallon container of milk with both hands.

"Well, I'm not the stupid one who wrote children's stories about a witch sticking little children in an oven," Christopher Osip remarked. "Now, *that's* what I call sick."

"That's different. *Hansel and Gretel* is a fairy tale, Daddy."

"What's so different about it?"

"Everything."

"Fine. Then I'll write a story about sticking a little girl in a pot or pan, with or without her homework. How's that?"

"You can't write, Daddy."

"What?"

"You heard me."

"I write reports every single day."

"That's not the same thing."

"Sure it is."

"Is not."

"If you're through with the milk, dear, please put it back," Harriet instructed her daughter. "And wipe that counter clean—thank you very much."

"I bet I could write the all-American novel in a weekend," Christopher boasted.

Both Vivian and her mother laughed.

"I bet you couldn't write a one-page letter without having Mom find twenty-seven thousand mistakes."

Harriet smiled but said nothing.

"Yeah, well I write reports all day long at work, and there are no mistakes."

"That's because you put it through spell-check, then have your secretary go over everything for you," Vivian concluded before finishing her glass of milk in several gulps.

"Hey, do you hear the way she's talking to her father?" Chris complained.

"I think you bring it upon yourself, dear."

"I think I'm putting you in the pot, too, Mrs. Osip. And you, *my little pretty* with the white mustache," Chris announced scaringly, his face scrunched into a frightful mask, "are going into a big double boiler. The bottom half," he threatened, starting after her.

Vivian ran from the room before her father could grab her. "Sick, sick, sick," she hollered from the hallway before climbing the staircase.

"You come back here this minute, young lady," Harriet called after her. "Bag off the table and up in your room. Then get started on your homework until I call you for dinner."

"Then tell him to leave me alone."

"Leave her alone."

Chris removed his briefcase from the table and quietly stepped behind the doorway.

Harriet shook her head and smiled.

As Vivian came back around the corner and into the kitchen, Christopher dropped his briefcase, grabbed and threw his startled daughter over his shoulder.

"Hey! Put me down," Vivian screamed. "I hate you both," she

hollered.

Harriet stuck both the schoolbag and briefcase into Chris' free hand.

"Can't write, huh?" the wiry man swore, heading up the stairs.

"I'm too big for this."

"Too big for your britches, you mean."

"I said put me down, stupid. Now!"

Christopher set his fresh-mouthed daughter down upon the landing and took her gently by the hair. "What's this?" he asked, touching the ornate yellow ornament at the top of her ponytail.

Vivian brushed his hand away. "It's mine."

"Obviously, it's yours, sweetheart. But what is it?"

"A Turk's head.

"A what?"

"It's a Turk's head hair ornament."

"Where did you get it?"

"An admirer," she answered evasively. "Like it?"

"It's beautiful, kiddo."

"It was made especially for me."

"That a fact?

"Uh-huh."

"Who's the admirer?

"Can't tell."

"Can't or won't?"

"Both."

"You're too young to have an admirer."

"Am not."

"Are, too."

"Well, for your information, I'm almost twelve, which means in another year I'll be a teenager, and then I'll have lots of admirers, and they'll drive you *crazy*—know why?"

Vivian's father shook his head. "Why?"

"Because."

"Because why?"

"Because Mommy says that's what happens when young men come courting."

"I see."

"But I'll tell you a little secret. Want to hear?"

Chris nodded.

"My admirer will be a much older man."

"Older than me?"

"Not that old," Vivian replied quite seriously.

"Oh. How old, then?"

"Never mind."

"Chris," Harriet called from downstairs.

"What?"

"I need your help down here with the salad."

"Be there in a minute."

"I don't want you helping her with her homework, hear?"

"I couldn't if I wanted to."

"Why's that, dear?"

"I'm too stupid."

Vivian giggled.

Harriet shook her head. "Just come down here."

"I'm comin', boss. And you, *my little pretty*," Chris announced in a mischievous taunting tone, crooking his finger threateningly before his daughter's face. "You're going to tell your mother and me all about this admirer of yours over dinner."

"Over my dead body, Witch Hazel," the young girl protested defiantly, straightening out her father's crooked finger.

"If need be," he swore with a grin.

"Sick. You're so sick, Daddy."

Chapter 13

It was the eve of Yom Kippur. Kalvin Matheson held a large canvas bag securely on his lap while smiling most happily.

"There's more money in here than I'd ordinarily need in a lifetime because I'm a very frugal man. But I do have extraordinary expenses, Nolan," he told the long-haired youngster restrained before him in the stone cellar. "Still, I must be very careful. I mustn't get greedy. Avarice would be very foolhardy. Instead, I've got to be patient in order to fool them all. That is, the insurance companies and the authorities," he explained as though the boy might possibly understand the killer's motivation. "That's where you come in, Nolan Andrews. Another seemingly random act. A victim out of thin air. Bizarre to be sure. The deed of an apparent madman," the lunatic cited deliciously.

The twelve-year-old wept uncontrollably as he stood naked, his body roped to a support column. Many lengths of clear, thinly tapered tightly-tied fly-fishing leaders dangled from the boy's hair as well as all of his fingers and toes, including the prisoner's penis and testicles. Sections of heavy rope lay flat upon the floor, fastened to and separating the ends of the leader material.

"It doesn't really matter much if you do or don't grasp the situation. You'll understand things better in just a little while. Later, I'll tell you all about Alvin. You'll like Alvin when you finally meet him. Then he can tell you all about me when you reach the other world. Do you believe in heaven and an afterlife, Nolan? You can nod your head if you do."

His mouth masked with a wide band of duct tape, Nolan Andrews' eyes pleaded for his freedom.

"Do you have a superhero or two, Nolan? Like Batman and

Robin? How about Superman or Spiderman? I had two heroes. Only they were as real as real can be. Not like that comic book stuff." Kalvin shook his head sadly. "They were both the real McCoy. Brilliant but crazy as they come. That was their downfall. Me? I'm just angry and lonely. But things are changing for the better. Look here." Kalvin held up a wrapped bundle of one-hundred-dollar bills from the bag. "In time, I'll cash in on another coup like this one. But for now, I'll put half of it down on Alvin's and my future. Know what I enjoy doing most, Nolan? Watching people tremble in fear before me like you're doing now. The eyes, Nolan. The eyes say it all. Wait. You'll see."

Kalvin got up to get his camcorder.

Nolan Andrews tried frantically to work his body free, but to no avail.

"This is only a temporary tomb, Nolan. It's simply a place to practice my craft. This way, I truly get to test the breaking point of both monofilament and fluorocarbon tapered leaders—their strengths as well as their weaknesses. For instance, did you know that their breaking strengths are really negligible out of water? In water, however, monofilament line absorbs up to thirty percent of its weight and therefore the knots become significantly weaker. The advantages of fluorocarbon are that it does not absorb water; too, the refraction index is far less visible in water, making it virtually invisible; also, it's abrasion resistant and positively indestructible when exposed to ultraviolet light. The downside is that it costs about three times as much as mono. But being that I plan to keep you high and dry, unless the crawlspace I stick you in later floods, I don't think it really matters much what leader material I use. Still, I like to experiment. Additionally, the leaders' lengths and strengths are serving as a series of clues, which I don't think the authorities are picking up on quite yet. But they will.

"Do you like Spiderman?" Kalvin called out from across the dark, dank, dusty space. "You're going to be fascinated by SpiderWire."

Chapter 14

Nolan Andrews' naked body appeared like a huge insect caught in a giant web. A vagrant had discovered the boy in the basement of an abandoned building across the street from the Long Island Railroad station in Riverhead. The derelict was still trembling when the detectives interviewed him. Not from the d.t.'s, but rather from what he had witnessed earlier.

"It's like I tol' the police. I crawled in over there to get out of the wind—got a bad cold—and there he was. Only I didn't know it was a person—a kid. I thought it was a big bug at first. I swear to God! I know that sounds dumb, but that's what I thought it was. I thought I was hallucinatin'. You know. Too much wine and booze, I guess."

"Did you see or hear anyone down there?" Detective York questioned.

"No, sir."

"How about before you went in or came out? Anyone at all?" York's partner asked.

The disheveled, filthy figure shook his head.

"Are you sure?" Brian Archer pressed.

"No, no one."

"Did you touch or take anything?" Gary snapped. "Any trinket or souvenir? Better tell us now."

"Are you kiddin'? I got the hell out of there as fast as I could. Went right over to that liquor store and had them call the police. They thought I was crazy at first, but then one of them finally came with me back there. 'See for yourself,' I said. He had a flashlight and put it on the boy."

"Come on over here," Gary ordered, roughly taking the man by the shoulder of his coat.

"Where are you takin' me? I didn't do anythin' bad. Hey! I don't want to go back in there"

"Shut up. You're not going back in there. Just stand right here and empty your pockets," he insisted, putting the man against a corner of the run-down building. "Do it."

"I didn't take anythin', I tol' you. Why are you doin' this?" the man whimpered, turning the pockets of his tattered coat inside out.

"Because you're a fucking whining wino. Pants pockets, too."

"There. See? Nothin'," he cried, angrily throwing down a book of matches along with a handful of snotty tissues. "I did nothin' wrong," he insisted.

"No? You were loitering and now littering. Now, get the hell out of here."

"Wait," Brian said, taking the agitated man aside. "Listen. My partner's had a rough time of it lately," he whispered. "Wife wants a divorce and everything he owns," he fibbed.

"Yeah, well that doesn't give him the right to push me around like that. I have rights," the man insisted.

"You're absolutely right."

"I may be a derelict, but your partner is derelict in his duty."

"Hey, that's a good one. Pretty damn sharp," *for a drunkard*, Brian wanted to add. "Didn't know you were a wordsmith, Roy."

"You can tell 'im I said so, too, for all I care."

"I will. And I'll even take it up with his boss. How's that?" Detective Brian Archer promised in appeasement. "And believe-you-me, he'll read him the riot act. Know why?"

The vagrant shook his head.

"Boss doesn't like him. That's why," Brian confided in all seriousness.

"I'm not surprised," the vagabond grumbled, picking up his matches and stuffing the pocket lining material back into his pants—straightening out the rumpled shoulder that Gary had ruffled along with what little pride the man maintained. "And I hope his wife *does* take everything he owns. Then he'll know what it's like," he resonated in a high nasal pitch before sneezing, whizzing and wiping his runny nose along the sleeve of his coat.

"You're probably right, Roy. Listen. I've got to ask you an

important question. And I want you to think real hard. All right?"

Roy Davidson nodded.

"Did you happen to see or hear a train go by around the time you had the liquor store owner call the police?"

"You mean the seven thirty-seven?"

"That's exactly what I mean."

"Sure."

"How come so sure?"

"Well, that's around the time I go to work."

"Work?"

"Yeah, work. Unless the police drive by, that is. Then I just wait for them to leave."

"And do what?"

"You know."

Brian thought he did. "Tell me anyhow."

"You gonna arrest me?"

"Not unless you murdered someone," the detective assured him.

"I ask the folks on the platform for spare change," Roy confessed.

"That's it?"

The man shrugged. "Sometimes a cigarette or matches."

"And you did that tonight, Roy?"

Roy nodded.

"Before or after the train pulled in?"

"Both."

Brian smiled and stuck the lining of the man's coat pockets back in for him. "So, then you saw all those people getting on and off the train tonight?"

"Yes."

"Did you discover the boy before or after the train pulled out?"

Roy Davidson looked around nervously. "After."

Brian took out a small pad and peered down at his notes. "Roy."

"Yes, sir?"

"You told the police earlier that you don't come around here often."

"That's right."

"Yet, you knew exactly—to the minute—what time tonight's train was due in."

"Uh-huh. 'Cause I wanted to be here and score some change. The schedule's posted right over there on the wall," he added defensively, pointing across the street to the newly renovated railroad station.

"But you were here much earlier. Yes?"

Roy looked around as if in search of the answer. "I hung around and drank a little wine while waitin' for the train. Not sure what time it really was. Didn't see the boy till I lit up a cigarette down there. That's when I saw him in the web."

But Brian was shaking his head, deciding to take a shot in the dark. "It says here in my notes that a neighbor on this block, who saw you loitering *hours* earlier, notified the police," he lied. "Yet you swore to the police that you just got here this evening, found the body, and reported it immediately."

Roy Davidson wanted to run. "Oh, you mean *early* this mornin' when I brought the newspapers in for Mr. Castro at the card store . . . and the corner coffee shop."

"Right. Early this morning," Brian agreed.

"Yeah, well. I take the stack of papers in, untie them, count and put 'em on the shelf."

"And how often do you do that, Roy?"

Roy shrugged. "Every now and then."

"What time this morning were you here, Roy? I want the truth this time."

"Five-thirty," he answered, staring down at the ground.

"Hang around after that?"

"Had a cup of coffee and . . ."

"And what?"

"Waited for the train."

"The early morning train."

Roy swallowed hard and nodded his head.

"And what time does that train arrive?"

"Six o-seven. It's posted over there on the wall," he repeated anxiously.

"And?"

"And I went over to the people to ask for change."

"Eastbound or westbound train?"

"Westbound. Toward the city."

"After that, what did you do, Roy? Oh, but before you answer me, I want you to note that my partner standing over there, all pissed off like he is, goes absolutely nuts if he thinks somebody's lying to us. By tomorrow morning when the stores open up, we're going to know where you were or weren't anyhow. So. Where did you go after that, Roy?"

Roy was staring westbound and wishing that he was far, far away. "I went into the basement of the building."

"And found the boy's body then and there. Didn't you?"

Roy nodded quickly.

"Why did you wait so long to report it, Roy?"

Roy looked over at Detective Archer's partner. "I was scared."

"Scared of what?"

"That the police might think I did it or know who did it and lock me up."

"So, what made you decide to finally report it?"

"Well, I waited around thinkin' that the guys might come back. Figured if I could identify them, there might be a reward. That it might be my ticket the hell out of here. But they didn't come back, and it was gettin' dark."

"What guys might come back?"

"Members of a gang I sometimes see."

"What gang?"

Roy Davidson shrugged. "Just some gang I saw a while ago. This summer. I mean, who else could have done that kind of thing to a kid?"

Brian smiled and shook his head in mild frustration. "Got anybody else in mind, Roy? Anyone getting on or off that train who looked suspicious? Anyone from the neighborhood?"

Roy shook his head, but leaned in toward Brian Archer, taking the detective into his confidence. "Not from the train or the neighborhood, Detective. But if I were you, I'd question that colored person standin' over there in the shadows. Stranger. Never saw him 'round here before. If you ask me, I'd say he has the look of a killer."

Brian looked over his right shoulder, taking in the figure standing on the platform. "Killer, huh?"

"Bet a belt of Bourbon on it."

"You would?"

"Absolutely. The police took mine away little while ago and never gave it back."

Brian grinned and called out to the man standing on the platform. "Hey, you! Get over here."

The imposing figure looked down and across the street at Archer like he was crazy. "Say what?"

"You heard me. Get the hell over here."

The man came bounding down the steps of the platform and across the street. "Yeah?"

In a state of uneasiness and confusion, Roy Davidson stepped behind Archer.

Gary York started walking back into their midst but was halted by his partner's gesture.

"You a killer?" Brian Archer asked the tall black man standing before him. "Better tell us the truth."

"Fuckin' A, I'm a killer," Justin Barnes admitted, going along with the program. "Why? Who wants to know?"

"Damn," Archer said, taking his wallet from his front pocket. "How much is a decent pint of Bourbon, J?"

"Sawbuck. Why?"

"Just lost a bet. Here," he said, handing over his card along with a twenty dollar bill to Davidson. "Half of this goes toward a hot meal, Roy. Promise me."

Roy Davidson was gratefully nodding and shaking Brian's hand.

"You hang around and keep your eyes and ears open. Your mouth shut. You learn anything, you give me a call. I'll see that you receive a little reward for your trouble—now and then. A big one if you help us find who we're looking for. All right?"

"Absolutely, Detective."

"Erase that last word from your vocabulary," Brian ordered.

"Oh, absolutely."

In a flash, the homeless man was gone.

"What the fuck was that all about?" Justin asked impatiently.

"Recruitment," Brian offered with a wink.

"Yeah, well, as I remember it, I had to go through several

interviews then sell my fucking soul to the devil before Theo *recruited* me."

"Yeah, well, as I recall, you had a five-course meal at Bella Sera and was offered a salary that rivals mine."

"Theo *did* recognize talent when he saw it; didn't he, Bri?" Justin grinned from ear to ear, displaying the whitest of white teeth.

"Can anyone join this circle jerk, now that that bum has gone?" York said, sauntering over to the pair. "You're such a soft touch, Bri."

"Well, that bum just confirmed the body was there prior to six a.m. this morning."

"I knew that prick was fucking lying. He know anything?"

Justin laughed. "Yeah, he knew he was gettin' a pint of Jack Daniel's. Hustled you good, Brian," he goaded. "Knows and saw jack shit, right? Tell 'im I'm right."

"Listen, had *you* spotted for what you are," Brian came back with a gun-finger pointed at Justin's head.

"And as attested to by our illustrious head of homicide," Gary unloaded and laughed, giving Justin both barrels—for what it was worth.

Playfully, Justin stepped back as though he had, indeed, been shot. "You guys are just plain jealous—" he quickly recouped "—that no civilian review board will ever be breathing down *my* neck. I simply don't exist. A nonentity. A phantom in the night."

"Oh, yeah? Not according to a couple of nosy newspaper reporters to who we have to keep spinning stories of our own to cover your ass," Gary reminded his cohort. "Hey! I have a great idea."

"What?" Brian asked with amusement, reading the ensuing humor holding in his partner's eyes.

"We have Justin kill the lieutenant. It's perfect."

The three of them laughed until it hurt. It was a good release for what had been raging inside them: the mounting anger at what they had witnessed earlier in the basement of the burnt-out abandoned building. The trio was inured to scenes involving murders of the most gruesome kind. Virtually everyone connected with their business grew accustomed to it—regardless of how heinous the act. The exception? The vicious and malicious killing of a child.

Chapter 15

Forensic pathologist, Marcus Ullman; hair and fiber examiner, Peter Danowski; serologist, Ian Quinn; forensic consultant and photographer, Nicholas Kemp; clinical and forensic psychiatrist, Otto Lang–M.D.; forensic psychiatric associate, Larry Silver–M.D.; knot expert, Ted Zimmer—along with Detective Lieutenant Ethan Powell, Commanding Officer of the Homicide Squad, Suffolk County Police Department, all converged within a corner of the brightly illuminated crawlspace within the abandoned building where Nolan Andrews' body hung suspended forward like a giant insect captured in a colossal web.

The gathering was unprecedented, simply explained away as a *'you have to be here to believe it'* scenario. It took a good part of the night to amass the host of professionals in their related fields of expertise. Ted Zimmer had been helicoptered up from Delaware.

Case Detective Brian Archer was informed by the lieutenant that all reports would be forthcoming the moment they were filed. Brian, Gary and Justin were still out scouring the neighborhood in the vicinity of the train station for a lead.

"Spider Hitches," the knot authority nodded knowingly, studying the series of wraps hooked to the overhead that suspended the twelve-year-old's body in a corner of the shallow space. "Nail Knots at the extremities."

"Including those attached to his hair?" the hair and fiber examiner questioned, taking an exemplar from the corpse's scalp.

"Nail Knots. Each and every one of them. Quite secure, in fact."

"Is the perp a pro with knots, or not—is what I need to know for openers, Ted?" Lieutenant Powell put forth directly.

Ted shook his head.

"How do you know?"

"Look for yourself, Lieutenant"

"Yeah, right. I wouldn't know a knot from a pretzel twist unless it was tied as such. "

Ted Zimmer smiled. "Come over here. This isn't brain surgery, Ethan."

The lieutenant crawled closer to the corner.

"Look at the wrap just below the hook here," the knot maven directed.

"What am I looking for?"

"Sloppy work."

"Looks pretty damn neat to me."

"To the naked eye, perhaps. Now look at it through the magnifier." Ted handed over the lens.

The lieutenant focused on the knot. "Yeah?"

"See how it's crisscrossed there?"

"Uh-huh."

"Sloppy. And again, here. See this one?"

The lieutenant focused on another knot. "Gotcha."

"Gotcha!" A blinding bright light from an electronic flash briefly added to the refulgence. Nick Kemp laughed, photographing the lieutenant holding and looking through the magnifying glass.

"What the hell are you doing?" Lieutenant Powell demanded to know.

"*Newsday's* front page photo for tomorrow morning; story on page three," the consultant/photographer kibitzed. "**New Homicide Boss: Trace Evidence with a Twist.** How's that for a headline? Or how about, **Getting Down and Back To Basics**?" he stated gamesomely.

"How 'bout with a picture of *my* body on page two, Nick?" Justin announced cheerfully, carefully reentering the space through an opening of crumbled red brick wall converging with a rusted out metal framework window. "I think this building is about to collapse."

"You're supposed to be out there, Barnes," the lieutenant snapped through clenched teeth.

"What, and miss this mass meeting of minds that truly matter?

Why, I ain't seen such collective talent since I served as tunnel chief for a think tank on how to make good our escape route out of the big house," Justin joked boisterously, referring to his prison stint in upstate New York, as well as Wyoming. "Or was it a stink tank—as us shitheads never made it past the sewer to the first plateau."

"Think you might hold it down a bit and let everyone do their job?" the top cop suggested with malice.

"Sorry, boss."

"Hiya, J," one of the two psychiatrists called over.

"Hey, Otto. How you been, man?"

"Been better. Is this a scene or what?"

"One for the books, for sure. Want my gut reaction on the unsub?"

"Sure. Shoot."

"Only a mother could love 'im," Justin jawed.

"Got that right."

"What kind of label you gonna attach to our lunatic, Larry?" Justin asked the other psychiatrist. "I mean, without the psychobabble."

"Gee, J. At first glance, your own dementia comes immediately to mind."

"That's what I like about Larry, fellas. Direct and to the point." Justin turned on his heels to face the serologist. "So, what are you doin' here, Ian? Peter prick himself or what? I thought they only called you out for half a pint or better. You here to collect blood, ask for donations, or simply take up limited space?"

"Nah. I thought we'd get lucky and maybe collect saliva from the knots our maniac tied. Gentleman here says a little lubrication goes a long way in securing them. We'll see," the man added pessimistically, working with gloved hands and a fistful of cotton swabs, carefully taking single samples and placing each within a rectangular box stacked with breathable containers. "Never saw such long hair on a young boy like this in my life. Like something right out of *Gulliver's Travels*."

"Who's the new guy, Marcus?" Justin pried, gesturing to the fellow next to the lieutenant.

"Ted Zimmer. Up from Delaware. Knot master," the crew chief replied.

"Ah, so you're the main man here, huh?"

Zimmer ignored Justin, continuing his conversation with the lieutenant.

"The master of 'beknottedness,'" Justin threw out for a rise—a little known reference attributed to the nineteenth century scientist and mathematician mentioned in the introduction of Zimmer's illustrated *Encyclopedia of Knots*.

The man faced briskly about. "You read my book?" the author questioned with some surprise.

"Nope, just peeked at some of the pictures," Justin remarked behind a big white smile.

Ted Zimmer went back to explaining why the killer had used a series of Spider Hitches hooked along the overhead beams in lieu of a more advantageous knot. The lieutenant was nodding his understanding.

"They're certainly simpler and faster to tie than say the Bimini Twist," Zimmer pontificated. "The problem is that the Spider Knot can cut itself if it's not properly executed. See right there?"

The lieutenant focused the magnifying lens on the line running from the boy's thumb to a beam above him. "Yep."

"I don't think time was a factor here," Justin interjected.

"Butt out, Barnes," Powell barked.

But Zimmer accepted the challenging remark. "No, let him speak; that is, if you don't mind, Lieutenant," the expert encouraged. "I'll give him just enough rope to hang himself," he quipped in a condescending tone.

"Fine," Powell acquiesced with a degree of disdain directed at Justin.

"Well?" Zimmer invited.

"Well, just look all around you, gentlemen. Four feet by what? Ten feet of fucking web: monofilament, fluorocarbon, and braid."

"Half these knots were tied elsewhere, Mr. Barnes," Zimmer explained. "Rather intricate knots at that."

"True—and where the killer had all the time in the world to tie them to the boy's hair, fingers, toes, tongue—even his penis and testicles. Nail Knots. About as secure a knot as you can manage, considering the diameter."

"Correct. But after he brought the body in here, he had to work fast in order to finish up and get out—so as to avoid detection. Hence, the Spider Hitches, which expedited the procedure."

"If he was so hellbent on getting out fast, he would have used an even simpler knot and hooked them to the overhead. Not to mention the time it took to tie in all these cross-strands. Scores of them. Look, I'm not saying he's an expert tier and knows knots like you. Call him an aficionado at best. But he's made it his business to know knots and their applications. He's already demonstrated that he has a definite working knowledge of both cordage and line such as this. What I think, Zimmer, is that you're so focused on these knots and what *you* might have used instead, that you're losing sight of the big picture that's staring you right in face. Knots connected to the killer's simple message."

"Which is?" the knot master asked curiously.

"That *quite* a web was spun."

"So, you're saying that he chose the Spider and Nail Knot for . . . for what exactly?"

"Theater," Justin answered in all seriousness.

"Theater?" Zimmer echoed.

"Theatrics," Justin expanded. "High drama."

Three of the men, working in the background, nodded and voiced their agreement. The others, exclusive of the lieutenant, kept their tongue.

"I think you're out of line, Barnes," Powell quipped. "Also, out of your league," he added for good measure. "Mr. Zimmer reviewed the other pics we have as well and feels, as I do, that the homicides are not necessarily connected. All right?"

Justin smiled. "Hence, we have what's known as the Great Divide, folks. But not to worry. Someone can simply ask the serial killer, nicely, when we nail 'im," he jabbed away in kind.

"That's only if that someone gives him half a chance," Larry Silver frowned bitterly, staring Justin in the eyes.

"Hey, that's not fair, Doc. I give 'em all a chance."

"That's funny because I never got to ask any one of them. Columba or Emery or Emery's accomplice."

"Larry's just sore, guys, because he looks at everything as job security," Justin explained in a hushed tone.

"No, no; I heard about you, Barnes," Zimmer admonished the

man.

"Dat right? All da way down dere in Delaware, did ya, Teddy? Well, don't believe everythin' you hear 'cause dat's what legends and myths are made of, my man. Oh, and before I forget. There's a Clover Knot on the back of the middle finger of the boy's right hand, in case you missed it. Look at it as a mnemonic cue reminding you that Nolan Andrews is his *fourth* victim. Note the number of knots and little loops that form it. Like an abacus, hotshot. Not another knot like it on any of the other nineteen digits—tied with fluorocarbon like on the broach of the Nathan woman. Subtle message for you there, butterfingers," Justin sallied, watching the knot wizard fumble for another of his lenses while scooting around behind the boy's body.

Several warm bodies moved in closer to the kid's suspended stark carcass.

Zimmer found and removed a jeweler's loupe from his vest pocket. "Jesus!" he suddenly exclaimed, holding the 20–power lens up to his eye.

"Let me know when Gary, Brian and I can tie the four cases to a single suspect, Lieutenant." Justin started to make his way back toward the opening. "Unless, of course, you still see things differently."

"Maybe, just maybe, these murders—if the knot even signifies what you think it does, Barnes—were committed by someone working in concert with the perp. Maybe even from another county or state," the detective lieutenant stated angrily, grasping at straws while trying to save face. "Ever think of that, wise guy?"

"Then maybe you should check out the state of Delaware, boss," Justin drawled. "Or better yet, why not get a second opinion from another knothead?"

Nick Kemp could not help but hide his laughing eyes behind a second Nikon camera as he snapped a series of close-up shots of the boy's middle digit.

Chapter 16

Christopher Osip had studied all the reports and evidence in great detail, writing then faxing over his own full-length report to Homicide, along with those of several colleagues, especially with respect to the killer's *web*. There was no question that the clover-shaped loops, knots and material found around the middle digit of Nolan Andrews' right hand were, indeed, distinct from any of the others affixed to the boy's hair and body. The series of wraps, which formed the Clover Knot in question, framed a formidable pattern in Osip's mind, for the tiny leaflets comprising the design were fashioned from fluorocarbon tippet material—not monofilament. Just as Justin Barnes had speculated, the analyst also believed that the four little loops signified victim number four. But the scientist now knew a good deal more.

What also fascinated the forensic investigator were the X-factors; that is, the lengths and diameters of the leader material the killer employed: 0X, 1X, 2X, 3X, 4X, 5X, 6X and 7X, fashioned from monofilament. Chris Osip grew excited and called a meeting.

"I'm not sure I follow this X business, Chris," Detective Archer said from his seat in a conference room as he stared down at a preliminary report.

"Let's just hold off on that for a minute, Bri," Chris Osip replied. "The lieutenant said he'd be right down." The assembled group heard footsteps and turned their heads toward the doorway. "Speak of the devil."

"I second that," Justin jeered.

"Got that right," Detective Gary York agreed with a smirk.

"Behave yourselves, guys," Archer warned.

The lieutenant entered the room and immediately took a seat. He looked exhausted.

"Sorry, boys and girls. The D.A. forgets that I'm as new as he is but still thinks Rome was built in a day. I told him we're making headway on this case and that I'd get back to him right after this meeting. Am I going to have anything *new* to tell him? Or should I just keep blowing smoke up his butt?"

"Is that anything like kissin' it, boss?" Justin blasted from behind a big grin.

Brian sighed deeply and shook his head.

"Because I can tell you before we even get started here that we at least know our boy can count," Justin pressed. "Think that'll make the D.A.'s day? You can tell him, too, that we're gonna nail this guy's ass to the wall just as soon as our illustrious leader wakes up and points the way. How's that for fresh information?"

"You know something that I don't know, Barnes? Or are you the one blowing smoke right now?"

"Lieutenant. J. Please, guys," Chris tried to intercede.

"*Several things* in answer to question number one, Lieutenant," Justin rejoined. "And *yes* to number two, 'cause when I blow smoke, bossman, you can bet your butt it's followed by fire."

"You're really full of yourself this morning, Barnes. Wouldn't you say?"

"I'd say we'd be further along the line if you'd pool your people and point them in the right direction instead of splitting the team and sending us off on wild-goose chases. You wanna tell the D.A. something? You tell 'im we got a solitary serial killer on the loose, but that you got us out there lookin' for multiple personalities."

"Justin," Chris pleaded anew. "Please."

From a front row seat, Gary York turned around and smiled with satisfaction, taking in every stone face in the room.

"Just who the hell do you think you're talking to, Barnes? Huh?" Powell demanded.

"A man with his head in the sand and his big donkey ass stickin' out, just askin' for a kickin'," Justin answered straightaway. "A man who's wastin' everyone's time and puttin' other lives at risk."

If Team Three could have read the color building and burning within the core of the lieutenant's body, radiating rapidly through his neck and face, they would have witnessed a shade of red as bright as the fire extinguisher hanging on the wall off the alcove. Both black men locked their eyes on one another in the heat of the moment.

"You know, I can have you transferred the hell out of here in a heartbeat, fella. You realize that? Insubordination. In front of how many witnesses?"

But Barnes was shaking his head. "No can do, boss. I don't exist. I'm a nonentity. You can have me removed from the team, but you can't have somebody who doesn't exist transferred. To the outside world, I'm just a private consultant."

Christopher Osip knew it was high time to earnestly interrupt. "GENTLEMEN! Please. With all due respect, sir, maybe this, uh, discussion could be put on hold till after my briefing. I believe the update here will help you decide the best course of action to take."

"Fine. We've wasted enough time already. Let's get started. Shall we, Barnes?" Detective Lieutenant Ethan Powell barked.

"Yes, sir," Justin agreed.

Another detective entered the room and immediately took a seat beside York.

"I'm sure by now that most of you have questions regarding the X-factors," Osip began. "First off, I want to explain that tapered fly-fishing leaders come in three different lengths: seven-and-a-half feet, nine feet, and twelve feet. The perp used all three lengths of varying X-factors to connect the victim's hair, fingers, toes, tongue, penis and testicles to overhead hooks. Common cup hooks made of brass. A multitude of the monofilament material, sold in individual packages, was employed. Also, four short strands of fluorocarbon tippet material of four different diameters were used to form the loops of the Clover Knot. First, we'll address the leader material.

"Now, tapered leader diameters are assigned X-sizes: 0X, 1X, 2X, 3X, 4X, 5X, 6X and 7X, representing thicknesses measured in thousandths of an inch—the X-reference making it a bit easier to follow. For example, a 1X seven-and-a-half foot tapered leader—ninety inches in overall length—is sectioned off as indicated on the chart up here." The scientist directed everyone's attention to the placard sitting on an easel before them.

1X

LENGTH OF SECTION IN INCHES	DIAMETER OF SECTION IN INCHES
24	.019
16	.017
14	.015
9	.013
9	.011
18	.010

"The diameter of the first twenty-four inches referencing the 1X tapered leader is point 019 inches; that is, nineteen thousandths of an inch. The next sixteen inches is point 017, et cetera, et cetera. X-sizes run between 0X to 4X with regard to those seven-and-a-half-foot leaders, 0X to 5X re nine-foot leaders, and 0X to 7X with respect to twelve-foot leaders—7X being the largest diameter and consequently the strongest leader. The end of a fly-fishing leader, the last and thinnest section, may be referred to as the tippet.

"What's interesting to note with reference to the three lengths of leader material is that the number four seems to have some significance here, too. In a systematic pattern, the killer spun his web, if you will, beginning with 0X on the victim's pinky, using graduated thicknesses of the mono material while working in sets of four before moving on to the next heavier-test leaders. The longer and stronger nine and twelve-foot tapered lengths were used to help suspend the body, along with SpiderWire, a super strong synthetic braided line, given its diameter."

Several detectives were buying into what Osip was selling—the idea that the number four might, indeed, be significant.

A female investigator nodded in agreement and commented.

"Could be a kind of accounting—accounting for the fact that we've had four murders in four months," the veteran detective tabled. "It seems that our guy, through the Andrews kid, is also giving us the middle finger, if you ask me. If the killer is one and the same person, this could be his way of keeping score, kind of like the notches made on some guns. My father used a file to cut a V-shape in the stock of his rifle whenever he killed a squirrel on our property. He called them 'fucking rats with tails,'" she expanded with a pretty smile.

"But why on the victim's third finger?" a skeptical detective sitting beside her threw out with a questionable look. "Why not the fourth digit if that number is so important? And why's it have to be a guy, Hanover? I know some pretty nasty broads out there on those mean streets. Even nastier than you," he rankled his partner.

"Because if it were a gal, Fuller, she'd have embroidered the number on your nuts," the seasoned detective swore.

"Might if she was as uptight as you, Lorna," the man retorted.

"Uptight's not my problem, mister; that is, if my partner were truly upright," she came back at him, slowly curling a limp forefinger downward into a fist.

"Then maybe *you* should drive next time out while *I* just sit back and relax," he suggested, navigating a palm across the top of his fiancée's knee.

Detective Lorna Hanover smirked. "We tried that once. Remember, sport? It wasn't me who ran out of gas," she declared, swatting his hand away.

"Girl just can't handle rejection," Detective Wayne Fuller announced in self-defense.

"No, it's a reject that I can't quite handle," the woman countered.

Several snickers surrounded the pair.

"This is what you give me to watch my back, Lieutenant?" Fuller feigned in framing his complaint.

"So try sending your partner on ahead, first," Ethan Powell suggested. "Then you can watch *her* back," he funned, relieved that the focus of ridicule had shifted to the rank and file. "How's that sound?"

"Works for me," the cop agreed, suggestively running a fingertip along the side of Hanover's thigh.

"Tell you what," the lieutenant reconsidered. "I'll give you Barnes for a week. Seven days with him, and you'll be begging me to have her back. Whattaya say, Fuller?"

"Nah, I'll work with what I got, thank you very much."

"That's what I thought. So, listen up, people. I'm still not convinced we're dealing with a single lunatic here. First and third murders strongly suggest an insurance angle. Second and fourth do not. You all know the bylaws and bywords of a homicide investigation. *Follow the money.* A middle-aged waitress, Denise Nathan, leaves her family a tidy sum from a life insurance policy. Salvatori Passaro, the uncle of Gretchen Bowers, suddenly disappears off the face of the earth after collecting on a hefty life insurance policy following his release from Pilgrim State. Two female victims, mind you. William Walker and Nolan Andrews show no definitive connection to those two cases."

"Lieutenant."

"Yes, Osip?"

"I haven't finished here."

"How much longer is this going take?" their commanding officer asked politely but impatiently, consulting his watch.

"Not five minutes, sir."

"Fine. Wind it up. Everybody here have a copy of your update?"

"They will have, sir," Chris acknowledged, anxiously tapping the stacks of papers on the table next to him that needed collating. "But first I want everyone's attention back up here."

The lieutenant leaned back in his chair and stretched. "Floor's all yours."

"Thank you. Now. What we initially found on the Nathan woman was a pin. A stickpin on the lapel of her blouse. A feathered stickpin—repaired with a single half hitch to hold a pair of tiny wings in place. We were not aware of its significance until Mr. Barnes followed up with the lab and found that the material used was fluorocarbon. A single loop finishes that wrap, encircling the head of the pin. Clarence Emery utilized fly-tying material involving one of his victims as some of you certainly recall.

"William Walker had a double loop of fluorocarbon tippet material affixed to the back of a resewn button on his shirt," Chris continued.

Chris turned a page of his report, paused and sneezed. "Excuse me."

"*Gesundheit.*"

"*Danke*. The Bowers woman had a bow in her hair, wrapped with fluorocarbon. We missed it because we weren't looking for it, tied off in a—" Chris held up three fingers and sneezed again. "—tri-knot. Justin Barnes found and noted them, also.

"And, of course, the Andrews boy matches the pattern perfectly. Kim printed out an Orvis catalog's Knotted Leader Formula for the three lengths and their corresponding X-factors from 0X through 7X, in addition to their approximate pound-test strengths in both monofilament and fluorocarbon. It's all there in the update.

"Oh, one final thing. Kim ran the probability of coincidence through Big Sister. Statistically," Chris turned another page, "the likelihood of coincidence regarding this theory is—well—to tell you the truth, I can't even read the number because it's got so many zeros," the investigator solemnly stated. "But let's just say for the sake of argument, that in terms of percentages, what we're dealing with here is more conclusive than DNA."

The lieutenant was rotating his head along his shoulders; first one way, and then the other. "Why wasn't this information given to me before the start of this briefing?" he questioned Osip crisply.

"You were in a meeting and told me you'd look at it later," Chris answered bluntly.

"But at the start of this meeting I asked you if there was anything new that I could tell the D.A."

"You asked *them*, Lieutenant, and I was trying to—"

The lieutenant put out the palm of his hand like a stop sign. "All right. Barnes. I want you working with Archer and York. Find the common denominator among these four murders—if there is one. The rest of you work the old files on Clarence Emery and Malcolm Columba. Report to Archer. Find the link. We're working on the assumption that we're dealing with a single killer. A serial killer."

Justin laughed aloud. "An assumption?"

"Don't push it, Barnes, or I'll put you with Hanover. Put her in charge of your sorry ass."

"Under or over Detective Hanover is fine by me, boss. That's if she don't mind." Justin grinned from ear to ear, staring down Fuller who was making a fist and a face.

"Mind? Why, I'd even sit in your lap and steer, J," Detective Lorna Hanover swore, calling their commanding officer's bluff, sending Justin an appreciative wink before turning around and facing her partner fully—making the sign of waving antlers followed by the protuberance of a long, pink tongue.

"Never mind," Powell recanted. "I want every swinging dick and damsel fully focused. Twenty-four/seven. Dos-à-dos your partner, Detective Fuller. Meaning, keep it in your pants till you're off duty. Let's find this fucker and fast."

Thirteen detectives, inclusive of their newly appointed commanding officer, rose to the occasion. Detective Yolanda Ivers helped sort and staple the updated report for the others, handing them out before heading toward the door and down the hallway.

Detectives Lorna Hanover and Wayne Fuller stood playfully back to back, gun-fingers propped skyward and at the ready before pacing off several yards. Elevator doors suddenly opened. Kim Archer appeared as the incorrigible pair turned, leveled their sights at one another, then fired.

"Oh, very sweet, you two," Kim said decidedly. "You should have had that showdown some years ago," she told the divorcé and divorcée. "You would have saved your former partners a great deal of grief," the computer maven needled, holding open the door for the frolicsome twosome.

"Nice work, Kim," Lorna said sincerely, ignoring the analyst's bedeviled remarks.

"Justin deserves the credit. Going down?"

"Just as soon as we wrap this up," Lorna decided, grabbing Fuller by the front of his belt and pulling him toward the waiting platform car—circling a tongue seductively around her full lips for Kim's benefit.

Wayne flashed his own tongue for the full effect.

"Licentious louts," Kim scolded sportively.

"What did she just say about us?" he questioned in mock confusion.

"That we're a pair of horny blunderheads," Lorna translated.

"I think she's got us pegged, partner," Wayne conceded above the sound of the buzzing alarm as the pair got into the elevator and Kim stepped out completely.

"Bye," Hanover waved to her colleague.

Kim smiled fondly, wiggling four slender fingers in parting as the doors closed and the pair descended. Taking in the tiny artwork painted upon each fingernail: pumpkins, cornstalks, a ghost, cat, and a witch riding a broom, the computer maven headed down the hall to find the lieutenant.

Chapter 17

"Hi, Daddy."

"Hi, kiddo."

"Want to hear what I wrote for school tomorrow?"

"Sure, but not right now, sweetheart. Daddy's very busy."

"I got an A plus from Miss Ellison on my last English assignment. Know what she said about my writing?"

"No, what?"

"She said, and I quote, 'You could be a writer one day.'"

"Me?"

"Not you, Daddy. Me!"

"Oh."

"Then she asked me if I had any help at home with my assignments, and I told her that my parents do *not* help me with *any* of my homework."

"Good for you, kiddo."

"What are you writing, Daddy?"

"A report."

"For work?"

"Uh-huh."

"About murder?"

"Uh-huh."

"Why do you always have to write about murder?"

"That's my job. That's what I do, kiddo. But sometimes I report on other things."

"What are all those X's for?"

Chris Osip looked up from his work. "Will you let me do this in peace, please?"

"Why won't you tell me?"

"Because it's not for your pretty little eyes or ears. That's why."

"Why don't you write about something nice for a change?"

"Like what?"

"Like a story with a happy ending."

"Many of my stories have happy endings."

"They do not."

"Sure they do."

"Do not. First, because they're really not stories. They're reports. Secondly, because the bad guys usually get away."

"That's not true."

"It is true. Mommy even says so."

"Does she now?"

Vivian nodded emphatically, unfolding her essay and placing it on the desk next to her father's papers.

"What else did she say?"

"That what you do is not a perfect science."

Chris looked back up at his daughter and smiled. "Would you like something very special?"

"What?"

"A good beating?"

Vivian laughed defiantly. "That's what a friend of mine said you people do to suspects. Well, not you particularly, but some of those you work for."

"Oh, really?"

"Yep."

"What else did this friend of yours say?"

"That when the police don't have all the answers, they make them up and make those they have in custody say things they want them to say. And if they don't, they're beaten up."

"Is that a fact?"

"If you had the facts, there wouldn't be a problem. Right?"

"Let me tell you something, Little Miss Know-It-All. When your daddy submits a report, it's filled with irrefutable facts that help the police find and put away the bad guys—sometimes for good. Know what irrefutable means?"

Vivian shook her head.

"It means that they're inarguably true."

"If your facts are inarbl–in-argu-ably true, then how come criminals sometimes get away with murder? How come sometimes murderers are later found to be innocent, Mister Big Shot? Huh?" Vivian stubbornly folded her arms across her chest. "Answer me that."

"Because the system isn't perfect. That's why."

"And aren't you part of the system, Daddy? Can't your ir-irre-irrefrutable facts—"

"Irrefutable."

"Can't your irrefutable facts sometimes be mistaken, mister?"

"You know, you remind me of this five-foot-two female defense attorney who I can't stand."

"Answer the question," Chris Osip's daughter demanded, stamping her foot down firmly upon the wood-planked floor of her father's home office.

"Yes, but not when the chance of error is one hundred billion, nine hundred and ninety-nine million and—"

"Ah, but still a chance of error, you will have to admit. So there. I rest my case."

"Listen, you little shrimp. I—"

Vivian snatched up the composition and walked away with the tips of her forefingers planted firmly in each ear.

"You're gonna cop the beating of your life, you little twit," her father called out with half a smile plastered across his face, gradually metamorphosing into a saddened frown.

Chapter 18

A cold November evening chilled Kalvin Matheson to the bone as he knocked and waited patiently by the front door of Emily Schroeder's residence. A moment later, the big woman answered from behind the thick horseshoe-shaped wooden-slatted portal.

"Yes?"

"Doctor Vale sent me over, ma'am."

"Who?"

"Commissioner Vale from the Center."

"What is this about?"

"He needs a favor."

"Well, what does he want?"

"Can you open the door so we can talk?"

"We can talk right here. What is it?"

"I'd rather do this face to face. We need to talk in private."

"Why doesn't he call me on the phone?"

"He tried. He told me your line is dead."

Emily Schroeder stepped back from the door and went over to her telephone. A moment later, she came back to the door.

"Who are you?"

"Kalvin Matheson, ma'am. You had my brother Alvin in your ward at Pilgrim State."

"You're his brother?"

"Yes, ma'am. Was. He's since passed on, as I think you know. I met you a few times before your retirement."

"If you're really Alvin Matheson's brother, take out your driver's license and pass it through the mailbox in the wall to your right. Then I'll open the door."

Kalvin reached for his wallet and did as the woman instructed. Sixty seconds later, he stood in the hallway of the woman's home.

"An old woman living alone can't be too careful, you know," she declared, punctuating her sentence with a single nod, handing Kalvin back his license. "Close the door behind you. You're letting out all the heat."

"Oh, you're really not that old, Mrs. Schroeder," Kalvin swore politely as he quickly pushed and closed the heavy door. "But believe me I know what you mean about not being too careful. Especially in this day and age."

Emily Schroeder impatiently waved away the comment. "It's got nothing to do with this day and age, Mr. Matheson. If you worked where I worked, you'd certainly know what I'm talking about. Actually, I'm a bit surprised that you don't—what with a brother like yours, may he rest in peace. Now, what's this business with Doctor Vale that he sends you out on a freezing night like this?"

Kalvin smiled boyishly. "First, let me respectfully say that it does have everything to do with this day and age, for today's your birthday, Emily. Your seventieth, in fact. And I brought you a present." Kalvin tapped his coat pocket. "Nothing elaborate. Just a little something for attending to my brother for all those years."

Emily certainly looked surprised.

"Secondly, Doctor Vale made me promise not to tell that it was he who gave me your address and phone number. But I thought I'd come by in person rather than call and have you tell me that you don't want any visitors or surprises on your birthday. How come you don't have a bell?"

"What?"

"How come you don't have a doorbell? I had to knock." Kalvin put down the collar of his coat.

"It broke a long time ago like many things around this place."

"It's nice and warm in here." Emily's visitor was walking up the hallway.

"Where do you think you're going?"

Kalvin stopped and turned around, standing in a better light.

"My God!" the woman exclaimed

"What?"

"You look just like him."

"Alvin?"

Emily nodded.

"We were identical twins. I'm surprised that you don't remember me." Kalvin grinned and dropped his chin upon a single vertical finger—the sudden noise of clicking teeth startling the woman.

"I don't know if I want you here, Kalvin. Why don't you just tell me what this is all about, then leave."

Kalvin nodded. "It's really very cold out there, but you're absolutely right."

The old woman stepped back as Kalvin reached inside his coat pocket.

"Here, please accept this. It's your birthday present. Go ahead. At least let me have the enjoyment of seeing the expression on your face when you open it. Come on, now. Before I leave."

Emily Schroeder took and shook the rectangular gift box. Something solid shifted around inside.

Kalvin headed back down the hallway toward the front door with Emily right behind him.

"Wait," she said with a tight smile, carefully lifting off the lid.

Kalvin stood staring up at the light fixture hanging from the cathedral ceiling. Three bulbs. Two of which were out.

In the poor light, the old woman peered down anxiously at the item.

"Like it?" Kalvin asked. "One size fits all. Got a ladder around here?" he questioned, staring back up at the fixture. "I might as well fix that while I'm here."

Emily began to cry softly.

"The attachments are in the other pockets of this coat," he explained quietly.

The big woman was shaking her head.

"What's the matter, Mrs. Schroeder? Really not into necklaces?"

Emily's hands were trembling. She lowered her frightened eyes from Kalvin back to the box containing the noose before she dropped it and started to run.

Kalvin grabbed and jabbed her twice with a stun gun as she flailed her arms about insanely. The third shock dropped the big woman to her knees.

"Guess I've got to press and hold it there firmly," he mumbled to himself, withdrawing the prongs of the weapon from her neck. "Now, to find a ladder when what I really need is a crane." Kalvin giggled. "Alvin, if you can hear me, just wait and see what I'll soon be sending over to the other side."

Chapter 19

Emily Schroeder's heavy frame hung high from a torn light fixture in the ceiling. Just above her body, three new bulbs illuminated the crime scene in a bath of intense lighting: four hundred fifty watts. Marcus Ullman's crew was carefully lowering the large woman. One of them handed Brian a noose hanging loosely from around her neck like a necklace.

"Why in the world would the killer bring a noose and separate sections of rope, and then hang her up there with electrical cord?" Detective Lieutenant Powell conferred with Archer and York.

"Electrical cord was probably an afterthought," Gary offered. "Who the hell knows? A traditional hangman's noose has thirteen wraps, not five," he reflected.

"So this is more likely him letting us know that Emily Schroeder is victim number five, figuring maybe he missed his subtle signature regarding the other four," Brian postulated, tracing the five turns of the hangman's noose with his fingertip. "Especially since we've mentioned nothing about knots to the media to date."

"Nor how William Walker actually died or how Gretchen Bowers could have," the lieutenant reminded them. "And let's keep it that way for the time being."

"Better Bowers' heart gave out first than to have continued suffering from asphyxiation at the hands of that conscienceless prick," the pathologist stated, trying to mitigate the horror in his own mind.

"So, what's the story here, Marcus?" the lieutenant pressed.

The man gestured to a half-eaten layer cake sitting in its box on a sideboard behind him. "Death by chocolate," he said with a straight face, making a conscious effort not to cringe before his crew and other colleagues as he heedfully removed the wire ligature from around the woman's neck. Ironically, Marcus Ullman never quite grew accustomed to viewing violent deaths in their surroundings. The good doctor was surely inured to bodies and body parts brought in for autopsy and examination: mutilated, dismembered, decapitated. Being physically present at a crime scene, however, unnerved the man to extremes. Black humor was the man's defense mechanism. "She may or may not have been dead before he ever got her up there, Lieutenant. He incapacitated her with a stun gun. See these marks? Another two here." Marcus was pointing to the burn marks along the side of the woman's neck. "Now, note these two one-inch circular contusions."

"Thumb pressure." Ethan Powell certainly did not need to be told.

"Of the most murderous kind," the forensic pathologist emphasized. "No gloves. Those curved cuts caused by the killer's fingernails dug deeply into her neck. Problem here is that any fingerprints are probably smudged with some kind of oily substance. See? Clever little creep that he most certainly is. Note the abrasion from the braided electrical cord above the bruises. Doesn't conform to the noose."

"Her sheer body weight probably pulled that fixture partway down like that," Gary speculated.

Brian nodded in agreement. "Perp discovers there's several extra feet of electrical cord up there to spare. Shuts off the power and uses the tool he cut the phone wire with to cut the length of cord he needs to suspend her; splices and reconnects the wire. Pretty neatly, I might add. Guy's in no hurry. Changes all three bulbs. Turns the power back on. And then it's showtime."

"Why the rope in two sections, apart from the noose?" Marcus questioned.

"Easy to carry in without being obvious," Gary figured. "One section in one coat pocket. One in the other. The noose presented to her as a present—sick fuck."

Several heads turned to review the gift box and light bulb packaging on the floor.

"But why all the antics?" Marcus pressed.

"High theater," Justin reminded everyone as he entered through the front doorway. "Man's a showman, like I said earlier."

Marcus shrugged indifferently. "Anyhow, I'll probably find the hyoid and thyroid damaged or broken. Tell you more when I have a good look at the windpipe and larynx . . . amount of force exerted via fractured cartilage, et cetera, et cetera."

"And the cake?" Powell questioned. "Any thoughts on that? Anyone."

"Oh, sure," Marcus answered up smartly. "Double-dark chocolate layered torte. Raspberry and vanilla. Removed from the kitchen area. Any latent print, reference that finger track through the swirl, belongs to Nick back there," he snitched.

The lieutenant scowled. "You mean the cake wasn't found here on the table?"

"Nope. Just her mail and eyeglasses—along with those two burnt-out bulbs and one good one. Nick brought the cake in from the kitchen while he was working," Marcus ratted out his friend and colleague.

"And what if she was poisoned, Marcus? Like the Andrews kid before he was suspended in a makeshift cobweb," the lieutenant fumed. "Then what?"

"Then I'd have to say the killer wanted to be doubly sure, Lieutenant," Marcus funned.

Brian, Gary and Justin looked at one another, smiled, and simply shook their heads.

"Nick seems pretty quiet back there," the pathologist persisted, glancing toward the kitchen. "He's probably still raiding the refrigerator. I was going to take the rest of the cake home if I finished up before him, but he insisted we share." Marcus frowned, examining the pinpoint hemorrhages surrounding the victim's dilated pupils.

Justin took in Emily Schroeder's ghostly pale countenance— the blue cast of her lips and tongue. "And where's the other sections of rope I heard tell of earlier? Or did it get moved around like the cake, fellas?"

Marcus hunched his shoulders. "Nick did the walk-through. Check with him."

Justin headed toward the kitchen.

Gary and Brian glanced at one another then back to the lieutenant.

"What?" Ethan Powell asked with annoyance.

"Why didn't you tell him?"

"Tell J what?"

"About the rest of the rope—laid out on the floor like a figure eight."

"Let him see it for himself. I want to hear what he has to say without *prefiguring* it. Get it?" Powell questioned half-jokingly.

"Cute," Gary grated. "Very fucking cute. Could mean nothing."

"Well, it sort of looks like a figure eight," Powell added. "Only I'm not really sure that it is, or what the hell it could possibly mean. But it's got to mean something." The lieutenant turned from Gary back to Marcus. "You keep your eyes open for fluorocarbon loops and knots, braid, or any of that monofilament leader."

"Will do, Lieutenant."

Powell headed toward the kitchen.

"Think maybe this *could* be two guys working in concert, Bri?" Gary questioned. "One with line? The other with rope or cord?"

"I don't know what to think anymore."

"Five fucking murders in five months," Justin mumbled to himself, coming back up the hallway with Nick and the lieutenant.

"What's your take on the rope, J?" Brian asked.

"Well, if no one accidentally kicked it with their foot because they had their eye on that fucking cake, I'd say our boy laid out the sign of infinity for us."

Gary considered the notion carefully.

Brian immediately nodded with certainty. "The five wraps in the noose represent victim number five. That rope back there really isn't laid out like a figure eight because the loops are extended, not crisscrossed."

"It just doesn't make any sense," the lieutenant snapped. "A figure eight *knot* might."

"But it's not a knot, Lieutenant."

"Again, it's not overlapping, like you would form a figure eight," Gary reinforced..

"Rather, both sections are lying perfectly flat. He's ruling out the number eight for us. Forming, instead, the sign of infinity. I think Justin's absolutely right."

Brian was nodding in total agreement. "The shape is elongated like the symbol. Definitely not an eight."

"So. Any further thoughts?" the lieutenant invited. "I'll listen to anything at this point, including why Nick, coming down the hallway here—looking for just deserts and just might get more than he bargained for—brought the cake to this table."

"Because I was hungry," the forensic consultant/photographer retorted with some irritation, standing there with two cameras strapped across his chest.

"You actually ate a piece of that goddamn cake?" Powell asked in disbelief.

"Yeah, and I had a glass of milk with it from the refrigerator. Took a piss in her toilet, too—*after* everything was dusted and photographed, Lieutenant. We've been here since eleven—that's a.m., in case you're interested—wondering when you were going to show your face so that we could finally take the body down as you insisted. Know what it's like trying to take close-ups while doing a balancing act on a stepladder?"

"You really ate a piece of cake taken at a crime scene?" he repeated.

"Cause of death is asphyxia, Lieutenant. Either by strangulation or hanging. Not poisoning like the Nolan kid. All right?"

"No, it's not all right."

"Then how about this? Is this all right?"

"What's that?"

"Foil ripped off from a corner cartridge of film."

"Film."

"For a camcorder. Same film I used when I did the walk-through."

"That's not yours?"

Nick shook his head. "I loaded before I got here. The rest are stills."

"Where'd you find it?"

"Under the front of the refrigerator when I dropped the cake fork," the criminalist confessed with a grin. "No sign of any photographic equipment in this house. Not even a Brownie or a box— meaning earlier types of cameras, Lieutenant," the man could not help but tease. "A bit before your time, I'd well imagine."

"Everybody's a comedian," their commander stated with annoyance. "Were you guys able to lift anything from the foil? Maybe my spirits in the bargain?"

The man shook his head. "Just a film of oil—like that substance we found on her neck."

"It fucking figures!" the lieutenant flared.

Chapter 20

Kalvin Matheson parked his dirty dark-blue Camry in front of the bishop's house on Calvary Lane in Lancaster, Pennsylvania. Carrying a large canvas bag in hand, he marched right up to the front door as if he owned the place.

Bishop John was not a bishop in the traditional ecclesiastical sense, but he was unquestionably more powerful than most prelates who supervised churches of considerable size. And although his worshippers were far fewer in terms of number, the man had more hard cold cash put upon the proverbial plate in a given month than most collection baskets drew in a decade.

"Do you have it?" John asked unabashedly.

"I wouldn't be here if I didn't," Kalvin declared, lifting and lowering the hefty bag as if it were an exercise weight.

"All of it?"

Kalvin Matheson hesitated. "Enough to whet your appetite if you satisfy mine," he hedged. "Then you'll get the rest. Not before."

"How much is in there for openers?" John asked coolly.

"Half a mil. Large bills."

John shrugged indifferently. "Well, you're here anyhow, so come on in and warm yourself by the fireplace. Put your offering down by the hearth, but not *too* close," he warned with a winning smile. "We wouldn't want your hopes and dreams going up in smoke, now would we?"

"Certainly not."

No sooner was Kalvin settled and comfortable when a man servant came forward for the bag.

"It's all right, Kalvin. Let Timmy take it. He just wants to be sure that—"

"Every dollar is there," Kalvin interrupted defensively.

"What you mean to say is half of what we agreed on is there, less interest charges, as I'm sure you realize that this first installment is a wee bit late. Immortality doesn't come cheap, Kalvin. And you do realize that you and Alvin are actually receiving two for the price of one."

"And well we should, being as we're coming in on this ground-floor opportunity."

But the bishop was shaking his head. "The ground-floor opportunity was months ago, Kalvin Matheson. I extended the deadline as a favor to you because you were having a little problem raising the cash, you said. You're getting a bargain here, and you know it. Think about it. Everlastingness."

It was now Kalvin who was shaking his head. "I'm not a fool, Bishop. Cloning is a far cry from Alvin and me living on forever. Cloning is not going to bring my brother back from the dead."

"Cloning, Kalvin, is about as close as we're going to come to creating another you and yours."

Again, Kalvin shook his head in disagreement. "Wrong on that count, too, Bishop. Twins are about as close as a creator can get to identical. Identical twins rule supreme," he added and smiled with satisfaction. "An artificial clone is essentially *less* identical than that."

"Only as things stand now, Kalvin. But in time, I can assure you that Alvin and Kalvin are going to come out on top."

"Maybe."

"No maybes about it. Science is providing a greater hope at this very moment than traditional religions could ever offer anyone in asking you to accept *their* doctrines based solely on faith. True?"

"Yet, you yourself offer up this packaged deal as a brand of religion. Do you not, John? Right down to your taking the title of a clergyman."

"But it's a package no longer shrouded in mystery and mystique—embracing both worlds, if you will. The physical as well as the spiritual. Science and religion standing side by side. Imagine. The miracle of creating the first human clone is about to be unveiled. Soon, there will no longer be a division of church and state. But rather a union. And may I remind you, too, that I was appointed, Kalvin. I assumed nothing on my own. Including my title." Bishop John sat down beside the new member. "Tea while we wait?"

"Sure. Why not? It's cold as death out there."

"I assume that Alvin's and your cultures have been delivered and stored safely?" John asked through a yawn.

"Yes, the lab is quite satisfied."

"Good. Relax and we'll enjoy a little tea and talk. I've got some very exciting things to tell and show you. You won't believe your ears, but you'll have to believe your eyes."

The bishop summoned forth his housekeeper and ordered tea and cake. Moments later, John produced a photo album. The man spoke in merely a whisper. Kalvin looked and listened intently.

Ten minutes later, the woman returned with a silver tea tray, set it down before the bishop and his guest, then immediately took her leave. John continued his talk between sips of Earl Grey tea and teeny bites of mini pastries, recounting a remarkable tale. When he finished, he closed and locked the album with a golden skeletal key.

"Can I ask you something personal, John? I mean, now that I'm almost a full-fledged member of the sect."

"You may ask," the official answered rather pompously.

"Malcolm Columba and Clarence Emery," Kalvin began. "Were they . . .? I mean, are they . . .? Well, you know what I mean."

John nodded. "They're here with us in spirit, Kalvin. In a short period of time, measured in a matter of years, not light-years—" the credible figure both boasted and beamed with utmost assurance "—their replication will live and breathe upon the face of this glorious planet forever. How's that for the short answer, Kalvin my friend?"

Tears filled Kalvin's eyes. "They were my heroes, John."

John put a comforting hand upon Kalvin's knee. "We know that, Kalvin. Believe me, we do. It's one of the reasons why you're here with us now."

Kalvin wiped his eyes on the sleeve of his jacket. "The bag of money wouldn't just happen to be the other reason, would it?" the recruit asked and laughed lightly, accepting a Kleenex.

"Only on account, Kalvin," John replied shrewdly. "On account of the fact that I like you," he furthered. "I trust you won't disappoint us, or yourself and Alvin, by failing to come up with the balance."

Kalvin peered down at the green marble tile floor. "I'm going to need some more time, John."

"How much time?"

"A couple of years. Maybe three at the most," he swallowed, raising his eyes pleadingly to meet his master's.

But the official was shaking his head, lips set tightly in disapproval. "Thirty days. Matters, as I just showed you, are moving along quicker than we anticipated. We're making quantum leaps, Kalvin. It's very expensive to run a lab like ours. We're not asking you to take a leap of faith, now are we? We're *showing* you the science."

"I need what little I have to live on, John. But I can get more. Please. It's just going to take awhile."

"I'll tell you what. Two months tops, plus interest, of course— so long as we can keep the freezer running," he funned. "The cost of electric keeps climbing, you know. We'll discuss the exact percentage after I speak to my superiors."

Kalvin nodded glumly. "Ask you something else?"

John sat motionless.

"How were you able to secure their tissues?"

"Columba's and Emery's?"

Kalvin nodded. "Yes."

The bishop leaned close to Kalvin's ear and whispered. "Columba gave us his cultures years before the drowning incident. We got to Emery in the nick of time, just before the fiery hell."

"Cremation?"

John nodded as his man servant entered and crossed the room.

"Half is there, Bishop; half a mil," Timothy stated.

"Yeah, like I'm really going to screw the pope," Kalvin kidded. "Hey, seriously; maybe you should surreptitiously try and sell His Eminence, too!" Kalvin jousted. "God only knows he has the money."

"How do you know we haven't?" the bishop questioned in earnest, politely dismissing his man servant with a hand gesture. "After all, we have to keep this battle of good and evil ongoing, or folks won't have anything left in life to either live or die for," he bantered back wickedly.

Kalvin put on an amused smile while his mind returned to matters of money, mercurially sending the madman between the errant poles of utmost concern and conviviality.

"Now, on a more serious note—take Timmy, for instance," Bishop John went on. "He's been with us since '67, Kalvin. Tim's in remission now, wanting only to serve."

"Will he be taken care of, too, John? I mean when the technology is proven and—"

"Last of his line, Kalvin. Just like you. All the man lives for is the day he dies," the bishop concluded in dead seriousness.

Chapter 21

Business at The Clubhouse Restaurant at Indian Island in Riverhead had slowed to a snail's pace simply because the game of golf was, for the most part, put on hold. The cold weather was taking its toll.

Justin Barnes watched as two diehards climbed back into their golf cart and huddled behind the Plexiglas windshield, seeking shelter from a gust of wind that ripped across a fairway. The otherwise richly-green expanse was now covered willy-nilly with thin patches of snow left over from the storm the week before.

Justin raised the collar of his coat and walked from the icy parking lot toward the wooden entrance ramp, up and into the empty restaurant.

Victor Gibson was standing off to the side of a counter, chatting away with his bartender, Hank.

"Open for lunch or closed for the season?" Justin called over to the owner.

"Jesus, Justin. We haven't seen you for a while," Victor said with surprise, walking over and extending his hand in a hardy, warm welcome. "You making any headway?" he asked, lowering his voice.

Justin's face gave away the answer.

"Come sit down. Social call? Business? You staying for lunch? Tell me. How about a nice bowl of butternut squash soup with shrimp, made fresh this morning? Marlow's been at it since eight a.m."

"Cup of hot black coffee and a rare cheeseburger is fine; fried onion. Got time to sit and talk?"

The proprietor turned three hundred sixty degrees, surveying the entire dining room before facing his first customer of the day. "I think so," Victor answered without change of expression.

"That's what I figured."

"Be right back. Sit anywhere you like."

Justin took a seat by a window overlooking the river. He watched the couple cuddled in the cart just a short distance away. The man was pouring steaming liquid from a thermos for the woman, the vapor rising between their frigid breaths and disappearing into vacuous space.

Victor returned from the kitchen. "Order's in. What's the latest? I know you guys got a serial killer on your hands."

Justin nodded. "You been doing like I asked?"

"Of course, I have." Victor reached inside a baggy pants pocket and handed over a folded sheet of paper. "The list keeps growing daily. Not by leaps and bounds this past week, however. That's for damn sure."

"How about the pro shop?" Justin questioned and gestured in the direction of the building beyond the wall of the bar area.

"Scott's keeping his list up, but he's only getting dribs and drabs as the season winds down. Most of the traffic's here in the parking lot. Folks tying in a round of golf with a round of beers and a bite to eat. I'll call and have him bring it over."

"Nah, don't bother. I'll go see him myself after lunch."

"J. I know you really can't talk about the case, but is there at least a new development? A hopeful sign? Something? You think the guy might really come back here?"

Justin shrugged. "You never know. We've got nothing concrete. It's just that it all started here as far as we know with Denise Nathan. And you're right. I can't talk about the case. But what I can talk about is golf. You're a golfer, Victor. How would I go about improving my distance drive? The long shot. I can't even put the ball out there two hundred yards. Yet, I see some guys drive two fifty—two eighty—like it was nothing."

"Well, you should really be talking to Scott about that. He's the pro. But I'll give you a tip or two. Number one, you've got to rethink, unlearn, then relearn that shot."

"Rethink?"

"Do you hit the ball with everything you've got?"

"Of course not."

"Why not?"

"Because I'd be sacrificing control. I'd be off in the woods someplace," Justin indicated, sending his arms in different directions. "You know the saying, 'Drive for show. Putt for the dough'? Well, I putt pretty decently, but I can't drive worth beans no matter what I do."

"Theoretically, a guy like you should be able to send the ball out at least two fifty against a driving wind. I see guys out there built like scarecrows who hit better than two hundred—and straight as an arrow."

"So what's their secret?"

"Weights for openers, J. Then a longer shaft for the wood," Victor said quite seriously.

"Weights?" Justin sat scratching his head.

"There are guys out there pumping iron today that wish they were built across the shoulders like you. Building up their strength so that they can really sail the ball. Next, Scott alters and outfits them with a wood that has a shaft at least three inches longer than what they're accustomed to. Your arm and club's a lever, J. The longer the lever, the greater the stroke. Hence, more speed. Finally, and most importantly, Scott teaches them how to control that powerhouse swing. When to accelerate. Smoother and smarter, et cetera. We've got a woman here who can send a ball out two hundred sixty yards, straight as an arrow, each and every time. Fact is you could blow her over with one good breath. But she can drive that ball from here to kingdom come. A controlled power stroke is her key."

"Huh."

"But that's where you separate the chaff from the wheat. You can have the strength of Samson, the best and longest club you can wield, but unless you can control that long shot, through instruction and practice, practice, practice, you won't ever make it out of the woods, J."

"What's your long shot? Consistently, I mean."

"Three hundred," Victor answered modestly. "Can't chip or putt worth a shit though. That's where my game falls apart." Victor laughed. "The game, as I know you know, will drive you absolutely crazy. I go positively nuts. I'm kind of glad I'm stuck in here building up the business. I see myself in some of the customers that walk through these doors after eighteen or even nine holes. Long pusses and frowns. 'We havin' fun yet, fellas?' Marlow and I always ask. If looks could kill."

"What about those two out there?"

Victor turned and leaned toward the window. "She's the one I'm telling you about. A natural. Shoots in the low eighties. Consistently."

"The guy?"

The owner shook his head. "Never saw him before. But from the looks of them, I think he's gonna be hangin' around here awhile." Victor straightened up and winked.

The young couple was kissing, holding onto their thermos cups in black-gloved hands.

"She single and mingle, or married and harried?" Justin pressed, admiring the attractive woman.

Victor looked at Justin keenly and grinned. "Just like you J, there are certain things I'm not at liberty to discuss."

"What if I told you that it's police business?" he put forth, putting on a silly grin.

Victor shrugged. "Then I'd probably have to tell you that she and her husband come here on the weekends. But you won't see much of him unless its sixty degrees or above. He hibernates this time of year. Thirty years her senior."

"I see."

"You're not suggesting . . ."

"No, of course not. Just being nosy is all."

"How about a hint, J. Any · progress being made? It goes nowhere. Not even to my better half. Promise."

"We're stymied, like I said. Working several angles."

The pleasant young waitress who had been Denise Nathan's friend appeared with Justin's coffee and burger. "Marlow said that Victor said that you like cheddar cheese, onions almost burnt, and coffee dark as mud. So, there you go, sir. Anything for you, Victor?"

"I'm fine, Rhonda. You know what? Bring me an apple-cinnamon tea."

"Coming right up." Rhonda took a bottle of catsup off a nearby table and placed it in front of her customer before returning to the kitchen.

"How's she working out, Vic?"

"Great. Not a whirlwind like Denise. But she's learning fast and very good with the customers."

"Saturn out front belong to her? Next to your SUV?"

"That's right."

"Her license on the list you just gave me? Wasn't on the first one."

"You're not serious, J."

"Every vehicle that comes in here. All right?"

Victor nodded with some annoyance.

"So, tell me more about that lovely looking thing heading for the fairway? You got *her* number, I'd bet." Justin grinned.

"On both lists I gave you."

"And that new BMW coupe over there?"

"That's hers. Irene Weinstein."

"She's a looker, Victor."

"Strange. No other car out there except yours and mine, Hanks and Marlow's, Rhonda's and Irene's. It's strange because I never saw her drive in with another guy before. She's always alone—unless, of course, she's with her husband. If not, she'd make it her business to meet some guy at the bar or at the driving range. Not that I'm out there every minute monitoring, mind you. But I've been pretty watchful since Denise."

"She come in here for lunch or dinner, or just golf and drinks?"

"All of the above. Hey! You tailin' her and this guy or what? He a suspect, J?"

"Like you, I never laid eyes on him before. Listen, you're doing a great job, Victor, and I appreciate it. Anything odd you see, anything at all, you let me know. Okay?"

"Absolutely. That going to be enough to hold you till dinner?"

"This is fine."

"Then let me let you eat in peace. Just holler if you need anything."

Justin acknowledged with a big bite from the burger. A dollop of melted cheddar cheese dropped to the dish. As he drank his coffee, he watched the couple in the golf cart disappear over a knoll.

The owner went back to chatting with his bartender. Rhonda came out of the kitchen, carefully carrying a cup of tea across the dining room and into the bar area for her boss.

Twenty minutes later, as Justin finished his cheeseburger, coffee, and the sports section of *The New York Post*, the couple in the golf cart came barreling back, traveling about as fast as they could safely navigate the snow-patched grounds. The cart stopped abruptly in the parking lot. The man got out and made a beeline for the restaurant. The woman quickly headed for her car.

An argument was the first thought that entered Justin's mind. Fright was the expression engraved on the male figure's face as he entered the building and hurried toward a pay phone between the two dining areas. Irene Weinstein and her BMW flew past the pro shop and vanished in a flash.

The stranger began arguing with the bartender who was on the public wall phone. Victor tried to intervene, and the argument grew louder.

"I want to report a body!" the golfer blurted aloud. "Now, get off that goddamn phone."

"What!? Where?" Victor Gibson demanded.

"Out there," the man pointed in a northerly direction. "Near the sixth hole. I thought it was a patch of snow at first—then a body in a sleeping bag as we—I mean, as I got closer. But she was wrapped in plastic."

"Who was?" Victor snapped. "Where's Irene?"

"I don't know any Irene," the man barked.

"Liar!" Victor declared, grabbing the man by the collar of his coat.

Justin Barnes stepped into the bar area and drew the pair apart as easily as pulling warm taffy.

"All right. Whoa! I said stop."

"Who the fuck are you?" the stranger screamed. "Hey! Get your goddamn hands off of me. I'm trying to call the cops. I said, let go."

Justin thrust a badge pinned to his wallet in the man's face. "'Where's a cop when you really need one', you're thinkin'. Right, fella? Well, here I be, sucker. Now sit the fuck down."

The man sat.

"I asked him where Irene was," Victor said excitedly, his voice trembling. "He may have hurt her."

"She's all right," Justin told him. "I just saw her hightail it the hell out of here."

The man started to get up to leave.

"I said, sit. ID. Let's have it. Tell me exactly what you found."

The man handed over his wallet. "I thought it was a little mound of snow . . . and then I thought it was a person in a sleeping bag. But she was like sealed in a sheet of plastic. Like they wrap boats. Only body-bagged. Can't think of the word."

"Shrink-wrap?"

"That's it! In white plastic. All shrunk up around her. Airtight."

Like your alibi? Justin considered. "How do you know it was a she?" He was studying both the man's driver's license as well as the frightened face.

The man looked down at the floor, then around the walls and ceiling. "I wasn't sure if it was an animal or person at first—or if it was alive or dead. I cut a slit in the plastic. I thought maybe she might still be breathing; but believe me, she's dead."

"How do you know that?"

"I was a medic in Nam."

"All right. Move your ass. We're taking a little ride."

But the man was shaking his head. "I've got to call a taxi and go home," Yancy Johnson pleaded. "I found a body and reported it to you immediately. I did nothing wrong."

Justin ignored the man's whining. "Victor, give us about fifteen minutes, then call this number if you don't hear from me before then." He handed the owner Detective Brian Archer's card. "Mr. Johnson and I should be back in a little while."

Yancy Johnson was still shaking his head. "I've got to get home."

"You got Irene Weinstein's number handy, big mouth?" Justin barked.

"I told you, I don't know any Irene—"

"Victor, call the pro shop and have Scott check his records and secure Irene Weinstein's phone number and home address. Then call her and tell her to stay put—that I'll call discretely in a little while. If she gives you any lip, tell her I'll be sure to pop in unexpectedly when I know her husband's home."

"All right, all right. I don't want to involve her," Johnson balked. "Please."

"She's already involved, asshole."

"She stayed in the cart. She didn't see anything. You *can't* say that I was with her. It's . . . it's—"

"I know, Mr. Johnson." Justin smirked. "It's par for the course," he punned. "Cooperate with me, now, and I'll see what I can do to keep her out of this. Jerk me around, and you'll both be sitting together in Yaphank until the wee hours of morning, giving several homicide detectives your collective statements until I arrive and peruse that information. And I'm a very slow but thorough peruser, Mr. Johnson. Got the picture? At that point, it'll be too late to help you out with a handicap. The press could probably print both your pics side by side in time for tomorrow's early edition," he exaggerated, holding up the man's driver's license to the skylight before handing back only his wallet. "You see, unlike most photo IDs from Motor Vehicle, you look exactly like yourself, Yancy. Matter of fact, I've got business there this afternoon."

"All right, all right, already," Johnson bellyached, giving Victor the woman's cell phone number.

"Call her for me, Victor," Justin repeated. "Tell her exactly what I said."

"You bet."

"Move it, Johnson," Justin ordered. "May I borrow that golf cart they rode in out there, Victor?"

"Of course, J. Anything you want."

Chapter 22

Detective Gary York joined his partner at the Indian Island crime scene. The forensic team was nearly finished, having reported their preliminary findings to Brian and Justin. Gary was being brought up to speed. Gusts of wind whipped a series of cumulus clouds across the fairway's darkening ceiling as the setting sun steadily descended behind a purple-gray horizon. The trio stepped back away from the body and talked quietly among themselves.

"Marcus believes the girl was unconscious but still alive when the bastard packaged her like a mummy right where she lies," Brian put forth matter-of-factly. "Won't know for certain till after the autopsy."

"Tied and shrink-wrapped her body right here," Justin reiterated, evidenced by the pieces of poly rope, shrink-wrap, and shrink-wrap tape forensics had collected. "But our killer would've needed an extension cord the length of Route 105," he hyperbolized, pointing out the distance to the nearest road. "Either that, or he'd had to have carried in one of those cumbersome containers of propane, which doesn't make much sense either."

"No, it doesn't," Gary agreed, "because he'd also need paraphernalia like a tank regulator, gas-fired shrink gun, hose, tools for the fittings and whatnot. And then he'd have to cart all that equipment back out again. Why would he do that?"

"I think *carted* is the operative word," Justin offered through a shiver from the cold.

"Yeah, but how?" Brian questioned. "Except for Weinstein's and Johnson's golf cart, there are no other tire tracks leading in from over there. Golf is pretty much over for the season. Those two lovebirds and another diehard duffer were the only holdouts. Besides, the course was closed yesterday. Furthermore, you can't get down here with a vehicle unless they open up that gate back there, which was locked until Nick had the County Parks personnel open it up for them. You think he just walked in from the road with all that stuff, J?"

"I think he *borrowed* a cart from the clubhouse last night. Two carts were left outside the building. The main entrance is always open. There's a shortcut under the 105 Bridge, along a footpath and through that wood lot, which is part of the route Yancy Johnson and I took back to the clubhouse. The path's just wide enough to accommodate a cart. The perp leaves his own vehicle back there at the clubhouse where it couldn't be seen from the road or highway, takes the golf cart and brings the girl over there, incapacitates her, then runs a hundred-foot extension cord from the golf cart to here. Next, he rigs an electric heat gun applicator with alligator clips to the cart's battery. He wouldn't need a tank of propane and all that paraphernalia as with a gas-fired gun. He sealed her up here in a matter of a minute or two."

"You think an electric heat gun running off a golf cart battery could generate enough juice to shrink that material?" Gary questioned skeptically.

"Yep. Because I made a couple of calls to a distributor and a boatyard in Aquebogue. The average thickness of shrink-wrap is six or seven mil and has a shrink temperature of two hundred and seventy-five to three hundred fifty degrees Fahrenheit. If you're wrapping a good size boat, you'd need propane to move the job along quickly. But a good hundred-and-ten volt industrial heat gun can produce an air flow temperature of up to a thousand degrees. More than enough to seal and suck her breath away. I'd say that sheet is what—maybe four mil tops?"

Gary smirked. "I'm surprised he didn't use clear plastic to enhance his enjoyment."

"You know, seriously, I thought about that. But the clear stuff's not that available and used mostly for displaying boats and such. Those white rolls are easier to come by and therefore harder to trace as is an electric heat gun. Also, a decent propane-fired gun with the accessories you'd need is a good six or seven hundred dollars. An electric heat gun runs about eighty bucks."

"And then you don't have all that other crap to carry around."

"Nor would he have to worry about anybody seeing a flame in the distance at that hour."

Gary and Brian were nodding in agreement.

"Although she was found completely naked, Marcus said there was no outward sign of sexual assault," Justin elaborated. "Poor thing couldn't be more than eleven or twelve."

Brian nodded, searching his troubled mind. "Know something?"

"What?"

"The kid looks kind of familiar."

"C'mon," Justin said, shuddering from the cold. "Her face *is* a bit dirty and distorted. They all start taking on a likeness if you let it."

But Detective Brian Archer could not shake the feeling.

"Earth to Brian."

"Oh, before I forget, J. Kim's got a lead on that rope configuration left behind at the Schroeder home. Seems the infinity symbol solidly fits your theory."

"Great. You can tell me all about it back at the car 'cause I'm freezing my fucking nuts off out here."

"What's the matter? No blood?"

"And that's another thing."

"What is?"

"The cocksucker's distancing himself from violent, bloody scenes to an almost . . . I don't know what the word is."

"Surreal?" Gary threw out.

"That's it. An ethereal quality. Airy. Spacey. Think about it. He changes his M.O. from bloody bludgeoning scenes referencing his first and second victims to bloodless murders. The spidery web with the Nolan boy first poisoned then placed in the center of it. The staging of the Schroeder woman, hanging high in her cathedral ceiling below a brightly lit space. This poor girl, sealed within a cloud-like shroud. Otherworldly, if you will."

Brian and Gary were staring at one another oddly.

"This guy's spooking me," Gary said of Justin.

"I guess I'm not making much sense."

"Yeah, you are, J. You didn't by any chance happen to speak to Kim earlier today and are just playing us like an instrument?" Brian questioned gravely.

"No, why?"

"You sure she didn't fill your head with talk about space-time continuum, or earthly beings being seeded by aliens from other worlds? Hey, I'm being serious here."

"Oh, shit. I knew the job would one day take its toll. I should have seen it comin'. Black woman being married to a white dude like you just pushed her over the edge," Justin teased. "Had I known you two were gonna tie the knot back then, I'd have warned her about these mixed marriages. But my black ass was in the slammer at the time you did the dirty deed. I'd have married her myself and spared her from this fate. She spends what? Seventy hours a week on that mainframe? She's finally lost it, Bri," Justin goaded.

"You know what's really spooky about Kim and you, J?"

"You mean besides us being both black and beautiful? Tell me."

"You're both on the same wavelength."

"It's a black thing, whitey. You'd never understand."

"You gonna listen to me, now?"

"Just as soon as my cock and balls stop feelin' like they've been shrink-wrapped. Gettin' mighty damn cold standin' out here in the open with this fucking wind picking up. Be dark in a few minutes."

Brian signaled for the forensic team to remove the body. He fixed his eyes on their crew chief. "You fellas can maybe help us account for all those knots in her ponytail, Marcus. Far more than six this time out. Either we're missing a few dozen bodies, or all those wraps, or weaves—or whatever the hell they are—mean something significant that we're overlooking."

"You can count on it."

"Not accounting for the fact that this crime scene is set around the sixth hole," the case detective concluded, turning to face the yellow pennant flapping in the breeze. The black embroidered number **6** stood boldly in its center. "I want every possibility explored."

The trio started for their cars parked in the distance.

"Hey! Do we ever let you guys down?" the pathologist called out. "Listen, it's not just us that you have to concern yourself with. It's Osip. I wanted him out here with us. He asked to be part of this team today. So where is he? Out looking for his daughter, they tell me. He hasn't even returned my call. Then I'm told not to call the house because his wife's home glued to the phone. He's not answering his cell."

Brian stopped dead in his tracks before he turned around and headed back toward the body. "Hold on, fellas," he called out to the team.

"Now what?" Justin complained, blowing and warming a stream of cold air through a tunnel of folded frozen fingers. "I just want you to know that I'm used to driving up to or at least parking *near* a crime scene. Not being told to leave the car at the clubhouse and walk back in half a fucking mile. I couldn't even borrow a cart the second go-around because suddenly they've *all* been stored away for the season. But just take a look at these other vehicles here. Look at Nick and the others keeping warm inside the van. What kind of shit is this anyhow? Suffolk County Parks people can't tell Homicide what to do. Hey! You guys listenin' to me? Do we have any clout around here or not?"

Gary walked up to Brian. "What's up, buddy?"

Brian was looking down at the body. "That's her."

"Her, who?"

"Osip's daughter."

"You shittin' me? You sure?"

"Pretty sure. I met her once at headquarters when Chris brought her in for a tour. Another time last year when I had to pull him away from her birthday party. Kim's godmother to the girl. I've seen pictures of her in Kim's album."

Gary knelt beside the body. "Oh, my God!"

Chapter 23

The sky was tinged with streaks of moonlight as dusk had long since disappeared, swallowed whole by the frigid night. Detective Gary York was at the wheel, heading the sedan back to police headquarters in Yaphank. Brian was busy explaining his wife's findings to Justin after having finally located Christopher Osip. The case detective explained Kim connecting two deceased serial killers with the company claiming to have successfully cloned the first human being. Clonite, Incorporated. The three men found it difficult to focus on the new development, as their thoughts kept returning to Osip's daughter, Vivian, and what Chris and Harriet were going through, for their eleven-year-old girl had been positively identified. Vivian Osip's body had been shrouded twice in twenty-four hours: initially in a sheet of white plastic by a madman, secondly in a black body bag by Marcus' crew. Although Justin never knew the girl, he was quite upset —being the first in authority to confirm and officially report the ghostly homicide.

"You with me on this, J?"

"Yeah. The company is into cloning. How does that compute?"

"It's about as close to immortality as one can get. But there's another group connected with them that Kim's concerned with, too. A religious sect bordering on the lunatic fringe. Reality. It founded Clonite. Clonite's research has appeared in scientific journals, and traditional newspapers have reported on their findings. Clonite's well respected and immersed in mainstream science."

"Respected, that is, until their recent claim," Gary elaborated. "Most experts are calling it a hoax. Others say it's quite possible, awaiting proof. Religion and science, J. Strange bedfellows. The two institutions have been connected since 1997."

"But now that Clonite's *supposedly* cloned the first human, Reality is taking on a new dimension. One of unparalleled proportion."

"And guess which two serial killers were associated with those two groups?"

Justin knew immediately. "Malcolm Columba and Clarence Emery."

"You got it, big guy."

The maverick was amazed at how Malcolm Columba and Clarence Emery had managed, even in death, to reenter his life. "How did Kim get a handle on this?"

"Wasn't hard. The symbol for infinity is Reality's logo."

"Clonite's been supporting them with dollars and a propaganda machine for the past six years."

"The beauty of their operation is that *faith*, for many, is no longer steeped in some sort of mystic belief or myth. A human clone has been created, or so they're telling the world. But Marcus and Peter spoke to people high up in the scientific community who say it's all bullshit, that Clonite will never furnish DNA proof, probably claiming at the last moment that the alleged parents won't submit to tests for fear the courts would take the child away, or some kind of crap like that."

"The collective beauty of their operation is that Clonite and Reality can sell their followers a bill of goods. And they are. Kim and Big Sister—God bless their processing souls—have begun to track huge sums of money from worshippers around the world. Kim believes that our killer could be a member of one or both of those groups."

In the backseat, Justin grew busy taking notes.

"Problem is that its members number in the thousands," Gary amplified.

"Can't Kim narrow the number down to those living on Long Island for starters?"

"She's doing just that, J. But nothing's turned up yet. We need Reality's and Clonite's confidential member/client lists. As we speak, she's running down leads through several large banks. Any big money transfer to either group from anyone living on the East End, and we'd be interrogating person or persons right now, by God. But the lieutenant's probably right. We're overlooking something from those early scenes: Denise Nathan and how she connects to Gretchen Bowers and her Uncle Sal. Him, we're missing all together. Vanished after cashing in. There's got to be more of a connection among Bowers' life insurance policy, Emily Schroeder, and Salvatori Passaro. Unfortunately, we're nowhere with that yet, either."

"Nowhere because we're trying to tie *all* the homicides together," Justin groused. "Salvatori Passaro holds the key to this. He and his missing million bucks. Cash on the barrelhead the insurance company paid out on Bowers."

"But Emily Schroeder and Salvatori Passaro had little or no contact with one another. He wasn't even on her ward."

"He's got to be our guy," Gary seriously considered.

"But it makes no sense."

"The dots just don't connect."

"Maybe because the guy's tying *us* up in knots," Justin suggested cannily.

"Like maybe the knots mean nothing at all."

"Other than a body count as you said from the onset."

"Yeah, like we really need a scorecard and a keeper."

"Why lay out the rope that way? Infinity. Reality. Clonite. Therein lies the connection."

"Maybe it's like Otto and Larry said in their off-the-record psychiatric profile. The guy wants to get caught. Only we're a little slow in figuring out the clues while he weaves his tangled web."

Justin leaned forward between them. "The guy doesn't want to get caught, but in the back of his mind he knows there's that possibility. So what does he have to fall back on?"

"The promise of immortality in case we body bag his butt."

"What if it isn't a symbol for infinity?"

"Maybe the guy's leading us in another direction with Vivian Osip as well."

"Look. Let's suppose Salvatori Passaro's disappearance is permanent. Let's suppose he was murdered for the money. Where did the dough go? In the hands of the killer who turned the money over to one of the groups in exchange for the promise of immortality."

"If all he wanted was the insurance money, J, why murder people who didn't have a dime? William Walker didn't have two nickels to rub together. Nor did Emily Schroeder—except for her house that's in probate. Nolan Andrews and Vivian Osip were kids. Denise Nathan leaves a goodly sum to her family that we're sure had nothing to do with any of this. We wasted plenty of time there. Bowers and Passaro at least fit the money mold. Pilgrim State Hospital.

"Maybe it goes back to what you said earlier, J. The killer wants to emulate Columba and Emery. It may be as simple as that. Maybe the money isn't necessarily the end-all. The guy just likes to kill. A million bucks is a bonus."

"He goes after Vivian Osip, a kid whose father's connected with law enforcement. It makes the perp feel powerful. Like his two heroes. He commits two murders at the Indian Island Golf Course, where he probably learned that Emery, like you did, J, had interviewed that flytier fellow from Eastern Flyrodders, where they hold their monthly meetings at The Clubhouse Restaurant. Two murders near and on the golf course; close to the water: Nathan and Osip. Walker at the Moose Lodge; spitting distance from the Peconic River, too. All too familiar themes if you ask me. I'm telling you, he's from the area. He knows it all too well. And I don't believe this Salvatori Passaro nut job did *any* of the killings like the lieutenant's speculating. Although our Mr. Passaro is quite capable of murder, he's not very smart. Whoever committed these murders is pretty damn bright."

"So, what do we do? Go to the founder of Reality who claims he was snatched up by aliens with almond-shaped eyes who told him that they seeded Earth with clones in the image of E.T.? That's precisely what he reported to the press, J. Talk about a reality check. The guy needs a shrink because he's definitely not wrapped too tight."

"I don't think you'd ever get through to a guy like that, Gary. Then again, your laundry man has almond-shaped eyes," Brian bantered. "Maybe you could dress him up in costume and bring him along as leverage. Anyhow, tell us how you two communicate, seeing as how neither of you speaks the same language."

"Yeah, but my Chinaman's certainly more down to earth, guys," Gary played along. "When I tell him I lost or forgot my ticket, which I somehow always manage to do, he says, '*Fruck* you' to my face, but nevertheless searches through scores of packages piled from floor to ceiling till he finds my shirts."

"What's your point?"

"My point is that I know what I'm dealing with, whereas this French fucker running things at Reality is a certified fruitcake from the word go, Kim says."

"What about that Manhattan-based chemist/director from Clonite?" Brian suggested. "She's a knockout from what I see in the papers. Single, too, I understand. Whattaya think, Gary?"

"Well, I could probably win her over in that department and let her have her way with me," he half-kidded. "But Kim tells me that the woman flatly refuses to give out any information on her clients. Period. Real hard-nosed. Not unlike the rep Kim spoke with at Reality. So, I was seriously thinking of infiltrating the fold. But at this point in time, the lieutenant put the kibosh on my flying to Bermuda where they're headquartered."

"Can't we just have their records subpoenaed?"

"Not with what we got right now, J. And that's nothing, with a capital N."

"Not to change the subject, fellas. But I just can't help thinking about Chris and Harriet. Anything we can do for them at this time?"

"Harriet's family will be flying in from Minnesota. Meantime, the neighbor next-door is holding their hand. Some of us will probably head on over whenever we finish up. It's going to be a long night. It'll be a madhouse for sure. Or should I say a sad house? I'll stop by after I drop Gary off and pick up Kim. J, you can come with us if you like. Either way, I'll take you and Gary back to your cars afterward. You decide. At least we got the chance to knock this business around somewhat."

"Well, at least the Osips have someone there with them now," Justin said with a heavy heart.

Chapter 24

Harriet Osip was standing and staring blankly at a kitchen wall. Her husband's hand was squarely on her shoulder.

"Why?" he asked the Lord. "Why did You let this happen? I always believed in You. Always!" Christopher Osip wept bitterly. "Never, ever again. DO YOU HEAR ME?"

"Shh, shh," Harriet interjected, placing a hand upon her husband's. Her whole body trembled.

"He allowed for someone to take our baby from us, honey. He took kiddo away."

"The bastard who took her from us will pay dearly," she promised, sitting down abruptly in a high-back chair—rocking gently to-and-fro before suddenly retching forward, falling to the floor on her hands and knees.

Christopher stared blankly at the ceiling, oblivious to his wife's dry heaving.

Kalvin Matheson rushed to help Harriet to her feet. Chris turned and looked vacantly at the two of them, sobbing uncontrollably.

"Walk with me to the living room, Harriet," Kalvin insisted. "I want you to lie down on the couch. Come on, now."

Harriet was shaking a head of messy curls. "Please go home now, Kalvin. You've done enough for us."

"I won't leave here until I know you're all right, Harriet. And you're not all right. Why won't you let me call the doctor?"

"Please."

Kalvin was wiping the spittle at the corner of her mouth with a paper napkin. "Come lie down, and then I promise I'll go."

Harriet allowed Kalvin to help her into the other room and over to a sectional sofa.

"Chris, bring Harriet a cold cloth for her head," he ordered.

Chris was holding onto the kitchen sink and would not let go. "My kiddo's gone forever, Kalvin," he cried out from the other room.

Kalvin came running into the kitchen and pried the man's fingers from around the rim of the stainless steel sink. "Get a grip, Chris," he whispered. "Your wife's shivering while burning up in there." Kalvin ran the cold water, soaked and wrung out a clean dishcloth. "Listen to me. I want you to be strong for her." He put his arm around Chris' waist and walked with him into the living room. "Sit down over here."

Kalvin lowered Chris to the club chair opposite his wife then went back to Harriet, folding and gently placing the cloth upon her forehead.

"There."

"I'm going to find out who killed her, Kalvin," Chris swore. "And then I'm going to hunt him down like an animal."

"And I'm going to help you if you let me. But first I want you two to drink and eat something. Not now, but maybe later. Build up your strength. I made soup and sandwiches. There's a meat loaf with gravy in the refrigerator I brought over, too. All you have to do is heat it up. I want Harriet and you to rest now."

"You're a good neighbor, Kalvin," Chris blubbered.

"Oh, I'm so much more than that, Chris. I'm your friend. I loved that little girl. Vivian and I were friends. Together, you and I are going to find out who did this."

"I'm very good at what I do, Kalvin. I don't know if you know that."

"No, I do. In fact, you're great," he stated most assuredly. "Vivian must have told me that a dozen times."

"Why did God let this happen?" Chris wailed, burying his face in a crooked arm.

"We'll find the son of a bitch—together, Chris," Kalvin repeated. "Now rest. Both of you. Please."

Chapter 25

As the computer maven for Suffolk County Homicide, Detective Kim Archer would ordinarily collect, analyze, and assimilate data, passing along the information through proper channels. Rarely would she address the teams of homicide detectives as a whole. Briefings were usually conducted by the detective sergeant or the case detective. Today, however, Detective Lieutenant Ethan Powell directed Kim to give the talk.

Kim hid her grief over Vivian Osip's shocking death and put on a brave face, lightly drumming four chewed fingernails upon an armrest in the lieutenant's office. "I know why you're having me do this," she declared.

"Oh, yeah?" the burly man replied and sighed with indifference.

"Yeah.

"Guess you're gonna tell me."

"Because both my dearly beloved Brian and Gary are afraid to get up there before the others and talk about extraterrestrials. You're afraid they'll laugh one of them out of the room. That's why."

The man smiled benignly and shook his head. "Your dearly beloved and his partner go where even angels fear to tread. You know that, Kim. Wherever destiny leads them, Lady Wizard. But I will admit this whole business does sound a bit *out there*. Doesn't it? However, the truth of the matter is that you're on top of this. You spoke to both Clonite and Reality. You can impart your impressions to the teams. They respect you."

"And that's another thing, Lieutenant. It was a mistake for you to have me contact Reality and Clonite and show them our hand," she said openly and honestly. "We could have poked around a bit first—sent Gary in undercover."

"I'm afraid that's where we disagree. It would have been a mistake *not* to put them on notice. We had five murders on our hands when you phoned them. Six as we shoot the breeze."

"But what did we gain? We got no cooperation from them whatsoever. You had me fax them an important piece of evidence: that photo of the rope laid out like Reality's logo. Well, I'd have run for cover, too, if I were running their show."

"The fact that they know they're being looked at as part of a murder investigation will shake their tree."

"Yeah, and maybe alert the killer that we're closing in for the kill."

"Well, I can see that this is getting us nowhere. What's done is done. Hopefully, they'll remain mute on that subject and contact us if they suspect anything."

"At a time when the eyes of the world are watching and waiting for news of Clonite's supposed success? Get real. Their PR department wouldn't bother calling us if they found a smoking gun in their janitor's hand. They'd probably have their lawyers and lobbyists explain it away as a setup."

"Listen to me. Marcus made some well-placed calls. This cloning claim will prove to be just one big public relations stunt. That's how this is going to wind up."

"So what! I'll let you in on a little secret. It doesn't really matter whether Clonite succeeds or not. Some group in the very near future is going to clone a human being if that company hasn't already. It's inevitable. What's important to both Reality and Clonite is that they're in the forefront at this moment. You're going to see their membership soar into the millions as profits climb into the billions. They could care less who they're servicing, just so long as the collection plate and the coffers are filled." Kim steamed, stewed, and then simmered there quietly in her seat.

"Kim, if we had anything concrete, we'd have their goddamn records in front of us."

"We've got *six* bodies, Lieutenant."

"Call me Ethan, Kim. Please," the man tried to placate with a polite and soothing tone.

"We've got six bodies whether I call you by your first name, your last, your title or the fool you really are for having me make those calls and tipping our hand."

The veins in the detective lieutenant's thick neck bulged. His jaw muscles turned to steel. "The only reason I'll let you get away with this *this* time, Detective Archer, is because you're a sister. Don't ever speak to me like that again. Understand?"

"The only reason you'll let me get away with anything is because you need me. Black or white has nothing to do with it—nor shouldn't. You made a bad call. Got it?"

"Got it. Now, get out of here."

"You still want me to deliver the Sermon on the Mount?" she questioned, standing still as a statue, her back to the boss, eyes brimming with tears that Kim refused to let him see. A pair of trembling shoulders nevertheless gave her away.

"Is that what this is really all about, Kim? Osip's family?"

Detective Archer focused on a spot above the doorway. "We're all family here, Lieutenant. Harriet is a friend. Brian sometimes flies model airplanes with Chris. Vivian was my godchild."

"Fifteen minutes, girl. Pull yourself together. Go wash your face."

Kim closed the door behind her and walked in a daze toward the lavatory.

Chapter 26

Virtually everyone sat taking notes as Kim Archer spoke to the assembled teams. Her husband stood off in a corner. Transfixed.

"Clonite is a Bahamas-based company founded by the Reality Movement in 1997, with offices around the world. We now have every reason to suspect that both Malcolm Columba and Clarence Emery were *deeply* involved with those two groups. The two men had connections to many cults, companies, corporations, and conglomerates both here and abroad as most of us know. Reality and Clonite are listed among them. Clonite enjoys global attention as we speak. And because of its affiliation with Reality, so does this Amsterdam-based movement, which boasts fifty-five thousand members of which a thousand reside in the United States. Clonite's clients are kept as secret as their laboratories. Now that they're on the brink of supposed success in claiming to have cloned the first human being, what those member/client numbers will rise to is anybody's guess, including the price tag for the privilege of immortality at some future date—whether it's true, or possible, or not. Rumor puts the cost at one million dollars for the promise of everlasting life when the technology becomes available and the procedure is perfected. In the meantime, one may have their healthy, living cells stored for a nominal fee of several hundred dollars annually, or avail themselves of several other services. None of which are cheap, I'm told."

Kim took a sip of coffee before continuing.

"Being that Clonite is involved in mainstream science, which it truly is, we have to take a good look at their agenda as it relates to its backer whom cult deprogrammers deem a most dangerous man. Dangerous because he has had thirty years to perfect his incredible story, coupled with a credible scientific firm to lend credence to his tale.

"That person is Hans Verber, a man who claims he was accosted and transported by extraterrestrials in 1973 to another place and time, commonly referred to as space-time continuum. That's spelled with two u's for some of us like me who can't spell worth a crap." Kim smiled uneasily. "Space-time continuum is just another way of expostulating Einstein's theory of relativity. Anyhow, it was somewhere along the line that Verber met four prophets: Jesus, Muhammad, Buddha and Moses—or so the founder claims."

Big smiles broke out all across the squad room.

"Christ, Kim. You sure it wasn't those four gentlemen from Verona?" a detective in the front row poked fun, trying his best to be funny.

"That's *Two Gentlemen of Verona*, moron," another mocked.

"Oh, yeah? Well, the four I'm talkin' 'bout are fake, phony, frauds. Because I was talkin' 'bout Verona, New Jersey and the Shepley brothers. Fucking psychopaths."

"Wrongo. They were from Tenafly."

Gigantic grins and light laughter filled the space.

"I think Verber left out Nostradamus and Gandhi," a voice from the back of the room boomed.

"Gandhi wasn't a prophet, Underwood."

"Yeah, well, he profited greatly, wise guy. You think you know some shit."

Ethan Powell seemed amused—antics that the commanding officer's predecessor would have put a stop to immediately. Then again, the men were justifiably blowing off steam, for many of them had worked closely with Chris Osip over the course of years, bearing the family's loss as though Vivian were their own child.

Kim waved for the group's attention. "You with me, people? Hello-o. Verber goes on to say the space aliens told him that they created life on Earth via genetic engineering, seeding our planet with clones left here many thousands of years ago."

At least a dozen men and two women in Kim's audience were rolling their eyes, smiling and joking. Detective Lorna Hanover from Team Three had all she could do to hold back a belly laugh. Finally, she could not contain herself and let go completely.

"Yeah, you laugh all you want, Lorna," an engaging youthful undercover cop dressed in raggedy jeans and a crumpled shirt interjected with a rather high-pitched pubescent voice. "But I'll personally attest to several space cadets who somehow infiltrated my wife's side of the family. Bad seeds—each and every one of them."

Lorna could barely catch her breath, her infectious laughter leveling all three teams. Ethan Powell's solid frame shook without expelling a sound. Kim nodded politely, and even her heartbroken husband, Brian, cracked a smile.

"May I continue now, please?" Kim asked civilly after everyone had more or less settled down.

"Hey, York," a veteran detective called over to Gary. "If you do go undercover, a party and costume rental place down the street from me carries Buck Rodgers, Flash Gordon, and Captain Video—all hanging in the window last time I looked."

"You're dating yourself, ol' timer," a rookie sitting beside him announced pleasantly. "The outfits you're referring to are actually from the *Star Trek, Starship Enterprise*. There's Captain Jonathan Archer—no relationship to Brian that I'm aware of—Sub-commander T'Pol, and Doctor Phlox."

"All right. That's enough from the Peanut Gallery, Clarabell," a detective sergeant remarked, trying to restore some order.

"There you go! We'll send Gary in as Clarabell's clone for the last laugh before he busts their asses."

Kim looked over at Ethan with a bit of irritation holding at the corners of her mouth.

"All right, troops," the lieutenant sounded, commanding their attention while wearing the hint of a grin. "Let's hear the rest of this fantastic voyage. Then we'll decide on a plan of action."

It was the first time the teams had heard their leader speak of doing anything collectively.

Kim nodded satisfactorily and resumed her talk. "Aside from the aforementioned background concerning the two groups, let's review what Big Sister has digested regarding a few important leads to date."

Whenever Big Sister was mentioned, it drew the detectives' undivided attention; for the personification of the mainframe was the teams' goddess of wisdom—Kim Archer, their practitioner of wizardry.

"As you know, a one million dollar life insurance policy on Gretchen Bowers has been paid out to a beneficiary, Salvatori Passaro, her uncle, a mental patient who was recently released from Pilgrim State Hospital. As you also know, Mr. Passaro has since disappeared without a trace. Denise Nathan's parents were the beneficiaries of a two hundred thousand dollar policy. No connection between the two families whatsoever. No connection between those families and the other victims except for the fact that Emily Schroeder was a retired psychiatric nurse from Pilgrim State. Inferences are yours, folks. Big Sister is still scratching her brain trust.

"Now, back to our first victim, Denise Nathan: murdered at Indian Island Golf Course, in Riverhead. Our last victim, Vivian Osip, was also murdered at Indian Island. Again, there's no connection among any of the victims insofar as we know. However, all were murdered in Suffolk County: five of them in Riverhead; one in Quogue. All bore those telltale loops and knots. With regard to the Schroeder woman, we note five additional wraps that form the noose that the killer never actually employed as such—along with a Clinch Knot comprising five loops in her hair. Marcus discovered that many loops were knotted in Vivian Osip's—" Kim's voice crackled "—were knotted in her ponytail."

The room fell still as death itself as a stream of tears ran down the computer maven's face and could be heard hitting her notebook from the first row through the last.

"Our serial killer is an experimenter. Growing bolder as he picks his victims. He thoroughly enjoys what he does. To help illustrate the point, it's been confirmed that the Bowers woman's eardrums were shattered. High frequency sound. As you heard, we believe he records his actions with a video camera, which accounts for no trophies that we know of. Doesn't need any. He's probably got it all on tape. He's not an expert with knots, we're told. But he is proficient.

"Justin Barnes' assessment of the killer, his profile if you will, is presumably on the mark. You can attribute it to J's years of *character study* on those mean streets." Kim labored a smile. "Nothing like what the public sees and hears in the movies or on the tube. J's not telling you how many times a day the bastard brushes his teeth, what kind of cologne he wears, or how he ties his shoes." Kim grinned, sighed, and shook her pretty head, for the latter reference alluded to Justin and the case involving Clarence Emery, whereby the maverick identified the disguised serial killer by his shoelaces, then shot him and his accomplice cold-stone dead in the line of *duty*. "No. Big Sister and I agree with J's assessment of the unsub being Caucasian, mid to late thirties, five-foot seven to eight, muscular build, a loner but a fun guy to be with if he wants to be, southpaw we're absolutely sure of now, a hero worshipper—which makes him somewhat vulnerable in that regard—and we believe we know the two who he worshipped and adored. Probably a closet homosexual, *I'll* throw in for good measure.

"And we all know that as the killing continues, the *bloody* business we first saw is on the wane—less gory, more bizarre. Make of it what you will. Let's recap. In sequence from victim number one through six: Denise Nathan, a vicious and fatal bludgeoning from behind; William Walker, blunt force injury to the forehead only to incapacitate the victim before the killer strangled the man to death with a garrote; Gretchen Bowers, heart attack brought on by sheer fright; Nolan Andrews, poisoning—shortly before the boy was suspended in a kind of surreal web; Emily Schroeder, incapacitated with a stun gun, choked to death, then hanged from a cathedral ceiling for show; Vivian Osip . . . immobilized, shrink-wrapped and suffocated.

"Here's what Big Sister has to tell us if you read between the lines. And I'll preface with and admit to a bit of subjectivity at this point in time. I say a *bit*, but the odds are in our favor by about a thousand to one that we're headed in the right direction by looking into Clonite, Reality, and the Columba/Emery connection as it relates to this case."

"Great," a hoarse voice sounded from the second row. "But you haven't explained this connection other than to tell us there is one. All you said was—"

"Laryngitis, Detective Tabor?" Kim Archer questioned.

"A touch," the man answered impatiently.

"Then save your breath while I unveil the *pièce de résistance*."

"Is that anything like disrobing?" Detective Lorna Hanover's partner, Wayne Fuller, asked excitedly, licking his lips lasciviously while darting his tongue in all directions.

"Yes, Wayne. But first you'll have to close your mouth, cross your legs, and sit on your hands," Kim gave back in spades. "You want to hit the lights and turn on the projector, Brian, seeing as you're standing over there doing nothing?" she addressed her husband in a manner of mild annoyance before pulling down an overhead screen.

Brian appeared out of sorts as he walked over to the projector, turned it on then switched off the lights.

"Good. Now, if you'll just focus it, dear. There you go. You see, ladies—" she said, winking at the two female detectives sitting on the other side of Wayne "—they *are* trainable."

Lorna Hanover and Yolanda Ivers both smiled and gave Kim a thumbs-up.

"So, if you'll note the configuration of the ancillary piece of rope the perp left behind for us at the Quogue scene. Not laid down as a figure eight as was initially thought, but rather as the symbol for infinity. Next one, Bri."

Brian hit the remote.

"This is the blowup of Clonite's logo you all received in a comprehensive report. And this is what Big Sister and I drummed up from a conference held in 1997, in Chicago."

All eyes were glued to the screen.

"What is it?" someone asked.

"The back of an invitation," Kim replied. "You'll note the symbol on the bottom."

"Infinity," Detective Tabor confirmed.

"That's why we have you with us, Danny."

"Yeah, but—"

"Hold your horses. Brian, wake up over there."

Brian pressed the remote.

"Note who the keynote speakers are. The first conference in the United States, introducing the collaboration of Reality and Clonite."

"Mother of God," Lorna said.

"No, Mary couldn't make it," Kim teased. "But messages from Jesus, Buddha, Moses and Muhammad's conversation with Hans Verber were promised later in the program, you'll note. Malcolm Columba and Clarence Emery delivered speeches marking 2003 as the year for the first human cloning, then sometime before 2035 when aliens will return to Earth. Columba's and Emery's thesis was, and I quote, 'Human cloning will become the key to human immortality when that day arrives.'"

"You think our serial killer attended that conference, Kim?" a senior detective asked.

"I'd bet good money he attended one of them, Eric."

"But suppose the killer just left that piece of rope to send us off on a wild-goose chase?" another seasoned detective asked.

"Frankly, Frank, I'm getting tired of hearing that," Kim complained. "I'm betting he didn't. Now, we may not be able to get our hands on Clonite's full and preferred client list, or Reality's register of members at this particular moment, but Big Sister is hard at work eliminating a number of people who attended those conferences through the years. Not necessarily dyed-in-the-wool members and clients, but rather prospective members and clients, journalists and authors, curiosity seekers, et cetera. Someone who attended a conference and signed in isn't necessarily a member of Reality's church or a customer of Clonite."

"How did we manage to get that particular list?"

"Public information, Danny. Also, there's a mystery man among us who applied a pressure point to some high official in government who applied pressure to a higher-up in Washington, who in turn made a call to Italy . . . could have been Verona, for all I know —" Kim winked "—who called the Netherlands, who then called Hans Verber in The Hague."

"So they're cooperating now?"

"To a degree, regarding the conference lists. But reluctantly," Kim clarified.

"How many signatures are we talking, Kim?"

"Six years worth, times however many states, countries and conferences. Several million names, maybe. I really don't know. The information is still coming in."

"And Big Sister's going to reduce that list to—what would be your guess?"

Kim had to laugh. "Let's suppose we suddenly learn our serial killer is bald and wears a pinkie ring on his left hand, coupled with our current profile . . . maybe two hundred fifty thousand names would be a conservative number. Who knows? Your guess is as good as mine."

"And maybe he didn't sign in or up at all."

"What do you want from me, Enrique?"

"How about a timetable."

"Several days. A week. A month. And that's if Big Sister doesn't blow a fuse before I do," Kim responded.

"What the hell's your brainchild doing back there, Kim? Paginating pages?"

"That's very funny, Owen. Paginating pages. I like that. But if Big Sister heard you, as sensitive as she is, she'd have your prick in the printer back there making carbon copies faster than we can multiply samples of DNA. How's that for an early form of cloning, dickhead?"

Half the troops were practically off their chairs or tottering on the brink.

Lorna was beside herself and practically in her partner's lap.

Then just as suddenly as the commotion began anew, it stopped abruptly—as if someone had hit a switch. In fact, someone did, indeed.

Christopher Osip crossed the threshold after turning on the lights.

Every face but one went to the ceiling . . . the walls . . . the floor.

"Why don't you take a seat, Chris," the lieutenant suggested.

Chris walked over to the corner of the room where Brian stood.

Kim continued her talk and the daunting task the three teams had ahead of them, especially with regard to a new twist in the case—both literally and figuratively speaking—concerning Chris' daughter. For not six, but rather two lengths of twenty some plaited wraps each were fashioned from the strands of shiny hair found in Vivian Osip's ponytail.

Chapter 27

Detective Gary York studied the woman seated behind her spacious desk as she carefully reviewed his application under an assumed name and occupation. She had not raised her dark eyes from the moment he entered the office, inviting the man to take a seat. Several minutes later, Pamela Richardson put the forms aside.

"A lawyer," she said and smiled brightly, taking in the applicant's handsome, rugged features.

"Was."

"Thinking of going back to it one day?"

Gary shook his head. "The only thing I want to practice is my game of golf."

"Do you play often?"

"Three, four times a week."

"And now that most courses are closed till early spring around here, what do you propose to do, Mr. Wright?"

"Travel with my clubs to where it's nice and warm."

"We have courses in Bermuda that are absolutely splendid. Are you aware of that?"

"Oh, sure. I read the brochure and other literature. I know that you're Bermuda-based."

"Maybe you'll get down there one day soon."

"No, I don't think so."

"And why is that, if I may ask?"

"I'm afraid of flying," he answered with a bit of embarrassment.

"Well, there's always a cruise ship," she suggested.

"No. Several of my friends went that route and got deathly ill recently. With the world the way it is today, I'd rather stay put in the good ol' USA. I'm going to spend some time in the Carolinas with friends, then work my way down to Miami."

"Mr. Wright, wh—"

"You can call me Gary if you like."

"Mr. Wright, why did you come to us?"

"You mean here to the New York office?"

"No, I mean our company, Clonite. What are you looking for precisely?"

Gary gestured. "It's all there in my application."

The striking woman leaned back in her leather chair. "Still, we like to ask. Often, people put down on paper what they think we want to read. That's why we like to have a private chat. One-on-one. I want you to open up to me, Mr. Wright."

"You feel I'm holding something back?"

"I didn't say that. Sometimes a person believes we can provide a service that we simply cannot deliver. We just want to be sure that we're all on the same page," she said with a slim smile, tapping his folder.

"I see. Some people delude themselves is what you're saying."

"Yes."

"Well, I'm not under any misconceptions if that's your concern. I understand contracts, and Clonite's is pretty cut-and-dried. And we're prepared to avail ourselves of your services."

"Wonderful. Then tell me why you're here. Please."

Gary sighed. "I guess I feel awkward saying it to someone's face."

The executive swiveled around one hundred eighty degrees, facing the wall. "How's this?"

Gary laughed. "Pretty funny. I'll give it a try."

Pamela Richardson slowly shook her head of shoulder length coal-black hair. "A shy lawyer. And to think I can't tell another soul because of our confidentiality clause here at Clonite."

"Better not."

"Please begin, Mr. Wright."

"You can turn around."

"You sure?"

"I'm sure."

When Richardson turned around, she was wearing a mask of a space alien with large almond-eyes. "Boo!" she blustered before lowering the plastic face.

Gary guffawed until his sides actually hurt. He wasn't acting at the moment.

"You see, I read your application very carefully, and I do pay attention, Mr. Wright. All right? I know you don't believe in extraterrestrials and our founder's story. Most people who walk through these doors do not. Humans, that is. Only kidding," she teased. "That's why we fly you out of here by UFO. Kidding, kidding. I just know you'd hate the altitude."

Pamela Richardson was nothing at all what the undercover cop had expected. Otherworldly, would be an understatement. Either she was one of the slickest salespeople he had ever encountered, or she was positively, certifiably nuts, the homicide detective swore as he came down out of the clouds.

"You're a trip, Ms. Richardson," he commented politely. "I mean that in the most sincere and positive sense."

"So then. Tell me what's in that handsome head of yours, Mr. Wright."

"Well, I was raised a Catholic, but I'm not at all a religious man. So I don't believe in Judgment Day—the rising of the dead and all that jazz. I do believe in science, however. Not Christian Science." Gary grinned. "There's no question in my mind whatsoever that Clonite has or will soon clone the first human being. The fact that your people have not documented their recent claim is of little concern to me because I know that Clonite is on the cutting edge. With regard to our current situation, I believe that my wife and I stand a good chance of having a child, with your help of course. Everything else has failed as I know you know from my file."

The woman nodded understandingly.

"Regarding the other issue, I know you're not exactly promising everlasting life like Reality; that is, immortality in the true sense of the word—today. My wife and I will, hopefully, through a happy and healthy child, live on forever in the heart of *that* creation. And that is all one can realistically expect at this time. Additionally, however, we would like to have our cells preserved while both of us are still in good health. If in the future, either of us ever needed and were candidates for new organ generation and transplant, everything would be in place. This other business of actually creating another Yolanda or me and downloading our memories if and when the technology becomes available, although intriguing, is a bit much for us. So at this point in time, we won't be subscribing to, or even entertaining that particular service. Not even on layaway," he joked pleasantly. "There you have it. Medical reports and all."

The director was studying her prospective client as a snake charmer would a viper. The man had all the right answers and no false hopes or illusions that she could immediately detect.

"And if we decided that your wife and you were indeed candidates for what you elected as outlined, do you have the monetary means to satisfy Clonite as stipulated in our contract?" the woman put forth bluntly.

Gary smiled. "I've saved a lot of money over the years by not flying or traveling via luxury liner," he teased. Pamela did not smile back. "The answer to your question is yes, Ms. Richardson."

"Have you discussed this with Yolanda?"

"All but the fact that I'm here today."

"And would she be agreeable—without reservation?"

"Absolutely."

"I'd like to meet her, Mr. Wright."

Gary was beaming. "Does this mean we're halfway there?"

"Just about," was the executive's succinct reply.

"Wonderful. How soon can we set this up?"

Richardson consulted her planner. "How about a week from Thursday? Same time."

"Fine."

"Are there any questions you'd like to ask me?"

Only about a million, Gary wanted to say. "I think I'll wait until Yolanda is here. Then we'll ask them together."

"Then I look forward to seeing both of you next Thursday."

The two stood simultaneously.

Pamela Richardson took the prospective client's hand firmly into hers.

Chapter 28

Detective Yolanda Ivers stared at Gary York incredulously. "Your wife?"

"Yep. I made an appointment for you and me to see Ms. Pamela Richardson, Executive Director for the New York Chapter of Clonite."

"You did what?"

"Next Thursday at three o'clock. And remember, you really, really want this child."

"A clone of you?" Yolanda laughed sarcastically. "A woman would have to be out of her mind."

"That's why I figure you're a shoo-in."

"Thank you very much."

"And I want you well-versed in all that in vitro, in vivo fertilization and reproductive cloning crapola by then. I want you to really know your shit."

"Hey, buster! I already got a partner. Remember? And so do you. On top of that, we've got a new commander who's still only tossing around the idea of sending in an undercover clown. You. Maybe. But he hasn't decided that yet."

"And if he does, I'll have had a head start."

"And if he doesn't?"

"It doesn't change a damn thing."

"Except for the fact that you'd better find someone else to host your party."

"There *is* no one else, Yolanda."

"Try an escort service."

"Listen. I ran this by Brian. We'll just swap partners for the day. No big deal. You'll be with me in Manhattan for a few hours on Thursday. Brian will hook up with Enrique for the afternoon."

"Oh, really?"

"Yes, really."

"And I'm just supposed to go along with this? What if something happens and I'm not where I'm supposed to be? Then what?"

"We'll have it covered. Believe me."

"Oh, I'm sure you will. But this is wrong."

"No, I'll tell you what's wrong. You recently made detective and you're scared."

"You're damn right. And I'm surprised Brian's even going along with this."

"Chris and Brian are friends. Remember? He'll do whatever is necessary to find this fucker."

"That's right. So I guess he'll go along with anything you say right now because he's vulnerable. Start taking things personally and you lose your competitive edge. You recall who told me that maybe a million times? You can remind him of that for me. Did you see Brian at the briefing? Did you see Kim? I mean really see them? Basket cases. Both of them . . . though Kim hides it, oh, so well."

"That's why he's taking a step back from this and letting me go in with you."

"Does Kim know about this, Gary? I want the truth."

"Kim's the one who's going to cover for us if anything comes up."

"Let me ask you something, Detective Gary York."

"Ask."

"Do you always use your friends?"

"Let me tell you something, lady."

"Tell me."

"You've got to learn the difference between friends and family —and fast."

"What exactly is that supposed to mean?"

"It means that Homicide's more than just a team. It's a family unit, Yolanda. You're part of that family now."

"And the lieutenant's the patriarch of that family, fella. With a job to do, just like you."

"The lieutenant's job is to let his detectives do their job."

"You sound like the kid who thinks he knows more than his parents."

"I know that the odds of catching this guy are nil if we don't have those confidential lists from Reality and Clonite. That's what I know."

"We don't even know if the killer's *on* any list."

"That's right. That's why it's important that I get in there now and start leveling the playing field. Starting with Clonite's client list. Not some 'enter-and-sign-in-please' list from some fucking conference six years ago."

"And how, exactly, do you propose to obtain that list? Or shouldn't I ask?"

"I think it's enough that you ask yourself if you really want to have a baby with me, Yolanda," the homicide detective stated with a big grin. "And it'll be your job to convince Ms. Pamela Richardson that we both want that more than anything else in the whole wide world."

Yolanda paced her studio apartment before she stopped, sighed and placed her hands firmly upon her hips. "Somehow I just know this is going to cost me, and I'm not talking gas and tolls, Mister Slick. If this gets fucked up, I'm going to put the blame on you. You got that?"

Gary grinned. "Sounds like family to me. Oh, and don't forget to pick out names for our future child. Male. Female. Maybe even twins."

"Don't make me puke."

"Well, if you do, don't let anyone there at Clonite think it's morning sickness, or you'll blow the whole deal," he declared behind a pair of laughing eyes.

"You know you're sick, Gary."

"That's *our* competitive edge, darlin'."

"What alias did you use?"

"Mr. Wright."

Detective Yolanda Ivers could not help but laugh in Gary's face. She grew even more hysterical as he set down a pile of clippings, booklets, medical papers, pamphlets, and finally a little pink and blue bound book of baby names.

"You're a rip, Mr. Wright. Title?"

"*Choosing Baby's Names*. Can't you read?"

"Your profession, I'm talking about; the title you handed Pamela Baby."

"Oh. Attorney; Mergers and Acquisitions." Gary handed her his bogus business card.

"Why am I not surprised?"

"Stick it in your memory bank."

"I know where to stick it all right, Mr. Wright. Where's Justin in all of this?"

"Packing for fairyland as we speak."

"Give."

"San Francisco. Satellite office of Reality."

"To do what?"

"Join the Church and come away with their current membership list."

"Jesus, Gary. Does the lieutenant know about this?"

"I keep trying to tell you. The lieutenant's in la-la land. We'd need a virtual army to track down just half the leads Kim's accumulating from here and abroad. We need to narrow the names of actual members and clients. Those who paid out big bucks. And we need it fast."

"And who's going to cover for J? I mean, this isn't going to be an afternoon stroll in the park."

"Nobody."

"Nobody?"

"He asked the lieutenant if he could go. Ethan said no. So he quit."

"What!?"

"Only he didn't quit. He's on his way to do a job, and he'll deal with the fallout later. He knows what needs to be done."

"He walked out?"

"In a matter of speaking. God, you're thick."

"Does Brian know?"

"He's the one who bought J the airline tickets, round trip, and Kim provided him with the necessary credentials."

"How can they do that?"

"Brian's the case detective, Yolanda. He does what he wants."

"But it's illegal."

"So's murder."

"What am I getting myself into?"

"The closest family you'll ever come to really know."

"Does anybody from the other teams know what Justin went and did but really didn't do?"

"No. No one knows but you, me, Enrique, Brian and Kim. And Brian wants to keep it that way for now."

"What's J's cover?"

"Mr. Fitch. Dumbshit nigger that he once was. But filthy rich. Shouldn't be too hard of a role for him to play."

"You guys are really too much."

"Wait. You ain't seen nothin' yet, Mrs. Wright."

Chapter 29

Kalvin Matheson gently tapped his foot against the bottom of the Osips' back door. Harriet was standing in the kitchen and immediately turned her head.

"God, you startled me, Kalvin."

"Sorry, Harriet. This is very hot." He took one step back on the stoop as she opened the door wide for her neighbor.

"What have you gone and done now?" Harriet remarked, staring down at the bubbling dish as he passed quickly into the kitchen.

"My special lasagna. Piping hot. Right out of the oven. Chris will probably be home soon. If he is or isn't, all you guys have to do is portion out what you want when you want it, set the oven to three-fifty for thirty minutes, then eat. That way, the rest of the dish won't dry out." Kalvin set the large Pyrex baking dish atop the center of the stove. "Got a pair of oven mitts?"

Harriet pulled a set from a cabinet drawer. "You're too much, Kalvin. You really are," she swore, holding back tears of grief.

Kalvin pulled on the insulated gloves, carefully lifting the steaming-hot glass container from its metal cradle, transferring the delicious-looking offering to a side burner. "There we go. Don't worry about the dish. Return it when you're all done. I'll just take the holder back for something else I'm cooking for your family." He giggled and held the stainless steel casserole dish cradle an inch above his head like a silvery crown. "King of the kitchen," he said proudly.

Harriet brought the tips of her fingers to her lips. "You're so silly," she said, trying to force a smile to keep the floodgates from opening once again. "I want you to know that you're a prince in my book, Kalvin. You really and truly are. Come here, you." She pulled Kalvin to her and gave him a peck on the cheek. "You're too good."

Kalvin feigned a frown, setting down the cradle. "A prince? Just a second ago I was a self-proclaimed king. Oh, well."

Tears suddenly formed at the corners of Harriet's eyes before they fell freely.

Kalvin stepped forward and put his arms around the woman whose daughter was three days dead. "Shh, shh," he said comfortingly. "There, there, now." He held Harriet close and kissed her hair gently above an ear while staring at a photograph of Vivian set within a magnetic frame attached to the refrigerator door. "I'm here for you, Harriet. Either here, or right next-door."

The woman trembled and wept bitterly in Kalvin's arms as Harriet Osip's mother and father hurried up the hallway.

"My baby was only eleven years old, Kalvin," Harriet bawled.

"I know, I know. We'll get him, Harriet. Chris and the others and me—if I can help in any way. We'll find him."

"Nothing's going to bring her back," she whispered through a shiver. "Nothing. But I want that bastard dead!"

"I know," Kalvin said quietly, embracing both Harriet and her parents as they tried to comfort their daughter. He peered between the two women's shoulders, focusing on another photo above the other on the freezer door: one of Vivian sitting before a bed of bright yellow summer dahlias, waving to him in her favorite yellow dress from across the family's well-manicured lawn. "I loved her, Harriet, and always will—as if she were my own daughter."

"You want to know a little secret, Kalvin?" Harriet asked, brushing aside her tears.

Kalvin held his tongue.

"She had a little crush on you. She couldn't wait for you to teach her how to fly-cast. That's all she talked about for days on end."

Kalvin seemed taken by surprise. "God's watching over her," he offered comfortingly.

"I know." Harriet heard her husband's car pulling into the driveway. "I know," she repeated softly.

"You're a good friend and neighbor, Mr. Matheson," Harriet's mother swore.

"He sure is," the husband seconded.

Kalvin affected another frown before the threesome. "But I keep getting demoted. A moment ago I was a king with a silver crown, and then a prince, and now . . . a good friend and neighbor. But you know something? I wouldn't trade your friendship for the crown jewels or an entire kingdom," he said, staring directly into Harriet's eyes.

Harriet surrendered a sincere smile. "Oh, he's so much more than a good friend and neighbor, Mom and Dad," she said without taking her eyes off the man. "He's like family. You do know that, don't you, Kalvin?"

Kalvin brightened. "Well, now that's better." He dabbed away at Harriet's tears before the pretender hugged and kissed them all goodbye, taking up and placing the cradle upon his head in a silly farewell gesture.

Chapter 30

On the top floor of a high-rise overlooking the Golden Gate Bridge, in a rather large and well-appointed office, Justin Barnes sat with a screener from Reality.

"Sir, we usually interview someone only after they fill out one of our applications. But I want you to know that I appreciate your candor and the courage it must have taken to reach out to us like you did."

"Yeah, well, courage I got plenty of, chief. But dat . . . what was dat? Can·dor? Don't know what dat be."

The tall bespectacled gentleman looked down his nose at the figure before him sporting a flashy purple satin suit.

"Frankness, Mr. Fitch."

"Frank, who?"

"No, no, no, sir. Your openness, in other words. Your sincerity."

"Oh, den you shouldn't be usin' dem fancy words if yo lookin' to be understood. See, dat be da trouble 'n dis world of ours today. Folks usin' dem five dollar words when da simple ones do jus' fine."

"Quite right. Quite right, sir. I guess you got me there."

"I don't mean no disrespect, chief."

"No, of course not. I didn't think for a moment that you did."

"See, dat's another thing."

"What is?"

"Folks not thinkin'. Shootin' off der mouths fo' they use der heads."

"Sir, tell me why you're here. Frankly. Openly. Sincerely."

"I wants to be a member of dis Church."

"Right. I understand that. But why, exactly?"

Justin Barnes leaned his muscular body into the man's mahogany desk. "Because I want to live fo'ever," he whispered. "Dat be sincere 'nough fo' yo?"

"Certainly is."

"Good. Now when do I rehearse?"

"Rehearse? Rehearse for what?"

"Fo' da choir. Man downstairs tol' me I could join da choir."

"Well, yes. But you're putting the cart before the horse, Mr. Fitch."

"Cart befo' da horse?"

"First things first is what I mean."

"Den yo should say what yo mean, chief."

"In your case, Mr. Fitch, I'll try and do exactly that."

"Good man. Good man."

"May I call you, Ed?"

"Fine by me, chief."

"Ed, do you truly believe in our spiritual leader's teachings and prophecies?"

"You mean 'bout brotherly love and everlastin' life?"

The screener nodded.

"Sure do. Dat's why I be here wif ya-all. I wanna sing in the choir, too. Know da song I wanna sing if dey let me?"

Alex Crawford shook his head.

"I wanna live fo'ever— Justin sang out loudly and off key "—I wanna learn how to fly. High! I knows ya-all know dat one. Dat's da one I hear downstairs."

"It's, 'I'm *gonna* live forever. I'm *gonna* learn how to fly.' There's an important difference," Alex Crawford pointed out. "It's the song from *Fame*."

"Right. Dat be like yo' national anthem. 'I'm gonna live fo'ev —'"

"Ed."

"Yes, sir?"

"Can you afford the initial contribution for the service you're asking our Church to perform? We'll talk about fees and such later."

"Sure can, chief. Matter o' fact, I got dis foldin' money burnin' holes in my pockets, right here." Justin stood and reached into the front pockets of his baggy purple pants and produced two thick rolls of one hundred dollar bills, which caused the screener's eyes to bulge.

"You're walking around with . . .?"

"Twenty-five hundred in dis fist, and twenty-five hundred in dat one—less one Abraham Lincoln dat da hot dog man downstairs done charge me—but from which roll I don't rightly recall," Justin elaborated, looking quizzically from hand to hand. "Ah, not da hot dog roll, chief, but da bankroll."

Alex Crawford smiled condescendingly. "Aren't you afraid that somebody might rob you, Ed? Flashing your money around like that."

"Well, da guy downstairs did exactly dat, chief. Robbed me! Charged me five dollars fo' one f'en frankfurter 'cause he couldn't make change of a hundred, he swore."

"I mean, rob you of *all* your money, Ed. Hit you over the head, or worse."

"Oh, dat's why I keep a few fins and a couple o' sawbucks tucked away in my shoe," Justin explained with a straight face, wisely tapping a forefinger to his temple. "Shoot, I hope to heck I didn't give 'im a Franklin 'stead of a Lincoln by mistake, 'cause I don't rightly recall takin' off *either* shoe, chief."

Crawford looked at the man strangely.

"Anyhow. Nobody gonna mess 'round wif or rob Ed Fitch. That thought wasn't goin' through *your* mind, now was it, chief?"

"Oh, no, heaven forbid."

"Good. 'Cause what I pay fo' is what I expect."

"Right, right. Absolutely, Ed."

"I ain't no dumbshit nigger dat folks is gonna take advantage of."

"No, I can certainly see that. Now, why don't you sit back down there and let me help you fill out this application."

"Cool. And jus' so we understands one another, I ain't puttin' down one thin dime till I sees da place, meet some o' da other members, and find out mo' 'bout da choir."

"I wouldn't have it any other way, Ed."

Justin put the two fistfuls of money back into his pants pockets and sat.

"May I say something, Ed? It's just a suggestion."

"Shoot."

"If you're going to walk around with that kind of money, why don't you keep the *small* bills in your pants pocket and hide those big bills on your person?"

"Person? Oh, I get'cha. Only problem wif dat is I can't get no five grand in these shoes. Not wif da corns *I* got, chief."

"Please call me Al, Ed. Everybody here does."

"Okay by me, Al."

Chapter 31

Kalvin Matheson drove his Camry five miles under the speed limit so as to avoid being pulled over by the police. As the killer signaled to make a right off of Northville Turnpike, he could not help but notice that his directional indicator was clicking and flashing quite erratically. It was not a faulty bulb or flasher as such, he recalled, for the same thing had happened last season when the weather turned bitter cold. Kalvin quickly sent his window down, shooting an arm out and upward into the frigid air—manually signaling a sharp-right turn.

"C'mon, c'mon." Kalvin panicked, frantically waving ahead the tailgating vehicle while continuing northeast toward Sound Avenue. When the couple in the sports car blew by, he immediately sent his window up and finally began to relax.

"Sorry about that," the madman said to the passenger lying silently on the floor directly behind him. "It won't be too much longer. Ten minutes at most. And if you think that felt cold, just you wait," he promised. "Damn directional signals. Never had an ounce of trouble with this car except for that crazy flashing. But only when it's extremely cold outside like this. As soon as the weather warms up a bit, she's fine."

Kalvin reached over and turned up the heat a notch.

"Comfy back there? Snug as a bug in a rug, I'll bet," he set forth excitedly. For that is exactly how his passenger was being transported—bound and gagged and rolled within a long length of carpet. "Come to think of it, I'll bet you didn't even feel that breeze.

"Hey, I'll bet you don't know that scientists use laser beams as hi-tech tweezers to tie the teeniest of knots in strands of DNA. Did you? I've used 0X tippet material to fool finicky fingerling trout, but that's about as thin as I'll go. Do you know that I know how to tie over forty different knots? Rope. Line. Cord. Thread. Leader and tippet material, too. You name it. I can tie the perfect knot. But I'll leave it to the science experts to unravel the mysteries of life and death.

"So, you're probably asking yourself. 'What is this all about? Why is he doing this to me?' Well, Rebecca. It's nothing personal. It's really all about survival in the strictest sense of the word. Everlasting life. You see, I know that upon your death, your husband stands to collect two million dollars—even though you're worth ten times that. I also know what's unique about that will and life insurance policy of yours. There's absolutely no problem in Phillip collecting if your death is natural or accidental. However, if you're murdered outright, or there is even the slightest suspicion of foul play, your insurer and lawyer won't pay out a dime until the matter is satisfactorily resolved. That's why this business has to be handled very carefully.

"No bludgeoning, strangulation, fright night, poisoning, hanging or asphyxiation. No, ma'am. Nothing at all like that this time out. You're just going to enter a walk-in freezer and not come out until your body is found when the owners return from their week's vacation. Very ingenious how I fixed the lock. Phillip will, of course, collect on your policy. But guess who Phillip's beneficiary will be in *his* last will and testament? Me! Not that I'd ever want or need the proceeds from that paltry life insurance policy of his. I'll bet you didn't know that *I* was the one you had to worry about—not Phillip, necessarily.

"And when I give a quarter of the money away to the charity of my choice, that's going to avert further suspicion, I'd well-imagine. All I need is a five hundred thousand dollar balance to secure a place for Alvin and myself for all eternity. Two for the price of one is what the bishop promised me. But I keep getting hit with interest and other ancillary charges, Rebecca. So I need a cushion should another unforeseen circumstance suddenly arise. They always do, you know. My home and property, too, need a face-lift, to be sure.

"Actually, I went to my partner, Sal, with the idea of begging, borrowing, or stealing the balance needed before thinking of you. However, upon his release from Pilgrim State, he went a little crazy with the monies we made together, wanting to invest most of his share in a rather risky real estate venture before I stopped him cold. And even with most of the balance of his half in hand and pocket, I'm still a wee bit shy because of all those nasty interest charges. So that's where you come in, Rebecca; otherwise, it would take every penny I have, and I still wouldn't be able to satisfy Bishop John and the folks at Clonite. I'd be left with nothing. But once I collect on your estate as beneficiary from Phillip's will, once all monies and properties are turned over to me, money will never, ever again be a problem.

"I guess you're wondering why Phillip would ever make *me* his beneficiary. Well, he married *you* for your money, deary. I know you know that. But he fell head over heels for me, that silly boy.

"Anyhow, my initial problem was how to leave you in that freezer and make it look like an accident. I can't have you writing on the walls, the floor, or even a side of beef saying that I kidnapped you and put you in there. Now, can I? Therefore, what was I going to do? I couldn't drug you because that would leave a trace. I couldn't afford to have a struggle with you. It had to be something, oh, so natural. So, I slept on it. The answer was staring me right in the face.

"Everybody has to go to sleep sometime, Rebecca. I bet you're so tired right now that that's all you really want to do. I've got this whole thing figured out perfectly. Where there's a *will*—as in your case a sizable sum that shall go to Phillip, and then to me upon *his* death, accidental or otherwise—there's a way."

Kalvin shivered deliciously.

Chapter 32

Yolanda Ivers sat across from the executive director of Clonite. Gary stood and left the room after giving his partner of the afternoon an affectionate hug and a reassuring squeeze upon her shoulder.

"Quite a guy you got there, Mrs. Wright."

"I'm very lucky, Ms. Richardson."

"Please. Call me Pamela."

"Thank you, Pamela. You do the same and call me Yolanda. I hate formality, if you want to know the truth."

Pamela Richardson smiled. "Yolanda. Truth, from this moment on, is what we have to share with one another. Woman to woman. Understand?"

Yolanda immediately nodded her head.

"You look nervous. I want you to try and relax. Everything is going to be just fine if we're truthful with one another. All right?"

"All right," Yolanda agreed, taking in a deep breath.

"Tell me exactly why you're here."

"I'm here for the most selfish reason in the world. I'm here to bring a baby into this world. Mine and Gary's. No one else's," Yolanda answered, staring the director directly in the eyes.

"And you considered and discussed fertility options with your husband."

"Yes, I have. We have."

"And?"

"And the closest we came to an agreement, that is before coming to you, was having my mother serve as a gestational carrier."

Richardson seemed impressed. "Your mother was willing to do

this?"

Yolanda nodded uncomfortably.

"What happened?"

"Gary did a one-eighty. He suddenly wouldn't hear of it and closed up like a clam. I tried to remind him that he would still be the donor, that it was still my eggs from my body fertilized with his sperm; that embryo transfer to my mother's womb was the only difference—that it would still be *our* child—that we'd be the biological parents." Yolanda paused and dabbed her eyes with a tissue.

"What was his reaction to that?"

"A lawyer?" Yolanda forced a little laugh. "What do you think? He looked into the law and learned that the child would technically be my brother or sister. My fucking *brother* or *sister*!" Yolanda repeated incredulously.

"By New York State law, that's true, Yolanda. The birth certificate is going to show your mother's name."

"That's totally asinine."

"I agree. However, the State of New York has a very strict statute regarding surrogacy. But I'm sure you know that you can opt to go out of state. No one is stopping you. Also, if you were to have the child in New York, you could arrange for adoption."

"I know, but that doesn't sit quite right with Gary. He says that in other states, you can petition the court beforehand and have the parents' names listed on the birth certificate. But not New York."

"He's right, Yolanda."

"It just seems so unfair."

"I know. But those laws were put in place for a good reason, following the Baby M case. I'm sure you're familiar with that battle as well as several other tragic stories involving surrogacy."

"Oh, believe me, Pamela, I am. And Gary realizes the bills were sponsored to address abuses. But our situation is quite different. Those bills that became law should be tailored to fit different situations. They should be amended as such. And as far as my mother is concerned, she has no ulterior motive other than wanting to be a grandmother."

Pamela reached across her desk and gestured for the woman's hand. The detective gave it willingly, praying that she had played a convincing role.

"I meet very few couples that have their heads screwed on straight," the executive director assured her. "Even fewer who are as well-informed as yourselves. If Gary wasn't so adamant about the laws in New York the way they stand, I'd push to have him reconsider and —"

Yolanda pulled her hand away and waved it like a flag. "It's not just the law with Gary," she went on. "It's this mother-in-law thing, too. You asked for the truth, so you're going to get it. I'll tell you what a chauvinist pig he can be at times. At times that I really need him. He told me, and I quote: 'Yolanda, darling; it's not this fertilization thing alone that bothers me. It's like renting a womb,' unquote. And then he laughed, thinking the whole thing was quite funny—using humor to hide his true feelings. Whenever I use the word *uterus* in front of him, he turns white as a sheet. That's what I'm dealing with. That's the man whose head you think is screwed on straight," she put forth bluntly. "He loves my mother dearly, but he just couldn't handle that . . . mentally."

Pamela could not help but smile. "I see. Now, let me ask you this, Yolanda Wright. Do you truly wish to avail yourself of our cloning procedure and to bring a healthy child to term? Not just to appease your husband but because you truly believe in our technology wholeheartedly."

"Yes, Pamela. I truly do. I ask just one thing of Clonite."

"And what is that?"

"To have our son or daughter genetically engineered so that it doesn't grow up to be a fucking lawyer."

The two women laughed for a full minute before the director asked Yolanda to fill out several green and white forms taken from a folder, promising her likely candidate, facetiously of course, that she would see what she could do about her personal request.

Suddenly, a fire alarm sounded in the hallway.

Chapter 33

Christopher Osip and his wife were sitting in their living room, both of them staring off into space. A moment later, Harriet picked up her crocheting. Chris absently turned an item over and over in his hand. Their combined activities did not lift the silence above the level of normal breathing.

Chris was the first to speak. "I've been meaning to ask you something."

Harriet kept her crochet hook busy, saying nothing.

"I'm talking to you."

Her hands stopped abruptly. "What is it?" she snapped.

"This," he said, showing her a yellow knotted hair ornament.

"What about it?"

"Did you ever see this?"

"No," she answered, returning to her busywork.

"I asked Vivian about this some weeks back. She told me an admirer gave it to her. Wouldn't tell me who."

Harriet just shook her head.

"No, what? No, you don't know anything about it? Or no, you don't care to?"

"Both. She's gone."

"I see."

"You see nothing. Never have," his wife barked. "If you weren't so goddamn suspicious and domineering—"

"If I wasn't so suspicious and domineering, what? She'd be alive? Is that what you're saying?"

"I don't know what I'm saying anymore. I can't even think straight."

Chris stood up and put the item into a pants pocket, then abruptly left the room.

Chapter 34

Gary and Yolanda hurried from the offices of Clonite, returned to their car, heading immediately for the Queens Midtown Tunnel.

"I can't believe you got it," Yolanda said excitedly.

Gary tapped his overcoat pocket.

"In there?"

He nodded.

"But I thought . . . ." Yolanda glanced down at the briefcase on the seat between them.

"There are hundreds upon hundreds of papers. I couldn't just walk out with the entire file cabinet."

"I don't understand."

"I located a computer file and downloaded it onto a disk."

"How?"

Gary grinned mischievously. "When the alarm went off, three warm bodies left the computer room in an all-fired hurry. Kim told me basically what and where to look for the back-up list. Just pray that the killer's surname doesn't run beyond the letter M. And that's if he even used his right name and not some fucking alias like us."

"M?"

"That's as far as I got—halfway through the alphabet to the middle of the 'M's. It's all I had time for." Gary smiled hopefully. "If we have to go back again, I'll make sure there's an air raid whistle sounded," he threw out half-jokingly. "After 9/11, I'd probably have the entire building to myself for the day. I hope Pamela gave us our next appointment in the early a.m.," he added with amusement.

"As a matter of fact, she did."

"All I really needed was another ten minutes. But maybe we'll get lucky with what we've got."

"I wonder how J is making out."

"He'd have called Kim, and she'd have called me if he had anything. You got some singles for the tunnel? Gave Ms. Pamela Richardson a cash deposit; she cleaned me out."

"I *knew* this was going to cost me something," she grumbled, opening up her handbag. "Don't you carry tokens or something? Flash credentials like my brother does on the train? Gotta get the lieutenant to get you an E-ZPass."

"Yeah, like I'm really in the city every day. And I thought your brother was still in the academy."

"He graduated last year."

"Where'd they put him?"

"Bed-Sty."

"Lovely area."

"Rathole"

"Sewer for a year or two at worst. He's a smart boy. He'll move up and out of there fast."

"I hope so."

"So, listen. We gonna have this kid or not?" he asked with a straight face.

"I'd throw myself off a bridge first before I'd ever let that happen."

"Should have told me sooner. We could have shot north to 59th Street instead of heading for the tunnel."

"I'm fond of you, too. Here, sport. That's all the singles I've got. Then again, you could crash the gate."

"Yeah, like I really need some more bells or whistles going off today."

"Which begs the question why you didn't tell me you had this evacuation plan in the works."

"You had enough to think and worry about without waiting for the alarm to go off."

"Pamela thought it was a drill."

"So did the folks in the computer room, until I told them I smelled smoke. Funny how the power of suggestion works. One guy actually pulled out a handkerchief and covered his nose and mouth— coughing his way down the entire staircase. The other two quickly followed on his heels."

"Did you pull the alarm, or have someone else on the inside do that for you?"

"Me. That is, after I set fires in two trash baskets in another part of the building."

"How did you behave in school when you were a kid?"

"Never caused anyone a moment of grief."

"Hard to believe."

"You know, after we get this disk to Kim, you and I can forget all about this cloning business for a while and just get it on in the backseat. Whattaya say?"

"Not if you were the last impostor on the face of this earth."

"I'm very fond of you, too," Gary declared and laughed wholeheartedly.

Chapter 35

Detective Lieutenant Ethan Powell waited impatiently in his office to update Team Three's lead detective and his partner.

Finally, Brian Archer appeared alone and took a seat.

"They got a body out in Mattituck. Walk-in freezer," Powell informed Archer. "And where's Gary?"

"He just called Kim and is heading in. Where in Mattituck?"

"Marty's Meats. It's a warehouse."

"I know it. Just off of Love Lane."

"Have him meet you out there."

"Will do."

"They're calling it a freak accident. Woman walked in, couldn't get out. Faulty lock or something. Rebecca Reynolds. Thirty-one. Furniture heiress."

"It's no accident," Brian stated with firm belief. "No way. Justin and Kim called it early on, Lieutenant. Our guy's gradually distancing himself from a physical hands-on form of bodily violence to a sort of surreal, hands-off kind of confrontation—meaning less and less tactile contact before murdering them outright. From brutally bludgeoning Denise Nathan with practically a goddamn boulder; clobbering then garroting William Walker; attempting to have Gretchen Bowers strangle herself with Constrictor Knots—causing her heart failure by blasting punk rock in her eardrums; poisoning then staging the Nolan boy like some sort of bug in the center of a giant gossamer web; hanging Emily Schroeder beneath a blinding light; shrink-wrapping and suffocating Vivian Osip, then freezing to death this Rebecca Reynolds woman."

"Maybe. Maybe not," Ethan wondered aloud.

"That bastard put her in there. I'd bet good money on it."

"You haven't even seen the body yet, Brian. There are no signs of any struggle, I'm told. It's like she finally gave up trying to get out of the freezer and went to sleep, they said. Besides, no knots were found, far as they can tell."

"Marcus there yet?"

"He's on his way. There's no hurry from what the coroner reported."

"Screw the coroner. I want to know what our M.E. says. Call Marcus again—and Chris, too, Lieutenant. Please. Tell them to step on it. Have the local boys back off. They probably contaminated the scene to high-heaven by now, but you can stop them from doing any further damage. Tell them what you think we got. C'mon, Lieutenant. Don't drag your feet on this one."

Ethan looked at Brian angrily. "Don't start—"

"No, don't you."

Ethan Powell put his hands in the air instead of around Brian's throat. "All right. I'll ride out there with you myself. Grab a car and meet me out back. I'll make those calls."

Brian grabbed his coat and headed for the stairs.

Gary and Yolanda were coming up the staircase as Brian was heading down.

Gary nodded an affirmative, not bothering to elaborate. "Gotta get this to Kim right away."

"You hear from J?"

"Negative. Wait for me. I've got—"

"We've got another one waiting for us in a walk-in freezer in Mattituck. Female Caucasian; thirty-one. Rebecca Reynolds."

"I certainly know *that* name. Furniture. Fame. Family fortune."

"Got that right. Lieutenant's coming with us."

"Oh, that's just fucking great. Yolanda. Go with Brian. I'll be right down."

"She can't come," Brian stated flatly.

"She's coming."

"Are you fucking nuts? The lieutenant—"

"I keep telling you, that's our edge, partner. And fuck the lieutenant. If he comes, tell him he has to behave himself."

"Hey, I'm the case detective—"

"That was then and this is now. I say she comes. Fill him in quickly, Mrs. Wright," Gary ordered, "before our figurehead god upstairs descends."

Brian mumbled something to himself as Gary continued up and around the landing. "I said go with Brian," Gary barked at Yolanda, before disappearing from view.

"You guys don't *really* alternate case responsibility, do you?" she questioned disbelievingly.

"Just the months with the letter r in them," Brian answered, holding up seven fingers. "It's something new we're trying out."

"You two *are* fucking nuts."

"That's how we—"

"I know, I know. I'm reminded constantly how *sheer* insanity is your leading edge."

"I was going to say, how we *keep* our sanity."

"And what do I say to the lieutenant when he asks me where I've been all afternoon?"

"How the hell do I know where you've been?"

"Are you kidding me? Why, that lyin' son of a—"

"Just fooling, Yolanda. Gary told me everything. You just touch your stomach tenderly and tell the lieutenant you were out looking for maternity clothes. He won't dare ask you another question. By the way. It's not Gary's, is it?"

Yolanda gave Brian a good punch in the arm.

"Hey!"

"Hey, yourself."

Brian's cell phone rang.

"Yeah, J . . . A to Z, huh? . . . Great, because Gary and Yolanda just got back with the goods and— Hey! Whattaya doin', girl?"

Yolanda had pulled the phone from Brian's hand. "We only got A to the middle of M on disk. So we might have to go back. Copy that, J?"

"Got it, kid. Gary's line is busy, so tell Bri to tell Kim I'm sending the list through in the next hour. She and Big Sister are going to be mighty busy. I'll be heading home tomorrow."

"Got it."

Brian grabbed back the phone. "Listen, J, we got another body in a warehouse freezer. Rebecca Reynolds. Furniture heiress. The lieutenant, Gary, Yolanda and I are heading out to Mattituck. You and Kim called it, fella. But the locals out there are calling it an accident."

"Accident, my fucking foot."

"I'll keep you posted. Between your list and half a one on this end, we may get lucky."

"I hear you, buddy. Gotta go. Oh, quickly; ask Yolanda if she picked out two names yet. One boy. One girl," Justin teased and chuckled.

"I'm right here, and I heard that," she chided. "Funny how word gets around so fast," the fledgling detective concluded, leaning further into Brian while purposely stepping on his foot.

"You did good, kid. Bye for now," Justin concluded.

Yolanda released her grip on the phone and removed her foot. "So how *does* word get around so quickly, Mr. Case Detective?"

Brian smiled. "Listen to me. The six of us, including your partner, have got to keep this among ourselves until the lieutenant comes to his senses. Shit. Here he comes."

"I thought you were getting the car," Powell groused.

"Phone's been ringing off the hook, Lieutenant."

"You can't walk and chew gum all of a sudden?"

"Gary's back and coming with us."

"Well, he better move his ass. Back from where?"

"You can ask him yourself," he gestured toward the top of the stairs.

"I'm asking you. You're the case detective, are you not? You should know where your people are at any given moment."

"Fine. Gary was taking a dump."

Yolanda lowered her eyes to the tiles.

Gary grinned anxiously, sensing the score. "Need more toilet paper back there, Lieutenant. What say we rock-'n'-roll?"

"Don't you have anything to do, Detective Ivers?" the top cop asked Yolanda.

"Sure do, Lieutenant. I'm driving you guys out to Mattituck," she answered up assertively.

"Oh, really?"

"My shoulder's been killing me since the moment I got back from the airport," Brian swore.

"And I've been sitting in rush-hour traffic for the past two hours since I left Manhattan," Gary told the truth. "My back is fucking killing me," he lied. "Spine's as stiff as the victim's, I'd be willing to wager."

"Airport? Manhattan?" The commanding officer looked from Gary back to Brian.

"You told me to get Justin Barnes out of your sight this morning, Lieutenant," Brian reminded the commander. "You took away his badge and gun; keys and the car. So, I dropped him off where he asked. The airport."

"And I was following up a lead which took me into the city. Hate that fucking hole."

Ethan Powell turned abruptly to Brian. "Did you send Detective York to Manhattan, Detective Archer? I want the truth."

"No, sir. I did not."

"Are you the case detective in charge or not?"

"Sir, we—"

"Answer me, damn it."

"Can we please continue this conversation in the car, Lieutenant?" Gary suggested. "Time's a wastin', and my back is killing me standing here arguing like this."

"What the fuck is going on here? I'm not stupid, guys."

"If you were stupid, Lieutenant, you wouldn't be sitting behind that desk commanding us. Now would you? Then again, you *are* going to be standing around in a fucking freezer in a month with an r in it for the next several hours. Damn, I hope that space is bearable because this back of mine just can't take much more," Gary went on inanely in doublespeak.

"You went to Clonite, didn't you?"

Gary said nothing.

"I want the whole story, York."

"En route, Lieutenant. Promise," he relented, knowing that truth-telling time was upon him.

"I have half a mind to take *your* gun and badge away this second."

"Or can you use the other half and hear me out? Yolanda told me you seemed like a reasonable man."

Detective Lieutenant Ethan Powell looked down at the rookie detective.

"Get the car. You're driving, Ivers."

"Yes, sir." Yolanda was gone in a flash.

The lieutenant fixed his eyes on Brian. "Barnes flew to California; didn't he, Archer? San Francisco. Reality, if I had to guess."

"You fired him, sir. He's a free agent," was Brian's straightforward answer.

The two men followed their commanding officer down the staircase, out the back of the building, then over to the parking area.

A moment later, Yolanda pulled the vehicle smartly up to the curb alongside the three men.

Chapter 36

Two crime lab vehicles were parked in front of Marty's Meats in Mattituck. A light snow fell as Detective Yolanda Ivers pulled just ahead of a County van and station wagon. The lieutenant got out and ducked under a yellow plastic CRIME SCENE ribbon, flashing his badge at an officer as he headed toward the side of the building. Brian and Yolanda followed on Ethan's heels. Gary hung back, looking down and all around him.

As Southold Town police covered the area from Laurel to Orient Point along the North Fork, the chief of police summarily greeted the three suits, foregoing any formal introduction for the moment.

Yolanda did not like the man, forming an immediate impression: abrupt, dismissive—with an air of arrogance. Portly. Sloppy.

"We've got things pretty much wrapped up here, Lieutenant. I'm afraid I haven't had the pleasure," he added, extending his hand. "Not officially, that is. We met briefly at the Peconic River Sportsman's Club. Manorville. Candidates Night. Our D.A. was the guest speaker that evening."

"Oh, yes," Powell replied taking and shaking the man's hand.

"Nothing's amiss here. Everything's pretty much cut-and-dried."

"Is it?"

"Absolutely. Our unit already went over everything. Your crew got here a little while ago. Come. I'll show you what we found." Chief Benjamin Greenly was about to lead the way when he turned and saw Gary York. "Hey, how you been, cowboy? Busy as a bee, I'll bet.

C'mon in, folks. Come. The Reynolds woman enters here—" he directed as from a script "—becomes curious, and decides to take a peek inside the cooler, over there."

"Freezer," Gary corrected.

"Right. Freezer locker to be precise. The door closes by itself. Let me show you. Fellas," he addressed Marcus' crew, "can you just step back a second so your lieutenant can have a look-see? Please and thank you very much."

"Chief. It's you who's in the way," Marcus' tool marks man set forth sourly. "We're working here. You can play with the door all you want when we're done. Meantime, I'd appreciate it if you'd give us a little space."

The police chief grew annoyed. "I don't know why they've got that lock taken half apart, Lieutenant. Faulty mechanism is all. Obviously worn. It was a freak accident. Shit happens. Our unit's been over that completely."

"Passed right over it is what you mean," the forensic scientist muttered, straightening up and pointing to a tiny, narrow metal strip, its end covered with a wad of grease. "Lock's been tampered with. See the filings?"

"Let me see that," Greenly grumbled.

"You're in my light, chief," the technician said sternly.

Greenly stood right where he was. "That could be from a wearing away."

The man simply shook his head. "Look. You're in my way. You're in my light. And now you're in my face."

"That lock is old," the chief said defensively.

The forensic specialist ignored him. "Lieutenant, I want you to see this for yourself."

Ethan Powell stooped eye-level with the lock. He did not have to be told. "Repacked."

"And recently. See how the oil's separated from the Lubriplate up here? Made to look like it's been there awhile. Then it should be down here, too. Note some older, heavier grease behind the mechanism. This piece has been filed down so it can't catch and hold here. We're going to take this lock out and back to the lab with us."

"Now, hold on just a minute," Greenly balked.

"Your guys vacuum here yet?" Gary interrupted, staring down

at the body in a corner by the door.

"And why would we? Besides, my people were told to stand down until your crew arrived," Greenly complained. "And if you must know, your boys haven't done squat except play with that lock. We could have had this area cleaned up and secured by now."

"Why would you even bother?" Gary challenged. "You're not treating this as anything suspicious, you're telling us. Right?"

"I'm saying that if we had, we'd be finished here. And those filings could have been from an earlier repair."

"Forget the filings for a moment, Ben. You say your unit hasn't vacuumed here. Correct?" Gary again questioned.

"That's right. And no one's touched the body except the coroner. No sign of foul play. She's just the way we found her. Lying there peacefully."

Gary shook and scratched his head in mild amusement. "Look around you. Lift up your shoe, Ben. All of you. Go ahead. Humor me." Gary lifted and removed his Loafer. "See? Cat litter."

Yolanda Ivers lifted and looked at the bottom of her shoe. "He's right."

The lieutenant and a detective from Greenly's team did the same.

"The sidewalk is covered with it," Gary explained. "Right on up the walkway."

"It's put down in place of salt or sand for ice and snow," Yolanda recalled aloud. "My grandmother uses it all the time."

"But much messier," Marcus mentioned casually. "Pulverized absorbent clay."

Two technicians lifted and checked their shoes.

"Come on, Ben. Get with the program," Gary coaxed.

Ben, like everyone else, had cat litter on the bottom of his shoes.

Gary stepped closer to the foot of the body. "But there's none of that shit on *her* shoes, Sherlock," he addressed the chief of police. "And you'll also note she has soles that collect shit and grit galore. Crepe. She didn't walk in here, Ben. She was carried in and placed here. The killer made those few scrapes and scratches there on the door to make it look like she first tried to pry her way out."

"Yeah, with this," Chief Greenly said, reaching into a long

canvas bag and removing a screwdriver sealed within a clear plastic evidence envelope.

"You don't put a few marks like that on a door you're trying to get out of and then retire to the other corner to take a nap. Door opens out, not in. I'm sure your guys didn't sweep her into that space, chief," Gary concluded.

"Well, this doesn't exactly fit your boy's M.O. either, Gary," Greenly challenged heatedly, not knowing what else to say.

"It does and it doesn't—" Gary proffered obscurely "—because maybe this one isn't supposed to."

"What the hell does that mean?" the chief of police pressed.

Gary York shook his head. "I'm not sure yet."

"That's what I thought."

Chris Osip stood and went over to the body. He knelt down beside the woman and began probing her blonde hair. Several strands at a time.

Brian went over to his friend. "Let's wait until we get her back to the lab, Chris. I'll help you. Too goddamn cold in here."

Chris looked up vacuously. "Think about how cold my poor Vivian is right now, Bri."

Brian looked over at his partner, but Gary simply shrugged.

Chris withdrew a tapered comb from an aluminum case then turned his attention back to the body, carefully pulling the coarser row of nylon teeth from the top of the woman's scalp down through her long, thick blonde hair. Searching for telltale knots.

Brian knelt beside him.

Gary stepped over, too.

Yolanda briskly wiped away the tears building at the corners of her eyes.

The lieutenant went over and put his arm around her. "Come on. You're gonna drive me home, Ivers. Let them work. Marcus can take Brian and Gary back in the van."

The tool marks man finished removing the lock mechanism and placed it upon a plastic sheet.

Ben Greenly ordered his crime scene unit and uniformed officers to help secure the area outside the building.

"Marcus," the lieutenant called over to the pathologist.

"I heard you. I'll see that Bri and Gary get back."

Ethan nodded. "Brian."

"What is it, Lieutenant?"

"Call Barnes when you finish up and tell him to come home."

"He'll be home by morning."

"No, I mean home where he belongs. I forgot that I can't fire him. He doesn't even exist. He's a fucking phantom. But he's *my* fucking phantom."

Brian nodded without looking up, carefully running the tips of his fingers through the Reynolds woman's hair. "After the body's removed, I want this floor vacuumed for trace, Ben. Especially these two corners." Brian gestured to both sides of the door. I'll wait for the bag."

"You got it."

"This is his handiwork," Chris said quietly. "I can feel it in my bones."

"I'm sure you're right, Chris," Brian said softly.

"Me, too," Gary swore. "Damn if I don't. Knots or not."

Chapter 37

Kalvin was furious to learn that the Southold police were holding Rebecca Reynolds' husband on suspicion of murder.

"Bunch of dumb hick cops!" Kalvin ranted and raved until he realized that his next-door neighbors might hear him. "How could the police possibly think that?" he whispered. "So close, Alvin. We are so fucking close. Fuckers!" he railed anew. "I had it all figured out. I gave Bishop John five hundred thousand dollars on account. He's the middleman between Reality and Clonite. Normally, the cost is a million bucks apiece. But we got two for the price of one. That's a bargain basement discount. Half a mil apiece for everlasting life, Alvin! But by January, he wants the balance paid plus exorbitant interest that just keeps compounding daily. What was I to do? I had a five-year plan and was going to pay Bishop John in installments, but he got impatient. I was even going to be a good guy and give a lump sum to charity when this was over. I had no choice but to work another score. Of course, I could just forget about you all together and worry about me, but I'm not like that, Alvin. I never was nor will be. Share and share alike. Brothers to the end. And that's the beauty of it. There doesn't have to be an end. The bishop showed me pictures. Told me secrets. Made me promises.

"In less than thirty years, Malcolm Columba and Clarence Emery's bodies are going to be reborn, their memories downloaded so that they'll live on forever as we shall, too. Not just as a clone of ourselves, Alvin, but actually *us*. It will take years of research and billions of dollars. The fee alone for such a procedure would be many millions to a client, the bishop said. But just like Malcolm and Clarence, those lucky stiffs—" he punned playfully "—we, too, will be among the privileged. And if I prove myself a worthy subject, Alvin, and work very hard for the Church, I could become an official, the bishop also said. Me! Imagine. You see, we were offered a bargain because we're identical twins. A twofer. But we have to be ready.

"Worse case scenario? We're cloned instead of being re-created —identical representations to be brought back into the world to carry on our lineage. The Mathesons. We have no offspring, Alvin. I'm the last of our line. How truly sad it would be to have it all end here like this. Therefore, I, the elder by a minute, had decided to underwrite one of the most important insurance policies of our lives. Think of it. Eternal life! Nothing ordinary or limited about that, dear brother," Kalvin went on maniacally.

"Now, if I was crazy, like Malcolm and Clarence surely were, I'd be out there right now collecting on double indemnity policies until I got caught. Sure. Maybe I'd have gotten away with it for a while if I wasn't rushed into it as I am this time out, but I'd also have red flags waving all over the place. Then what? Where would I be? In a cheap wooden box six feet under the ground, or perhaps a pile of ashes like Clarence Emery, I mean to tell you, Alvin.

"Well, I really went on and on there, didn't I? Usually, I carry on like this with you at graveside. God only knows what kind of listening equipment they might have out there these days—especially now that their inquiry might eventually lead them to us. Not as a matter of mere formality regarding an accidental death at Marty's Meats, but rather a full-blown murder investigation. It could get quite interesting, Alvin."

Kalvin sighed from sheer exhaustion, yet thinking quite carefully about his next move.

Chapter 38

Kim Archer walked briskly into Ethan Powell's office, closed the door behind her, pulled a chair around next to the lieutenant, placed a printout along with other papers on the man's desk, and then plopped her thin frame into the seat.

"You look like shit," Ethan said.

"Warmed over," Kim added from extreme weariness, but with her eyes set afire.

"Got good news?"

"Our president announced the capture of Saddam Hussein."

"Terrific. Now tell me something I don't know. Something on our local front, please."

"We got us two possible suspects plus a most promising candidate that just might prove to be pure gold."

"That's three out of how many hundreds or thousands, Kim?"

"Three surnames, all beginning with the letter M for openers."

"You found no one from A to L?" he asked incredulously.

"Not connected with Clonite because I'm working the list in reverse. But I ran Reality from A through Z, and guess what?"

"What? Why you're still sitting here with me instead of back there with Big Sister?"

"To get you motivated while I run the rest."

"Wrong. We don't have the time or manpower to waste tracking down *all the usual suspects*, Detective. The way this works is we run the names first. All of them we have. And *then* we narrow it down to the likeliest. Understood?"

Kim impatiently tapped a finger upon the printout. "It's very *un*usual for all three names to show up on both Reality's and Clonite's lists *and* the lists of names I cross-referenced that we now know to be affiliated with groups connected to Malcolm Columba and Clarence Emery. Radical religious cults."

"It seems to me the psychopaths who join those kinds of organizations are going to turn up on many lists, probably including the Most Wanted. Get my point, Kim? If you reach, you're going to wind up grabbing at straws."

Kim restrained her impatience. "One guy works for the Suffolk County Parks. Disgruntled. Criminal record. Tax evasion. The second is a lawyer. Practices in Queens. Lives in Nassau. Defended some of the members and clients of both Reality and Clonite in addition to one freak from the Circle of Friends. Remember that lovely cult, Lieutenant?"

Ethan grinned. "I'd definitely put him ahead of the Parks guy."

"The third man's unemployed. Has been for the past decade. Living off his bank account. Most of the money's gone."

"I haven't got time for this, Kim. And neither have you. See me after you back-pedal through Clonite's list of the names you do have. L to A. Perhaps you'll turn up a Supreme Court judge. Maybe then I'll pay attention," he funned.

Kim ignored the remark. "He sold insurance. Life insurance, Lieutenant."

"My brother-in-law sold life insurance—and my sister a bill of goods in the bargain. Or was it car insurance? Anyhow, you take your life in your hands when you ride with him. Come to think of it, he sold her both policies before he knocked her up."

"His twin brother—"

"Ah, now we're getting somewhere. My sister has twins."

"Identical twins. Alvin and Kalvin Matheson."

Ethan scowled. "Don't leave anything out, Kim, because the devil is there in the details. Run A through L re the Clonite list, and then come see me. Now, out! I'm very busy."

"Alvin Matheson was committed to and died in Pilgrim State Hospital—where Gretchen Bowers' uncle, Salvatori Passaro, was committed—where Emily Schroeder worked as a psychiatric nurse. Are you listening to me, Lieutenant? Life insurance policies were paid out to parties closely related to the victims—"

"They usually are, sweetheart." Powell smiled politely,

pointing to the door.

"—Nathan's family and Bowers' uncle. The third settlement is in a holding pattern and would benefit Rebecca Reynolds' husband handsomely if suspicion of foul play went undisputed by the insurance company and her estate attorney. In the event of Phillip Reynolds' demise, a will leaving assets of well over two million dollars falls to a second party who *coincidentally* underwrote Phillip Reynolds' initial life insurance policy. Kalvin Matheson. I believe he went about killing the others not only for the thrill of it, but to throw us off track. That's his pattern. Motive? Money to pay Reality, Clonite, or both for the promise of immortality, would be my guess."

Ethan Powell was now listening and creating creases in his face. "I don't know, Kim."

"You don't know?" She laughed sarcastically. "Want to know where this guy lives? Quogue. Right next door to Chris Osip. Kalvin Frederick Matheson. They're neighbors!"

"What? Yeah, Kalvin. I met him with Gary—the day after Osip's daughter's murder. The evening after you and Brian dropped by their home. Gary and I were there consoling Harriet and Chris when the guy brought over a six-foot hero. Helluva nice fella." But the lieutenant was also thinking back to something that Justin had stated at the start of the investigation . . . *the knots the killer employed with regard to his victims . . . the very knots Columba and Emery had used on some of their victims . . . knots not necessarily employed in the same fashion, but the same knots nonetheless . . . as if the killer had access to the files.*

"Kim, was Chris involved in the Author/Teacher cases; Columba/Emery respectively?"

"Involved? Obsessed would be more like it."

"Pics? Blowups?"

"Analyzed and wrote detailed reports regarding every nuance. He's the best at what he does, Lieutenant. He really is."

"Ever take work home with him?"

"I'm not his keeper. But I'd imagine. You know. When you're working 24/7."

"This is too good to be true, Kim. An incredible piece of teamwork, girl."

"Well, you're relatively new here, Ethan. So we wanted you to look good your first time out," she teased, thrilled that the man was finally coming around.

"I fought you guys tooth and nail."

"So, you'll make it up to us," she said with a bright smile.

"Christ!" Ethan grabbed the phone.

"May I ask what you're doing?"

"Chris and Harriet. They could be in danger."

"Got it covered."

"Covered how?"

"Hanover's watching Harriet and the house. Chris is still at the lab. Brian and Yolanda are on their way out to Quogue to surveil Matheson. Maybe pick him up for questioning; with your permission, of course. Harriet has an appointment at the funeral home for last minute arrangements."

"Chris or Harriet know what you got?"

Kim shook her head.

"How sure are we about this guy?"

"Big Sister gives us sixty-eight point five percent odds as it stands. And that's without Clonite's A to L client list," she added through a smile. "Percentage either goes up or down after we go in."

"In where?"

Kim smiled. "Those kinds of questions are questions you'll have to ask and answer for yourself from this point on, Lieutenant. I only take you to the threshold."

Ethan Powell nodded knowingly. "I understand. But I still want you to run Clonite's list back to A, Detective."

"That goes without saying."

"Anything else you care to share?"

"Sure. Welcome to our family, Detective Lieutenant Powell."

"Carry on, Detective Archer."

Kim stood, gathered up her printout along with the other papers, pushed the chair back to where she had found it, saluted smartly, then turned and left the office, closing the door quietly behind her.

"Yes!" She beamed with certain satisfaction. "Yes!!"

Chapter 39

Kalvin scooted across the backyard and around the hedges to the Osip home. Harriet saw him from the kitchen window and waved, then unlocked the back door. Kalvin tripped coming up the steps and looked away in embarrassment.

"My God, Kalvin! I don't think I've ever seen you in a suit before." Her eyes were red from crying.

"I'm taking a little trip, besides the one on your steps." He laughed nervously, closing the door behind him.

"Listen, I hate to be abrupt, Kalvin, but I've got to run to the funeral parlor with an album and—" Harriet Osip began to sob.

Kalvin rushed to her side with a sheet of paper towel pulled from the holder above the sink. "There, there," he said softly. "Want me to go with you? I don't have to leave for another hour or so. I'll drive you there and back. How's that? But first I've got to stop off at the bank."

Harriet blew her nose and shook her head. "No, I'll be all right."

"I'll tell you what. I won't leave till after lunch. This way neither of us has to rush."

"No. I'll be fine. Really. You've done so much already. Chris and I are truly indebted to you."

"Nonsense."

"No, it's true. You're one of the finest people we've ever met, Kalvin Matheson. I mean that."

"Thank you, Harriet. That means a great deal to me." Kalvin looked down at the photo album on the table. "Pictures of Vivian?"

Harriet nodded.

"I have some pictures of her I'll share with you and Chris at a later date."

"Of Vivian?"

"Yes," he said rather sheepishly. "She was like a daughter to me, you know. I don't have any children, nor ever will." Kalvin hung his head sadly. "Anyhow, I'll let you get going. Oh! Reason I came over. Can you tie this tie for me? I know Chris isn't here, or I'd ask him. He did it once or twice for me some years ago. Windsor knot. My favorite."

Forcing a smile, Harriet reached for the colorfully loud tie, adjusting its length beneath his collar. "Lean forward, please. You tie your own shoelaces, Mr. Matheson?" she asked teasingly.

"Barely," he confessed jokingly.

"That's what I thought. Where're you headed?"

"Out of town. Business trip. But I'll be back in time for the funeral service tomorrow."

Harriet nodded solemnly. "Are you sure you don't have a woman you're seeing secretly? Keeping things from me, mister?"

"Not on your life."

"Want me to look in on Poochie?"

"I was hoping you'd ask. Saves me the expense and trouble of bringing him to the kennel, which he hates. And he'll love you for it. You know where the key is."

"Raise your head. There," she said, drawing the knot. "You handsome devil. Yeah, I think you've got a date with a lady friend."

"I'd tell you if I did, Harriet," he swore.

"Do you have a tie clasp, Kalvin?"

"No, I just tuck the ends inside my shirt like this."

"Wait. I'll be right back. Don't go anywhere."

"Harriet, I'm holding you up."

"Stay put."

Harriet disappeared upstairs to the bedroom and opened her husband's black leather jewelry box. She picked through two Timex watches, a Seiko, and several sets of cuff links before finding one of her husband's tie bars lying next to the yellow knotted hair ornament he had questioned her about the other night—worn like a badge of honor whenever Vivian put her hair up in a ponytail—the distraught woman recollected.

But why is it buried at the bottom of Chris' jewelry box? Harriet wondered. "Strange," she mused aloud.

Chapter 40

Detective Brian Archer stealthily made his way through Kalvin Matheson's messy backyard to the Osips' manicured lawn. Detective Yolanda Ivers pulled her cell phone from her shoulder bag, then called and spoke with the funeral director at the chapel before speaking to Harriet. Next, she called Kim at headquarters.

Kim picked up immediately. "Yes, Yolanda?"

"Matheson's gone. Vehicle, too."

"And Harriet?"

"She's fine—still at the funeral parlor. She said she spoke with Matheson just before she left the house. He told her he was going to the bank, then out of town on a business trip. Didn't say where. Said he'd be back in time for the funeral service tomorrow. She'll be looking in on his dog while he's away."

"Where's Brian?" Kim asked with concern.

"He's just checking next-door. I'm heading across the yard now. Hold on a second. I see him, and he's fine."

"Does Harriet know what's going on yet?"

"No, I'm sure not. I had to tell her something with all the questions I was asking. So I said Brian was looking to ask Matheson a few questions concerning a lead on a robbery/homicide some years back near where he was employed. I figured Brian could tell Chris what's really going on; that is, if we inform him at all at this point."

"Good girl. Let's keep it that way for now."

"Anyhow, Harriet says he's wearing a dark gray two-piece polyester suit with a white button-down collar shirt and a hellacious pink polka-dot silk tie; black socks and wing tip shoes; beige raincoat with bone-colored buttons."

"Quite the powers of observation Harriet has. She gets that from living with a man concerned with such detail."

"That's what *I* said; only *she* said she couldn't help but notice because she practically had to dress him. He had her tie his tie for him in a Windsor knot."

"Oh, this guy is both sick and fucking slick, Yolanda."

"Tell me about it. Hanover was waiting by a window, just itching for him to make the wrong move. Listen, Brian said you already have the make, model, and plate number of the car."

"Yes, indeed."

"We should put out an APB; description, outfit and all."

"Already have. Updated as we speak."

"Really?"

Kim could not help but smile. "A complete ID of the weasel and his wheels, right from the wizard's fingertips—with orders to keep our suspect under surveillance, Yolanda. Nineteen ninety-three dark blue Toyota, Camry XL. New York plate, **A**lpha, **F**oxtrot, **R**omeo 3511. We want to know where he goes and why."

"What about the lieutenant?"

"Got him on the same page with us."

"Thank God, Kim. No, I take that back. Thank you. The lieutenant finally saw the light?"

"That and my baby browns. Men just can't resist them, although most black men tell me it's my butt." Kim giggled. "Just don't tell Brian I ever said that."

"I'm not saying a word," she swore through a laugh of relief, confident that their case was drawing to a close.

"Not saying a word about what?" Brian questioned.

"Here, it's your wife." Yolanda handed him the phone.

"Yeah, Kim."

"Lieutenant's cool with everything so far. He just gave us a green light."

"What did you do? Flash your butt?"

"What's Yolanda doing? Writing you a note?"

Yolanda grabbed the phone back. "I said nothing," she swore.

"I believe you, honey. I guess it doesn't really matter if they're black or white or purple."

"Got that right. Men will always be boys."

"Amen to that. Listen, I think someone should go in now, while Matheson's away. We may or may not get a warrant with what we've got. Tell Brian to think about that and give me a call later."

"Wanna say good-bye?"

"I gotta run. Watch his back but not his butt."

"He doesn't have one."

Kim laughed. "See, you're lookin', girl."

"Bye."

"Over and out."

"What? She's too damn busy to talk to me?"

"Not while she's sitting on the lieutenant's lap."

Brian rolled his eyes and shook his head. "Will you just tell me what she said?"

"That you should think about breaking and entering while the prick's away."

"What else?"

"That you have a really nice butt."

"She did not."

"No, she did." Yolanda's big blue eyes danced away devilishly in her head.

Chapter 41

Pennsylvania State Police, working in concert with New York authorities, reported the vehicle in question as leaving a Tudor home on Calvary Lane in Lancaster. Personnel in an unmarked vehicle and a traffic/weather helicopter were told to track the suspect's route and maintain land/air surveillance with a command center in Philadelphia. Once it had been established that Matheson was in all likelihood heading back home, New Jersey and New York State Police maintained a watchful eye. Kalvin was traveling northeast on Interstate 195 and was not expected to arrive on the East End of Long Island for several hours at the earliest.

In Quogue, two men had surreptitiously entered the home of their suspect. The only set of eyes that beheld the unauthorized intrusion belonged to Kalvin's collie.

Later that same evening in Lancaster, Justin Barnes paid Bishop John an unexpected visit.

"Tea?" the bishop asked politely through tightly clenched teeth.

Justin shook his head and removed his jacket, taking a seat on the couch directly across from the man setting himself into a leather armchair.

"We really never, ever see anyone without an appointment, Mr. Barnes. Timmy said you were rather rude and quite insistent."

"True. Timmy got his nose a bit out of joint, so I promised to remove it from his face altogether if he didn't let me in to see you."

"You know, I could and should call the police."

"One's right outside your door, Johnny: a state trooper waiting to take me to a chopper. The sooner you and I talk business, the sooner I'll be out of your hair."

"The only reason I'm seeing you is because Timmy said it has something to do with a Mr. Matheson."

"The only reason you're seeing me is because a high ranking official in New York told you it would be in your best interest to do so."

"New York muscle does not intimidate me, Mr. Barnes. Neither does a state trooper sitting outside my door. Now, I know Suffolk County is having their difficulties, and that they're trying to secure the client list from Clonite. But I can't help you with that."

"I'm not asking you to. I'm just asking about one particular client."

"This Mr. Matheson, I presume."

"That's right."

Bishop John was shaking his head. "I'm afraid I'm not at liberty—"

Justin started laughing, raising his hands high above his head before bringing them down hard upon both knees with a slap that made the bishop flinch.

"Oh, it's good to be afraid, I want you to know. Keeps the senses sharp, Johnny."

"It's Bishop John to you, Mr. Barnes," John said haughtily.

"Well, Bishop John. If you were affiliated with one of the mainstream churches, you'd be stepping aside right now." Justin reached for his coat and produced a folded photo and several documents. "That you, Johnny boy? Santa Fe? Eleven years ago? I know newsmen who'd print and air that story in a heartbeat. And I'm not talking about the *Enquirer* or *The Star*."

The bishop studied the items and Justin for a good moment before he spoke. "Tell me exactly what it is you want to know, Mr. Barnes."

"Now, there's a change of heart if I ever saw one. Why don't you first dismiss Timmy for the evening, John? Before he gets an earful."

"I have no secrets from Timmy, Mr. Barnes."

"Yeah, but I do. And if they get out, I'll have to come back here and redecorate this place."

Tim stood by defiantly and awaited his instruction.

"You may have the rest of the evening off, Timmy," the bishop said anxiously.

Without a word, Timothy disappeared up a carpeted staircase to his room.

"I just want you to know that *that* man has terminal cancer, Mr. Barnes," Bishop John spoke in a hushed but firm voice.

"I'll let you in on a little secret, John," Justin said hardly above a whisper, tapping the cushion next to him invitingly.

The bishop stood and took a seat at the other end of the couch, waiting with apparent interest mixed with apprehension. "Well, what is it?"

Justin leaned in close. "I really and truly couldn't give a good fuck about Timmy and his big C, John. You can keep that pic and copies of those so-called sealed court papers as a constant reminder of your past. I've got triplicates."

Chapter 42

It was in the wee hours of the morning when Kalvin Matheson was suddenly pulled over on Sunrise Highway in Suffolk County, boxed between two sedans. Two men got out of their respective vehicles, and Yolanda immediately slid behind the steering wheel. Brian flashed his badge while Gary flooded the interior of the Camry with a beam of light.

"Oh, my God! What?" Kalvin shrieked after sending down his window.

"Wrap all ten fingers around that steering wheel and keep them there." Detective Archer pulled open the car door. "I want you to slowly step out and come with us, Kalvin. We have some questions we'd like to ask you."

"What kind of questions?"

"Get out."

"Am I under arrest?"

Detective Gary York consulted both his calendar watch and partner. "It's now a.m. and still a month with an r in it," he said with a slick grin. "But I'll defer to you, good buddy."

"If you come with us voluntarily, you're not under arrest," Brian answered their suspect. "If you don't, you are. How's that, fuckface?"

Kalvin was pulled from the car and searched.

"If you're taking me someplace, I first have to make a call. I know the law."

"Yeah, but do you follow it, Kalvin, is one of the questions we'd like to ask you," Gary toyed vociferously, turning the man around abruptly and placing him in handcuffs.

"I thought you said—"

"We don't want you picking your fucking nose."

"I have a puppy at home that has to be walked."

"And I'm sure he's just as cute as you."

Gary put Kalvin into the backseat of his sedan, next to a slouched-over, snoring figure.

Yolanda awoke, nodded, got out, then took off alone in Brian's vehicle.

"Where are you taking me?" Kalvin demanded.

"For a joyride. Then maybe the Crossbar Hotel. Depends how cooperative you are."

"Poochie's going to pee all over the house."

"And you in your pants when you see your accommodations."

"But I'm cooperating."

"Quick question, Kalvin. Where'd you get that great looking tie?" Brian asked.

"Probably from some fag shop in the Village," Gary answered for their collar.

"Nah, Bishop John likely bought it for him as a gift for spending all that money," Brian bantered.

Gary slammed the car door and grinned from ear to ear. "Like I said, Bri, from some fag shop."

Justin sat up straight and wiped the sleep from his eyes before slipping a powerful arm around their prime suspect.

Chapter 43

"**N**ot a shred. Not a fucking thread," Detective Troy Anderson of Team Three reported to Brian Archer via cell phone.

"What?"

"The place is clean."

"I can't believe you found nothing."

"Well, we're not Marcus and company, Brian. Just a couple of guys who happened to be in the neighborhood and popped in for a look-see. But when we heard what the deal was and the time we had, Eric and I spent the better part of the evening going through everything. And I do mean *everything*. Believe me, we'd have found something besides a bunch of books on alien beings, cloning, saltwater and freshwater fly-fishing, and crime stories."

"Then he's got to have a safe house. Some building. Storage shed. Something."

"Now, dog hair we can give you by the bagful. But not one strand of it found on any victim. Not a single fiber from his carpets. No cat litter. Nothing."

"Makes no sense."

"I just heard that Marcus and the boys didn't do so hot with his car, either."

"You heard right. Whattaya make of all this, Troy?"

"There's nothing on the bodies or their clothing to link the son of a bitch; nothing on that rock, garrote handle, duct tape, mono, fluoro, braid, rope, cord, shrink-wrap, or any fucking thing to connect him to the victims. What do I think? I think the guy's somehow connected to this from what Kim found out, but that we still got a serial killer loose out there. That's what I think."

"That's what I was afraid you'd say."

"Maybe, just maybe, if Marcus and his crew along with their box of toys and bag of tricks had gone in, they'd have turned up something. Who knows? But I tend to doubt it."

"Well, we sure as hell aren't headed back there with any warrant now."

Troy chuckled. "Nope. Instead, we might have been served with one ourselves last night."

"How do you mean?"

"Well, Eric got off his hands and knees for just a second to stretch his legs when suddenly the security timer light comes on in Matheson's living room. Eric drops back down on all fours. So the dog thinks he wants to play and starts going nuts. Next thing you know, Harriet's at her window, peeking through the blinds toward the house as Chris rolls into his driveway at midnight and sets off Matheson's motion detector between the properties. Guess she figured the headlights spooked the mutt. But Eric was sure she'd check on the dog again, or worse yet, call the police. I had to keep reminding him that we were the police and that I'd handle matters if anyone came to the door." Troy laughed. "You know how crazy he can get when he bumps heads with the local boys."

Brian laughed, too. "Listen, you guys did what you could. I gotta run. But thanks."

"Yeah, for nothing."

"We'll figure this fucker out, Troy."

"Of this, I have no doubt."

Chapter 44

Detective Brian Archer went in alone and initiated the first interview, interrogating their suspect within the confines of the infamous 8 x 8 foot claustrophobic space at police headquarters in Yaphank. Brian felt it prudent to start off in an area back in time.

"Look at me, Kalvin. We know that you attended conferences in San Francisco and New York City. Conferences held by Reality and Clonite. We also know—after speaking with several individuals—that you felt, shall we say, a reverence toward Malcolm Columba and Clarence Emery."

"So? Is that against the law?"

"No, of course not. But murder is."

"And what does that have to do with me?"

Brian studied his suspect for a moment before continuing. "That you're misguided, perhaps, in who you choose to worship is what it has to do with you."

"Really?"

Brian nodded. "Really."

"And who or what do you worship, Detective?"

"God and country."

Kalvin Matheson laughed. "God and country. Good for you."

"Pretty square, huh?"

"Let me tell you something about myth and religion."

"All right."

"Your God, your religion, you accept purely on faith."

"True enough."

"My religion stems from pure science. Stem cells, *perhaps*, are my ticket to immortality. I don't put my faith in something I can't see or touch."

"I understand what you're saying, Kalvin. May I call you Kalvin?"

"You pull me out of my car in the middle of the night, take my personal effects, refuse to allow me to make a phone call, which I'm entitled to by law, and you want to get chummy?"

Brian minded the hatred building in Matheson's eyes.

"You're going to have some lawsuit on your hands, I hope to tell you, Detective," Kalvin threatened. "Archer is it?"

"Why don't you tell me how this religion of yours works."

"Works? It would take the rest of the morning and well into the afternoon."

Brian smiled. "We've got the rest of the day and into tomorrow, if need be, Mr. Matheson."

Kalvin glared. "I know exactly how you guys operate. I know all about sleep deprivation, intimidation, starvation tactics, and so forth. Even the themes you use. I know what you people did to Malcolm and Clarence."

"I see you were on a first name basis with those boys."

"Those boys earned my respect. They were brilliant."

"And now your two heroes are gone forever."

"That's where you're wrong, Archer."

"Then why don't you enlighten me. Or do I have to attend those conferences and lectures to learn what you already seem to know?"

Kalvin sneered. "I had to pay good money to know what I've come to know—and you want the information for nothing."

"Suit yourself." Brian got up to leave and let the suspect sit and stew. Part of the drill. "I'll just let you dwell on things awhile."

"Wait a minute."

Brian sat back down.

"Do you really wish to be enlightened, Detective?"

Brian remained mute.

"I'm going to have to take you back in time, thousands and thousands of years."

"Begin at the beginning, Kalvin," the lead detective invited. "I'm listening."

"But not with an open mind, your body language tells me,

Detective Archer," the detainee vented with irritation.

Brian unfolded his arms from across his chest and relaxed.

"That's a bit better." Kalvin placed his elbows on the table and interlaced his fingers as if in prayer. "Many thousands of years ago, extraterrestrial beings from the planet Elohim, the eternal planet, created all life here on Earth."

Brian did not so much as blink.

"Through the years, they visited and cohabited here with humans. There are many allusions to this in your bible, Detective, along with scores of references and other recorded writings of their travels across the skies on chariots and pillars of fire, or metallic mushroom and seemingly saucer-shaped clouds. Quite reminiscent of the UFO phenomenon we read and hear about even today. Angels descending from the heavens, Archer. *Angelos*, from the Greek word meaning messenger."

Brian pulled his chair a little closer to the table, taking down notes.

"Ever read *Chariots of the Gods* by Erich Von Däniken, Detective?"

Brian shook his head. "No, I haven't."

"It's an interesting book written in the late sixties. Its very first paragraph asks us to reconsider the belief that we're the only form of intelligent life in the entire solar system. Pretty presumptuous of us. Think about that. It really got *me* to thinking. And I haven't stopped. I read everything on the subject that I could get my hands on. Then I heard and read about Hans Verber. In 1973, he was picked up by aliens and chosen as an ambassador, a modern day prophet. He founded the Reality Movement the following year. Twenty-three years later, in 1997, he founded Clonite. I attended two conferences and was truly moved. I read all his books and literature. Astonishing. I see a hint of skepticism on your face, Detective. I was skeptical, too. Believe me. But after exhaustive research, I've come to the conclusion that everything the man says is true. But I still play devil's advocate— challenging everyone and everything. Do you know why I do that, Detective?"

"No, why?"

"To expose the dissemblers who surround our leader. Hypocrites who pay nothing more than lip service to this great man."

"And what do you do when you've exposed them?"

"I report it to our bishop in Lancaster. Bishop John."

"And?"

"And he deals with it."

"Deals with it how?"

"I'm not privy to that information."

"Couldn't this Bishop John of yours from Lancaster be a dissembler?"

Kalvin shook his head emphatically. "Absolutely not. I thought he was at first. But then he told and showed me many things."

"What kind of things?"

"Things that will come to pass."

"Like what?"

"Like Malcolm Columba and Clarence Emery returning from the dead."

"And you believe this?"

"I know it to be quite possible."

"How?"

"I saw with my own eyes what steps are being taken to ensure this. How their living cells are being prepared in a laboratory to bring them back to life. Not in a hundred years from now, but in a few decades."

"Wow!" Brian went along as best he could.

"Wow, is right."

"Where's the lab?"

"That's kept secret. I'm sure you can understand."

"Are you going to return from the dead one day," Brian asked with a straight face, "like Columba and Emery?"

"Yes," Kalvin Matheson responded. "Indeed, I am. That's why, for the first time in my otherwise miserable little life, I am not afraid of dying. I'm not afraid of the unknown because I now know my destiny."

"That being immortality?"

"Yes. Everlasting life."

"Explain something to me, Kal."

Kalvin smiled. "Oh, so now it's Kal."

"A clone of you or Columba or Emery, or anyone for that matter, would not really be *you* or *them* in the flesh, so to speak. But rather a likeness . . . a similarity. Same DNA, granted. But a reproduction nonetheless. A carbon copy at best. Not the original."

"Correct. Not until our memories, feelings and emotions, along with our environmental surroundings are downloaded into the mix, which will happen one day, I can assure you."

"Can you now?"

"Absolutely, because within the next thirty years, perhaps even less time at the rate genetic technology is advancing, we'll have the possibility to live at least ten times longer than what you would normally expect: seven hundred to maybe twelve hundred years. But to ensure everlastingness in lieu of longevity, diseases notwithstanding, I'd recommend having your cell tissue stored with the people at Clonite. You get what you pay for, Detective Archer."

Archer read Matheson's mercurial temperament like a well-calibrated thermometer. The man now sitting before him was calm, relaxed, and confident. The detective decided to take their conversation along a different tact. The transition, he knew, would have to be as smooth as glass.

"Cost beaucoup bucks for that, I'll bet."

"Come on, Detective. It's like the advertising slogan for L'Oréal. You simply say to yourself: 'Why? Because I'm worth it,'" Matheson offered in an affected, effeminate tone, grinning from ear to ear.

Brian took the chancy step.

"But how does an ordinary person get that kind of dough?"

"By any means possible, I would imagine," Kalvin answered slyly.

"How did you come by that kind of money?"

"By-and-by," he responded evenly.

The question was out there, but Brian knew that no straight answer would be forthcoming. "Care to elaborate?"

"How I came by the money is my business," Kalvin snapped with a degree of anxiety.

There was no turning away from the line of questioning, Brian decided. Not unless one wanted to go back to pussyfooting around, he concluded then and there.

"Kalvin. You haven't worked in ten years. You have sixty three hundred dollars left in your savings and checking accounts combined.

Your home is valued at one-forty, if you're lucky, because it's in disrepair. You have no other equity. Where did you come up with half a million dollars; that is, half the down payment to Clonite? Hard, cold cash. How and where do you think you'll come up with the balance of another five hundred thousand to pay off Bishop John? Less, of course, the thirty thousand you withdrew from you account yesterday morning."

"You believe I'm that serial killer, don't you?"

Brian shook his head. "No—not believe it, Kal. I know it."

"Then prove it," Kalvin said belligerently. "Go ahead."

Chapter 45

Detective Gary York consulted with his partner before entering the interrogation room. Matheson raised his head from the table and opened his bloodshot eyes. Gary looked as though he had just stepped off the cover of *Gentleman's Quarterly*, closing the solid steel door behind him.

"Gee. You look tired, Matheson."

"I know what you're doing, and I'm afraid it's just not going to work."

"What am I doing?"

"You know damn well what. Keeping me up all night and day. Trying to intimidate me. Depriving me of my rights."

"And what rights are those?"

"I have the right to an attorney."

"You're not even charged yet, so—"

"So then let me go. I have a dog that has to be walked and fed, and a church service and funeral to attend."

"Your neighbor is taking care of the hound."

"You spoke to Harriet?"

"Yes, and you know goddamn well she's not going to let the dog take a leak and shit in your house, or go hungry. So just relax."

"So, I guess Poochie has it better than I do for the moment." Kalvin brooded then suddenly laughed out loud.

"Let's see if you're still laughing in the next several hours."

"I told you. I know the games you people play. And it's simply not going to work."

Gary pulled back a chair and took a seat at the small table across from Kalvin. "I'll let you in on a little secret, Matheson. It doesn't matter what you know or don't know about any games. It doesn't change a thing. Get it?"

"What am I supposed to get?"

"That you're going to confess."

"Confess to what exactly?"

"To the murders of Denise Nathan, William Walker, Gretchen Bowers, Nolan Andrews, Emily Schroeder and Rebecca Reynolds."

Kalvin was surprised that the detective failed to mention Vivian Osip. *Is this some sort of stupid trick?* he wondered. *Surely, they had to believe that if I killed the others, I had to have killed Vivian, too. Surely, they uncovered the telltale knots in her ponytail. Surely. Or was having lived right next-door to the Osips for all those years too incredible for them to comprehend that fact? Surely. Maybe Chris has told everyone that it just isn't possible.* Harriet, Kalvin knew, would not believe her ears with regard to what the police suspected. *Surely it was just an oversight on the detective's behalf not mentioning Vivian,* Kalvin decided. *Still, how very odd.*

"I don't know a single soul you mentioned, Detective."

"That a fact?"

"Not that I recall."

"Do you recall underwriting a life insurance policy for Phillip Reynolds."

"No, sir. Wait! Phillip. Yes, of course. Is Phillip a suspect, too, Detective?" Kalvin asked as if the news were new to him.

"Not as far as we're concerned, he's not. Just you, Kalvin. Southold cops have arrested Phillip for her murder, which I'm sure you know. You killed Phillip Reynolds' wife to collect the inheritance."

"Now, hold on just a minute, because I'm quite confused."

"Really?"

"Yes, really. You're saying Phillip's wife, Rebecca, left monies to *me*?"

"To Phillip."

"But you just said . . . ." Kalvin feigned confusion and scratched his head. "If Phillip's the beneficiary, then I would assume that everything goes to him."

"You didn't let me finish. I was about to say that in the event of his demise, a portion of the estate goes to you. Well over two million dollars, in addition to their home and property valued at just over three point five million." Gary smirked. "I suppose you didn't know that."

"No, I had absolutely no idea. As a matter of fact, I didn't even want my name as beneficiary on Phillip's life insurance policy, which he had me write years ago. I told him to take me off of it because, as the underwriter, I thought it a conflict of interest. Mr. Morely, who was my boss, said that the face value of the policy—just a few thousand dollars as I recall—posed no problem. You can ask him. I'm sure that he'd remember. So, I don't see what all this has to do with me."

"Because you were planning to kill Phillip Reynolds in short order, knowing a bonanza would be coming your way. Just like you killed Gretchen Bowers and made her uncle disappear—like the money—after he collected one million greenbacks upon her death, following his release from Pilgrim State. Salvatori Passaro, Kalvin. A fellow inmate of your brother's at the hospital."

"I don't know any Passaro. And I never heard my brother speak of him."

"That so?"

"Yes, that's so."

But the detective was shaking his head. "First, the murder of Denise Nathan at Indian Island, knowing her family would be bequeathed a tidy sum, but unconnected to you in any way, shape or form. Very clever, Matheson. Next, a random murder near the Moose Lodge to further complicate matters for us: William Walker. Then you figured it was time to cash in by killing Gretchen Bowers. I guess Nolan Andrews was another of your random killings. Emily Schroeder was employed at Pilgrim State Hospital during the years your brother was committed. You figured you'd have us off on another wild-goose chase while you sat back with half a million bucks over the next several years. But Bishop John got greedy and moved your timetable up, so you needed another score as part of Clonite's package deal. One million dollars in two installments plus interest at usury rates. The balance of five hundred thousand plus penalties to be paid by the end of January. That would put you in the red. Hence, Rebecca Reynolds. But as soon as you learned you botched that job and they arrested Phillip, you decided to wipe the slate clean and settle up with the bishop in case we nailed your ass. You withdrew thirty thousand from your account yesterday morning, collected Salvatori Passaro's share from his niece's policy—by hook or by crook—drove back up to Lancaster and paid Bishop John the final installment, plus interest. And so here you are."

Still no mention of Vivian Osip, Kalvin thought. *Clearly not an oversight. What is this detective's game?*

"Not unlike the bishop, you, too, got greedy—like they all do, Matheson. When you weigh the equity in your home and property against the mortgage, well, it doesn't leave you very much. Certainly not enough for counsel to defend six counts of murder one; seven when we find Passaro's body." Gary let the last lines linger there a moment for the suspect to digest. "It could carry the death penalty if you're convicted. But you figure you're covered. Right?"

Kalvin Matheson could not help but smile. "Think you got it all figured out, don't you?"

The detectives pretty much felt that they had. Needless to say, they would have to prove those allegations. York knew they would be hard-pressed to find Matheson's safe house, or Salvatori Passaro's body for that matter.

"Yes, Matheson. We do."

"Proving it will be another matter, though. Won't it? And seeing as how I did nothing wrong, you won't be able to."

"Is that a fact?"

"If you had the facts, Detective, instead of a lot of speculation, you would have charged me by now."

"Well, before I lay my trump card on the table, screwball, I thought maybe *we* could strike a deal."

"A deal?"

"Sure. You're a wheeler-dealer. No?" Gary York sat back confidently, the tips of ten fingers placed firmly together to form a pyramid.

"Did you ever stop to think that maybe this Sal somebody, this uncle who you said collected a million bucks before he disappeared, might be the one you're after? Or how about Phillip? Although I really don't believe he'd harm a fly."

"You mean just like Harriet Osip wouldn't believe you'd ever harm anyone? Especially her daughter."

Kalvin looked the detective dead in the eyes. "Of course I wouldn't harm anyone. Not in a million years or for a million dollars or for any amount of money in the world, for that matter."

"How about for the promise to *live*—not for seven hundred to twelve hundred years—but *forever*? Would you kill for the privilege, Kalvin Matheson, believing that one day both Alvin's and your cell tissues, safeguarded by Clonite, will be genetically engineered when the technology becomes available and that the two of you shall be blessed with immortality, just like Malcolm Columba and Clarence Emery? Would you murder men, women and children for the right of passage then? Bishop John told us everything about Alvin, Kalvin."

Kalvin could not hide the mounting anger coursing through his body and his brain. *What had happened to Bishop John's promise of anonymity?* he wondered. *Two for the price of one. 'Confidentiality is our hallmark,'* he had been assured by the representatives of both Clonite and Reality.

"Don't have an answer for me, Mister Life Insurance Man? What's the matter, Matheson? You look a little pale. You didn't think Reality and Clonite would cooperate with us? This is a murder investigation. All bets and promises are off. And that's not the half of it. I haven't even turned over my trump card yet. Wait till you see that beauty. So tell me. Want to hear the deal?"

Kalvin regained his composure. The police were full of tricks and quite deceitful he knew from having read many newspaper accounts through the years. True crime stories were among his favorite. He followed them like sheep follow their shepherd. He was not going to fall for one of their ruses. He recalled how they had forced several suspects into confessing. A Marvin Tolliver in particular —arrested and convicted for the murder of his parents, which he probably did *not* commit. The games the police played with others simply would not work with him, he swore, for he was wise to their ways.

"For my amusement, Detective, let me hear what it is you have to say."

"It's very simple. You sign a full confession admitting to the murders of Nathan, Walker, Bowers, Andrews, Schroeder and Reynolds. In exchange, we give you a pass on lethal injection. You'll spend the rest of your natural life in prison. We also drop the attempted murder charge re Vivian Osip. It doesn't help your situation, of course. But it spares the state and the Osip family the ordeal of a trial. That poor girl's been through enough. Don't you think?"

Kalvin looked at the detective as though he were positively crazy.

"If on the other hand, you want to opt for the needle—realizing, of course, that it takes about a decade because of all the appeals—rather than wait for the Grim Reaper to appear at your cell door when you're old and gray, we can help arrange for you to end things shortly. The choice is yours. It's perfectly understandable that you'd want to go to sleep sooner than later with peace of mind that you and Alvin will someday be off and running. And if Clonite *does* come up with the technology to create another *you*, before you're scheduled to be executed by the state or make it into your nineties, well, you could always visit yourself in prison. How's that?" Gary offered and laughed good-naturedly. "Poor Alvin, though, will have to go it alone, I'm afraid."

"You're a very sick man, Detective."

"Yeah, but I never murdered anyone in cold blood. Simply shot them cold-stone dead in the line of duty. And I didn't get off on it either. That's the major difference between us."

"Vivian Osip is dead, Detective. I don't know how you could defile her memory like you're doing. Her mother just went to the funeral parlor yesterday to finalize arrangements. Do you have any idea what that poor woman is going through?"

"Yes, Harriet, indeed, went to the funeral parlor to bring a photo album along with some of Vivian's effects. All part of *our* arrangement, here, Matheson," the detective downright lied. "Closed casket from the get-go. Chris insisted on it. Harriet and he couldn't bear to look at Vivian lying there and say their final goodbyes. We took advantage of their wishes. The medical examiner said it was the thick white mil plastic that insulated and protected her; the surrounding cold that actually saved her life, slowing down her respiratory system. She had no pulse. Clinically, she was dead. When you sealed her fate and thought you had sucked the last breath out of her body, Matheson, you inadvertently created a little tear in the shrink-wrap. Enough to sustain her. If you want to know the morbid truth, we all thought she was dead when we found her, including EMS. We informed Chris and Harriet immediately. There was no need for Chris to come down to identify her because several of us knew Vivian from family functions. But he came anyway and left with a broken heart. Not five minutes later, the M.E. comes running out screaming that there's been a miracle. To make a long story endless, she was in a coma for three days before she came around. We almost lost her. But God wouldn't let that happen. The God you don't believe in, fuckface. Vivian told us everything she could remember. That's when we learned it was you. A little too late to save the Reynolds woman. But not too late to save the day."

"How could you not tell Chris and Harriet their daughter's alive?" was all that Kalvin would give him, although the sweat on the suspect's brow told York so much more.

"That's something we really had to struggle with. Believe me. We had a lead on you but couldn't prove squat at that point. I told you we almost lost her. She was in guarded condition and started to slip away from us. If she succumbed, we'd have next to nothing. We had to get her testimony come hell or high water. If Chris and Harriet were in the picture, we would have lost that opportunity because Vivian was extremely weak. Vivian's parents and doctors—had they had her instead of us—unquestionably would have kept us at bay. A parent's and physician's prerogative. Powerful medicine," Gary swore. "The M.E. said that we might lose her at any moment. The prognosis did not look good. For admittedly very selfish reasons, we decided that taking a chance on hearing and recording Vivian's *complete* deathbed testimony rather than the likelihood of getting nothing at all in her weakened condition was a no-brainer.

"We've kept the truth from Chris and Harriet for a few reasons. One: There's been very little change since her relapse; loss of oxygen to the brain brought about by your actions, not ours. So if she does fail, those two torn souls won't be put through double torture. Two: If Chris knew right now that it was you who did what you did to his little girl, he'd find a way to kill you himself. Believe me he would. That would be bad P.R. for us, to say the least. Just for the record, I promised my partner and myself that I'd do everything in my power to see that you do at least a decade on death row before they sterilize the needle if that's to be the outcome. Needless to say, you'd be on suicide watch 24/7 so you don't escape us through an early death. If not the needle, like I said, you'll receive life in prison without the possibility of parole till death do you part. Three: As I already mentioned, you'll spare all parties concerned the ordeal of a trial. But if it has to come to that, even with her audiovisual testimony having been taken at bedside, Vivian may still have to appear if she's well enough. That's up to the judge. Either way, it's going to be very tough on the family. But you wouldn't know about that because you don't have a family and because you're already dead inside.

"So, Mr. Kalvin Matheson, serial killer *not* so extraordinaire—unlike your two heroes that you worship and adore—what's it going to be?"

Wide-eyed, Kalvin leaned against the back of his chair, handcuffs stretched straight upward, palms cupped and clapping loudly. "That was an extraordinary performance, Detective whatever your name is. Only Vivian would never say whatever you said she said because I'm innocent."

"Detective York's my name."

"York. York. But of course. Detective Gary York. I remember reading all about you in the papers. Rumor has it that you misrepresented yourself as an attorney for the accused. Right here in this very room, in fact. What was the suspect's name?" Kalvin racked his brain. "Ah, yes. Howard Mills. Accused of murdering all those prostitutes back west. He had his younger brother help him dispose of the bodies. Some say *he*, the younger brother, was the one who actually killed them. But Howard took the fall. I can't remember the brother's name offhand. But I know he's dead. You tricked Howard into signing a confession by passing yourself off as his attorney. Very sneaky." Kalvin smiled. "They call you The Closer, don't they? Yes, I remember. Oh, will you do me a favor and close the door when you leave here, Detective?"

Gary was livid but hid it well. "I'm so glad you remember Howard, Kalvin. You're going to be joining him one day. He can tell you all about waiting to die on death row."

"Then maybe I can arrange for him to meet someone from Clonite before it's too late, Detective *Dork*." Kalvin could not help but giggle.

"You just think over what I said." Gary got up. "Next time I see you, I'll have a pad and pen in hand."

"And why is that? Is it too hard for you to remember an order of fish and chips, side of coleslaw, and a bottle of Bud?" Kalvin positively roared—quite proud of himself for not having caved before the veteran homicide detective, knowing that Malcolm Columba and Clarence Emery would have been very proud of him, too, and would maybe one day get to tell him so themselves. "And if somebody doesn't take me to the bathroom soon, I promise you that I'll piss and shit in this corner like a mistreated dog. I swear it."

"And I promise you that I'll come back here and clean it up with your fucking face."

"Wish I had that on audiovisual, tough guy."

"You're gonna wish for a lot of things before I'm through with you, Matheson. Believe me."

Chapter 46

Literally hundreds of people had attended Vivian Osip's wake, church service and funeral. Afterward, fifty or so mourners accepted the invitation back to Chris and Harriet's home for salads, soups and sandwiches. Most were law enforcement personnel. When family, friends, relatives, colleagues, and neighbors had finally left, Kim and Yolanda helped the heartbroken woman finish cleaning up in the kitchen. Apart from returning to the Osip home immediately following the funeral to console and comfort the grieving couple, Brian went upstairs with Chris on police business in order to secure photographs and videos of Vivian's last birthday party necessary to the ongoing investigation. Kim and Yolanda remained downstairs with Harriet.

"You know what's amazing to me?" Harriet sobbed, wringing her hands in an uncontrollable manner.

"Tell me," Kim replied, embracing the woman in an attempt to comfort her.

"The children! All the chil-children who came. I never knew she had so many little friends. Some of them so young . . . to think that their parents would even allow them to attend. I saw a busload of them from the school enter and leave the cemetery."

"Vivian was very popular," Kim said, wiping the tears away from her own eyes. "So much so that the school set up grief counseling for all grades. She was loved by everyone, especially her teachers. She drove them crazy as you well know, but they adored her, Harriet. She'll be sorely missed." Vivian's godmother managed a little smile in order to hold back the floodgates.

Harriet suddenly dropped to her knees before Kim could grab

hold of her. Yolanda quickly stepped forward, and the two detectives pulled the distraught woman to her feet.

"I want to die and be with her," Harriet whispered eerily in Kim's ear.

"Stop it!" Kim practically shouted, taking her friend firmly by the shoulders, then back into a pair of comforting arms.

"I want God to take me to her, now! I can't bear this another second."

"Come over here with me," Kim ordered. "Over here and sit down."

Kim and Yolanda led Harriet to the kitchen table and sat her down gingerly.

"Now, I want you to listen very carefully to what I have to say," Kim insisted.

But Harriet was shaking her head back and forth hysterically.

Both Kim and Yolanda each pulled up a chair, then took and held Harriet's hands.

"My poor ba-baby." The woman wept bitterly. "My darling little girl."

"Shh," Yolanda comforted quietly. "Shh."

"She's with the angels, now," Kim breathed the words and firmly believed them with all her heart.

"But I wa-want her here with me, or-or I'll gladly go to her," she pleaded, sobbing and rocking herself backward and forward before the Formica table.

"I said that I want you to listen to me," Kim demanded.

Upstairs in the study, Chris wrestled with Brian's request.

"I'm not stupid, Bri. You're holding something back."

Brian was shaking his head.

"Yes, you are. If there's something in those pictures, *I'll* find it. Just tell me what it is we're looking for. Please. I can help. You know I can."

"The D.A. doesn't want you near this case."

Chris laughed. "It's my daughter, for Christ's sake, Brian."

"Your daughter's dead, Chris. Your wife's coming apart down there. She needs you. We're handling this."

"I thought you were my friend."

"I am your friend."

"No, you're not."

"I'm also a homicide detective, and you know that I have a job to do here."

"What I know is that it's gone to your head."

"Please don't make this any tougher than it already is, Chris."

Chris got up from his desk and handed Brian a large Manila envelope. "Everything you asked for is in there. Now, go."

"Not just yet."

"What now?"

"I have some questions."

"You sound like you're on the job."

"24/7, buddy."

"What is it, Brian?"

"You take work home from the office from time to time?"

"I wouldn't get half of it done if I didn't."

"Pics included?"

"Sometimes. Gonna put that in your report—friend?"

"Did you ever bring home crime scene photos of Columba's and Emery's victims?"

"Where's this all leading?"

"Answer the question."

"I don't like your tone."

"I don't like your hesitation."

"Let me ask *you* a question. You ever bring work like that home? You and Kim? Sit around and speculate about this and that?"

"Off the record, yes."

"Then what's your fucking problem?"

"Problem is you got a kid that—"

"Had a kid."

"Is there any possibility Vivian could have gotten her hands on those photographs?"

Chris was shaking his head.

"Perhaps showed them to someone who might have shown them to someone else? Know what I'm getting at here, Chris?"

"I want you to leave."

"I thought you wanted to help."

"By dragging my kid into this—who I just put in the ground

two-and-a-half fucking hours ago?"

"See what I mean, Chris?"

"See what?"

"You can't be objective about this. And no one's expecting you to be. That's why the D.A. on down wants you on the sidelines. Get the picture?"

"Yeah, I got the picture, all right. And you got yours. All of them. Now, get the hell out of my house."

"I love you, too, Chris," Brian Archer said, trying not to take things personally, for he understood the situation perfectly—or so he wanted to believe.

Brian descended the spiral staircase, walking into the kitchen to collect his wife and Yolanda, but the latter shook her head.

"I'll stay here awhile and help Harriet finish up."

"How will you get back?"

"Hitchhike if I have to. Go on, now. You go back with Kim. I'll be fine."

Kim grabbed her husband by the arm and headed for the door.

Brian looked back at Harriet. "Catch you later," he said awkwardly.

Harriet did not look up.

"Come on." Kim escorted Brian through the kitchen and out the door.

Once outside, Brian questioned his wife. "What was that all about? Why's Yolanda hanging around?"

"It's called a suicide watch. Ever hear of it?"

"You're kidding?"

"Some detective you are. I see you got what you wanted," she said, staring down at the envelope. "You have a good talk with Chris?"

"Yeah."

"And?"

"And I think I'm beginning to form a picture."

"You think Vivian showed Matheson some pics she shouldn't have?"

"Either that, or he found them for himself."

"You think Chris suspects Kalvin?"

"You kidding me? He hasn't got a clue. He's just upset that his good neighbor was a no-show and is still wondering why."

"It's better this way for now. Don't you think?"

"What I think is that I'm on the verge of losing a friend."

"It's just temporary. Believe me."

"Here." He handed her the keys. "You drive."

"Why?"

"I've got to sit and think."

"About what exactly?"

"About how we're going to pull this off," he mumbled.

"You kidding me? You and Gary are the kings of con."

"Don't kid yourself. Matheson just put Gary's shit out on the street."

"Well, you guys just pick it up and put it right back in his lap."

Kim unlocked the car, slid behind the wheel, started the engine and immediately shot away from the curb before Brian could secure his seat belt.

"You headed for a fire?"

"Behave yourself."

"I forgot to ask you. You run the rest of the list—L back to A?"

Kim looked at her husband curiously. "You asked me that before, and I told you yes."

"No, you didn't."

"Yes, I did. Ask Yolanda."

"I will when I see her. So, what did you find?"

"Twelve possibilities from five boroughs. Scores more who are scattered throughout the United States. Two good leads in Kenya, if you'd like to make the trip."

"Seriously."

"I'm being serious."

"How does our dirty dozen fair?"

"Compared to Matheson? *Dozen* hold a candle," she punned playfully.

"Cute."

"I think we got him, Bri. I really do."

"Big Sister says . . .?"

"She says, and I quote, though weakly translated, 'Feed me anymo' *in·fo·ma·tion*, and I'll blow a gasket if I had one because I'm on overload.'"

"Sounds a bit like Justin when he's mad."

Kim laughed. "How's he doing?"

"Waiting in the wings."

"He got a plan?"

"Believes he does."

"Doable, you think?"

"You really never know with him. He flies by the seat of his pants."

"Yet he manages to land on his feet."

"He's been lucky in the past. We've all been lucky. I don't want him hurt. This Matheson prick is slick."

"You can't hold that dirtbag forever."

"Tell me something I don't know."

Kim grinned. "How about the lieutenant's assurance that we're close to securing subpoenas for the lists we're already in possession of. Less, of course, the balance of Clonite's client list."

"Who cares—if we got what we think we got?"

"We care, because you never know who or what might turn up. Once everything's nice and legal, you'd be surprised who or what could come out of the woodwork. Folks suddenly tend to cooperate."

"Too bad we can't . . . promote Justin's way of handling matters—if and when this business comes about."

"You know better than that, husband o' mine. Justin's method is a powerful tool for us. He's our secret weapon, sweetheart. Our justice system needs an edge these days when you're dealing with scum like Columba and Emery and maybe Matheson."

"It's the maybe, baby, that bothers me."

"Why? Nothing's going to happen until we're absolutely positive."

"What worries me is if we have to let Matheson go. He'll disappear and kill again. This is not just about money, especially now that his plan is in play and paid for. Bottom line? He's a vicious, sadistic stone-cold serial killer. If he confesses, we can't just execute him on the spot. And once he's arraigned, he's off-limits to us. But you can bet your pretty little butt Chris would find a way to get to him and kill him if things ever got that far along the line. What Gary told Kalvin is true. You know that. Chris is cunning and resourceful. Right now, he has his blinders on, thank God."

"I'll go you one better."

"What's that?"

"Harriet just told Yolanda and me that she hates her husband. She's blaming Chris for what happened. She said that if Kalvin showed her more than a passing interest, she'd ask if she could move in with him and the dog. That's if she doesn't go and kill herself first."

"Harriet said that?"

"There's more. She said she's had a crush on him since the day he moved in next-door ten years ago, and that Vivian secretly wished Kalvin was her father since she was nine. She went on about how Chris is married to his work, rarely finding time for his family."

Brian simply shook his head and smirked. "Remind me to tell the prosecutor not to call her as a witness—that is, if it ever gets that far."

"If it does, I just might kill Matheson myself."

"Boy, if any civilian ever heard the two of us."

"Oh, you might be surprised, Brian, my love."

Chapter 47

The lieutenant hung up the phone in his office and waited. A detective went downstairs to get Justin, had him sign in officially, and then escorted the irritable soul into the commanding officer's chambers. Ethan Powell dismissed the detective.

"Take a seat, Barnes."

"What's with all this happy horseshit? I gotta sign in now?"

"We can't be too careful at the moment. Yesterday, one of ours spotted an undercover reporter milling about the lobby."

Justin laughed.

"What's so funny?"

"One of ours . . . one of theirs." Justin was shaking his head. "A fucking reporter? Kind of like a security cop but with a pen in his pocket instead of a gun in his holster. So what?"

"A pen with poison ink that could find its way into tomorrow's print. That's what."

"I thought these guys were in our corner."

"You're so fucking naive. The guy is freelance, and he's good. He's out there trying to make a name for himself. You won't read about yourself in *Newsday*. But you could wind up as a feature story in *The New York Times*. So, we do everything by the book, for now. You sign in just like any other civilian. You're a consultant on this case, remember. When we call you. So make out like *I* called *you*. Now, what is it that you want, J?"

"A raise."

Both men laughed.

"Tell me why you're here. But before you do, I'd just like to tell you that there are times I wish I had your job for what you're getting paid. Today is one of them."

"Yeah, well, I'm sorry that you have to sometimes *earn* your salary, bossman."

"I'm your lieutenant. You'll show me that respect."

The maverick smiled broadly. "Yes, sah."

Ethan Powell shook his head. "One more time. What the fuck do you want?"

"Access."

"To what?"

"Not to what—but who."

"Then, who?"

"Matheson."

The lieutenant laughed heartily. "You're out of your fucking mind."

"That's why I'm your *número uno* hombre, my man."

"No fucking way, José. Forget it."

"Matheson is our knot man."

"Maybe."

"Maybe I can find out more."

"Oh, you want to interview him?" Ethan said sarcastically. "I thought maybe you wanted to waste him in there. Silly me."

Justin put up a single digit. "One hour with him. Not a minute more."

"Not one second," the head of homicide swore.

Justin sent his frustration through his nostrils. "Look."

"I said forget it."

"I'm a member of the team. Team Three. Remember?"

"You're a consultant on this case, period."

"Is that your final answer?"

"First and final."

"All right then."

"All right then, what?"

"I'll just have to find another way."

"Another way to do what?"

"Elicit the truth from that lyin' sack of shit."

"I see. You think you're gonna get what Brian and Gary have failed to get thus far."

"They've got their ways. I've got mine."

"We don't need another murder on our hands."

"I wouldn't lay a finger on him. I swear it."

"So why don't you pass along your strategy to your two pals?"

"Because you gotta be black and beautiful to win that fucker's dark heart." Justin smiled most winsomely, displaying his pearly whites.

Ethan smiled back. "Then maybe *I* should have a crack at him."

"You too ugly, boss. I mean, Lieutenant. Suspect see you, he die o' fright."

"Then our problems would be over, provided he's our man."

"If you give me an hour alone with him, I could practically guarantee your problems would be over."

"That a fact?"

"Give me the opportunity."

"Out."

Justin got up and left the office quietly. Too quietly, in fact, for the lieutenant's comfort and peace of mind.

Chapter 48

Detective Kim Archer studied the DNA information on her monitor for a good minute before she slipped on her hands-free headset and called the lab. Thirty seconds later, she was speaking with one of the forensic scientists familiar with the case.

"Quentin."

"Hey. What's up, Kim?"

"How many knots did you guys find woven within Vivian Osip's ponytail?"

"Forty something. Why?"

"Go find out exactly. I'll hold."

"Kim, I'm working on the Reynolds case. Priority. Let me get back to you."

"I need to know now, Quentin. Please. It'll take you but a minute."

"Hang on, pest."

While Kim waited, she brought up a diagram of a double helix, rising digitally from an enhanced image of a pair of chromosomes. Big Sister graphically unraveled the tightly wound package while the computer maven split the screen and compiled the building blocks of life, enlarging the components: cells–more chromosomes–genes–DNA base pairs. The four bases of a nucleotide.

"Kim?"

"Right here."

"Forty-six. Two strands equally braided. Twenty-three, and twenty-three."

"Remind you of anything?"

"Like what?"

"Like what you guys work with when you're not busy playing solitaire or Scrabble," she answered knowingly.

"Jesus, Kim!"

"Twenty-three pairs of chromosomes."

"Forty-six in all."

"Half from the mother."

"Half from the father."

"Like he's mapping out a genetic code."

"Know what I'm thinking?"

"That this is one big fucking puzzle."

"Yeah, but how do the pieces fit?"

"I don't know."

"You mean the wizard hasn't got a clue?"

"Very funny, Quentin. Let's see if Big Sister can crack this code, if there even is one."

"Do you know what letters to assign the base pairs, Kim?"

"I think so."

"**A** always pairs with **T**. **G** with **C**."

"**A**denine. **T**hymine. **G**uanine. **C**ytosine."

"Plus sugar and phosphoric acid."

"Shit. Which would make forty-eight."

"Only if you add those two molecules."

"Hold on a sec." Kim flashed her fingers across the keyboard and brought up the additional information. "Let me work with this awhile," she said excitedly.

"You do that. Listen. Call me if you got any questions. Sorry I tried to brush you off, but we're really busy."

"With the Reynolds woman, really—or a hot Scrabble game, Quentin?" she teased with good reason.

"No. The Reynolds woman. Honestly. But while I got you, does Big Sister have time for *Newsday's* JUMBLE? Just one five-letter word, Kim. I got the other three. Besides, Matheson's on ice, so to speak. Right?"

Kim sighed. "That's cheating, Quentin, but go ahead."

"I just can't seem to unscramble S-I-F-I-N. "

Kim saved her information then switched to an electronic Game Menu: **Build Word List.** She entered the five letters. "F-I-N-I-S," she decoded and spelled out in a flash.

"What?"

"*Finis*."

"They're supposed to be ordinary words, Kim. Not foreign. Says it right here."

"It is."

"F-I-N-I-S?"

"Yes. They're three pronunciations, Quentin. First is fin´is; accent on the first syllable. Second with the i's pronounced as long e's and a silent s. And the third—"

"Whoa! That's *fini*, you mean—with four letters—spelled f-i-n-i. And it's French; meaning finished or done."

"But F-I-N-I-**S** is Middle English, meaning end or conclusion."

"This isn't fair. I'm supposed to unscramble four *ordinary* words," Quentin repeated, "then arrange the circled letters to solve the puzzle. Maybe it's a misprint. Maybe they mean finesse. You know, like a kind of clever maneuvering."

"What's the caption beneath the cartoon?"

"WHY THE NOVELIST VISITED THE CEMETERY," Quentin read from the puzzle's furnished clue.

"TO FIND PLOTS?" Kim both asked and answered immediately and most mischievously.

There was a moment of silence before the man went berserk. "You just ruined my puzzle *and* my morning, Kim! You do *not* call me if and when you have a question. Ever! Hear? I can't believe you did that, Kim Archer. Wait till I tell Brian. You spoiled everything. I would have gotten it, damn it."

"I'm sure you would have, Quentin. But we'd all be dead and buried by then," she taunted.

"I hate you!"

"Maybe you can help me with this **A_T_ G_C_** enigma after you calm down and clear your head. Just don't go on to a game of Scrabble with the boys and forget about me. All right?"

Quentin hung up the phone in a huff.

Kim laughed loudly, removed her headset and went back to staring at the double helix.

Chapter 49

S eated before Big Sister, Kim toyed with the initial letters of the four base pairs found in nucleotides, one of the building blocks of DNA.

"**A** always pairs with **T**," she reminded herself. "Adenine. Thymine. **C** with **G**. Guanine. Cytosine." At. Act. Tag. Cat—the computer maven threw up on the screen, arranging and rearranging letters to try and fit or form a pattern. "But Matheson has a dog. A collie named Poochie. Too, it has its proper tags. Nothing remarkable there," Kim chattered to herself. "So let's try this."

She played with prefixes and suffixes. "*Ade* and the suffix *nine*. *Thy* and *mine*." Backwards and forwards she ran them. Inside and out. "Nine lives? Phooey."

Guanine. "What the hell's a *gua?*" She giggled. "And *nine*, appearing for a second time, totals eighteen and means absolutely nothing to me, Big Sister, dear."

Cyto. "A combining form—meaning cell. Or from the Greek: container, receptacle, body. Hum."

Sine, as a prefix, led Kim through a conundrum of triangular measurements. As a suffix attached to *cyto*, it spelled out, "One of the fundamental components of RNA and DNA," she read aloud through a yawn. "Big deal!" she finally said in sheer frustration after juggling the periodic table of elements.

"Back to square one." The wizard withered after another grueling hour of fuzzy mathematics in addition to unscrambling and scribbling scores of numbers and letters. Kim took a ten-second break, rubbed her eyes and threw the monitor a K-I-S-S. "**Keep It Simple, Stupid**," she said quite loudly in lieu of leaving her seat to go splash cold water on her face.

Two paired knot-braided strands of hair, representing 46 chromosomes of DNA in her goddaughter's ponytail, seemed about as complicated as it was going to get, she somehow sensed. Matheson's madness appeared limited to his knots. In-your-face antics, not abstractions, was what the serial killer was all about, she was beginning to believe. Still, Kim trifled with series after series of numbers and names and street addresses. Acronyms and anagrams.

Nothing registered nor raised a red flag.

For several hours, Kim ran Big Sister through a series of codes and signs . . . returning to the elongated three-dimensional model of the double helix . . . its paired rungs connecting the two strands like a spiral . . . staircase.

"Jesus, Joseph and Mary!" Kim suddenly realized the connection. "Oh, dear God! Brian! Lieutenant! Gary! Yolanda!" she shouted.

Yolanda and Gary were not around. In their stead appeared ten detectives, gathering around the screen, staring at it vacantly, wondering what was going on but knowing that whenever Kim sounded like Sheena, Queen of the Jungle, sacred ground was being covered quickly.

Seconds later, Brian and the lieutenant loomed over everyone else's shoulders.

"Make a hole," a detective sergeant ordered, and several suits stepped aside for the lead investigator and the head of homicide.

"What is it, Kim?" her husband asked excitedly.

"Look," she said. "Just look."

"I'm looking. We're all looking. We've been looking at that all goddamn day. A double helix. Two strands of DNA. Now, tell us, please, what we're supposed to *see*," he sallied.

"Look from the top down to the bottom of the model. How it tapers to the cell. Look at the rungs or steps."

"Like a ladder," someone said.

"Not like a ladder, Eric," Kim challenged.

"Like a staircase," another answered.

"A spiral staircase," Kim clarified.

"Yes," Brian mumbled, beginning to unravel the enigma. "Top of a staircase . . . descending to a cell . . . or cellar. Matheson's nucleus."

Kim nodded satisfactorily. "Good boy."

"But . . .? What cellar?" the lieutenant asked in confusion. "Do we know where, Kim?"

Kim looked over her shoulder at her husband. "Well, tell him."

Brian looked from the screen to his wife then back to the screen with a sense of uneasiness imbuing a vaguely familiar feeling, when suddenly it hit him like a ton of building blocks. "Like the winding staircase leading from Chris' study . . . Harriet and Chris' spiral staircase," Brian said dumbfounded. "Chris designed it to represent a double helix."

"Exactly," Kim said excitedly.

"That's right! Some of us were up and down that serpentine staircase today, consoling Chris and Harriet—right after the funeral," a detective declared incredulously. "I never thought of it in those terms —just some weird avant-garde architecture."

"They have a double helix staircase in the Vatican museum," Gary recalled.

"That's very much how Chris fashioned his own fancy staircase—" Brian elaborated "—only on a miniature scale, of course. The fascinating thing about it is that the people going up, *pass*, but never *meet* those going down."

"The double helical structure of a DNA molecule," Detective Lorna Hanover remembered from a science class in college.

"What I'm thinking," Kim Archer proposed, "is that maybe Matheson brought some of his victims—like Gretchen Bowers, Nolan Andrews and Vivian—down to Chris's cellar—where he'd knot their hair or prepare that intricate web. *That's* his safe house. Can you think of a better one?"

"Right under our fucking noses," a cop blew. "I'll bet no one here checked it out because no one saw a need to. Vivian Osip's body was discovered shortly after she went missing. End of search. Otherwise, we would have turned Osip's house upside down."

Two detectives nodded in agreement.

"Now, hold on a second," Lieutenant Powell enjoined. "The only opportunity that Matheson might have had to enter that house was when Chris was at work, Harriet out shopping or at her garden club, and the kid in school. The problem with your theory being is that there was always someone in the house, Kim. Vivian Osip would be back from school by the time her mom left for the supermarket or club. The lab said it would have taken someone many hours, if not days, to construct the web with just the preliminary knots alone before the Andrews boy was murdered and his body moved to that abandoned building in Riverhead. It's just not feasible."

Kim hit a few keys and glanced up at her husband before she spoke. "Big Sister and I have a theory about that, too, Lieutenant," the wizard practically whispered, biting a fingernail.

Ethan Powell looked at her keenly. "Care to share?"

"It's just a theory," she retreated.

The lieutenant waited.

Brian had the distinct feeling he knew where his wife was headed.

"Denise Nathan, William Walker, Emily Schroeder and Rebecca Reynolds were killed on a Sunday. Gretchen Bowers, Nolan Andrews and Vivian were murdered on a Wednesday. Vivian may have let Matheson into the house."

"That's the most ridiculous thing I ever heard you say, Kim!" a veteran detective in the group declared. "I've known that girl since the day she was born. I know how she was raised."

"And I was her godmother, fella," Kim reminded the man and everyone present.

"Some godmother," he mumbled beneath his breath.

"I think you're way off base with this call, Kim. I really do," another commented, shaking his head in disbelief.

"Oh, how I wish I were. How I wish I were."

Yolanda appeared from around the corner. "God, what a gloomy group we've got here. Tell me we've got another murder while that fucker's sitting in solitude back there."

Kim forced a smile and shook her head. "You find out anything?"

"I checked with the school and two of his teachers. Lorna and Wayne interviewed a dozen kids there."

"Two of whose teachers?" the lieutenant snapped.

"Nolan Andrews'," Yolanda answered. She turned back to Kim. "You were right. Vivian absolutely knew and hated Nolan. She swore she would kill him one day soon. She even told him so in front of several classmates—and that she had a secret admirer who promised to help her do it."

A senior detective scratched his head. "Then why would the Andrews boy go to that house?"

"Whose house?" Yolanda asked.

"Osip's house," Brian replied.

Yolanda looked from the group to Kim who flashed her fingers across the keyboard. Everyone watched the screen as the double helix suddenly spun toward the foreground before rotating three-dimensionally. A spiral within a spiral reappeared.

"Osip's winding staircase—" Yolanda suddenly realized "—leading from Chris' upstairs study, circling down to the landing off the kitchen . . . next to the basement door."

"Maybe the boy was lured there by Matheson," someone suggested.

"Where's Chris Osip now?" the lieutenant asked.

"I think he's left the lab and headed home."

"Call him on his cell and tell him we're sending Marcus and a crew over there immediately. We'll meet them."

"I don't think that's a good idea, Lieutenant," Brian spoke up.

"And why's that?"

"Because of what we might find in Chris' presence. If that is Matheson's safe house, so to speak, we'll probably uncover pics or videos of his victims, and God knows what else he's got hidden down there for safekeeping. We don't need Chris or Harriet around for that. They're at wit's end as it is and quite unstable. On top of that, we don't want them to know we're holding their good friend and neighbor just yet. They'd probably blow whatever time we have left to hold this creep. Chris would want to shoot him on the spot, and that's if he could even gather his senses, while Harriet hires Matheson a lawyer the caliber of F. Lee Bailey. That would be Dunn or Profeta, or both of them. The best of the best. We'd be opening up a kettle of worms."

"Well, what do you suggest?"

Brian glanced at Troy and Eric. "We wait until Chris returns to work tomorrow. You can bet your bottom dollar he'll leave the house early and be gone most of the day. He's pumped. Yolanda will find a reason to get Harriet out of the house. Then we send in Marcus and a crew. Troy and Eric will escort them."

Detective Lieutenant Ethan Powell was emphatically shaking his head. "Sorry. No can do."

"Why?"

"Why? Will someone who still has his or her faculties intact explain it to him, please."

But no one said or moved a muscle.

"I don't believe this."

Finally, one of the senior men stepped forward.

"Ah, a fellow detective with a brain in his head."

But the man firmly took their leader by the arm and walked him away and out of earshot. The detective spoke and the lieutenant listened before he blew.

"Are you fucking crazy!" the commander shrieked.

"You didn't give the order," the detective sergeant explained. "In fact, you said no dice in front of a dozen witnesses, if it ever comes down to that. In the event that this bites anybody else in the ass, you wash your hands of it. And my suggestion for next time is that you turn and look the other way. Troy and Eric are very good at what they do, Lieutenant. They've elevated it to an art form."

"But a break-in," Powell steamed, "in broad daylight?"

The man grinned. "Well, I guess you never worked robbery, hey Lieutenant? Look, it's not like the Mills case. This is a case of a few colleagues paying another a visit."

"Unannounced. And letting in—"

"The cleaning crew or whoever. Couple hours. They find the evidence they need to hang this guy, and we go from there."

"Go where?"

Detective Sergeant Carter shrugged. "Guess you gotta talk to Brian and Gary 'bout that. I don't know nothin'. Never even had this conversation with you, Lieutenant. I wouldn't ask them 'bout *where* or *what*, though. Funny how the less you know, the more you learn. Strange how this business really works. Well, excuse me. Gotta get back to the Team that I never left."

And with that announcement, the seasoned detective sergeant stepped back to the group.

Chapter 50

Detective Yolanda Ivers begged, pleaded and cajoled, then practically dragged Harriet off to exercise class. Two minutes later, half a dozen men wearing coveralls, jeans and work gloves stepped from a Surround Sound Systems vehicle. The six labored theatrically in carrying a large, empty carton to the front door. Shielded from the street by the big cardboard box, Eric Bokina picked the lock then invited his partner and Marcus' crew across the threshold and into the Osip residence. Marcus Ullman and his hair and fiber expert, Peter Danowski; serologist, Ian Quinn; along with forensic consultant/photographer Nicholas Kemp, crossed the room and directly descended the cellar stairs. The men exchanged their canvas work gloves for latex, confining themselves to the area as instructed.

An old Underwood typewriter sat on a corner table. Troy, Eric, Marcus, Peter, Ian, and Nick immediately went to work: searching, photographing, measuring, jotting down notes, collecting and labeling samples, working with a Reflected Ultraviolet Imaging System tool in lieu of chemicals and messy telltale powders, passing a lint roller across the back, arms and seat of an old upholstered chair, vacuuming along the base of a workbench. Dust, cobwebs and more dust among the clutter were everywhere. In the far corner of the cellar, there stood a massive open cabinet.

"I never knew Chris and Harriet drank fine wines," Nick commented, carefully removing and examining a bottle from a rack of over a hundred clarets.

"He just collects and stores them. They don't drink the stuff," Marcus explained.

"Ever?"

"I don't know about ever. Probably every now and then. Chris resells them for a small fortune after several years," the pathologist elaborated.

"Wow—look at that whopper over there!" Troy exclaimed. "I never saw a wine bottle that size before."

"Methuselah."

"Who?"

"Methuselah. Holds six liters; roughly six-and-a-half quarts. Equal to about eight of those regular bottles. That next one down in size is called a jeroboam; holds half that amount. He's got some magnums sitting over there."

"Methuselah, huh?"

"Yep, but not the largest bottle they make."

"What's that smaller one?"

"Jeroboam, then magnum—right down to your ordinary 750 milliliter bottles—like those reds in the rack."

"That big one doesn't seem too practical to me. You'd probably need two guys just to steady and pour it without spilling."

"They're usually just for show—although Chris had one delivered to a party once."

"Hey, Nick. Take a peek over here," Ian called out.

Nick walked over with his camera in hand. "Don't they ever dust down here?"

"It's a cellar. Not a finished basement. And you should talk."

"Listen. I'm the neatest guy I know for a bachelor."

"You're a slob."

"Hey! I resemble that remark."

"Got that right. Whattaya think?"

"Looks like a feather."

"No shit, Sherlock. What kind of feather?"

"I don't know. What goes with a good wine? Duck or goose feather, I guess."

"This is the guy they send us in a pinch?"

"Hey, I'm retired from all this shit. All right? I'm just a consultant these days, like Justin. Well, not exactly like J. I only shoot pictures," the photographer needled in kind. "I take a few pictures when you guys call me. What can I say?"

"Whether or not this is a feather one might use for fly tying is what you could address."

"You could use any fucking feather for fly tying, birdbrain."

"Take your pictures then step aside, please. This guy can really grate on your nerves."

Peter walked over and collected a single white, black-rimmed feather. "It's from the Lady Amherst pheasant. The smaller dun colored feather attached behind it, called a gimp feather, is especially used by freshwater fly fishermen for trout. See?"

"I never worked in a space so dusty," Nick groused. "Even that abandoned basement back in Riverhead was cleaner than this place."

"That abandoned basement had wind whipping through it at twenty knots. You were working in a crawlspace with broken windows and you didn't complain."

"Maybe that's what I should do with my apartment."

"What? Break out all your windows and let the filth fly out?" Eric goaded.

"No. Abandon it all together," Nick answered with a straight face.

"Bingo, fellas! Look what I got," Troy said excitedly, pulling out a large quarter-inch plywood sheet from behind an old workbench. "Tapered leaders . . . in monofilament." Stapled to the back of the board hung an assortment of 0X through 7X leader material wrapped in clean, clear cellophane packages, along with tiny spools of fluorocarbon tippet material.

Peter stooped to examine the display. "In seven-and-a-half, nine, and twelve-foot lengths," he read from the packets, noting each neat row. "Yep, this is where he must have prepped the web re the Nolan boy."

"Any of you guys know if Chris is into fly-tying?" Eric questioned rather suspiciously.

"No way. Nohow," Marcus answered abruptly.

"How do you know?"

"We'd know. That's all."

"Well, Nick didn't know he stored fine wines," Troy countered.

"That's different."

"Why's it so different?"

No one from Marcus' crew seemed to have a suitable answer.

"All right, let's not jump to any conclusions," Marcus

reproached. "Chris occasionally flies indoor model airplanes with Brian. Apart from wine, that's Chris' only other hobby—if you can even call it that. The man's a workaholic. So, enough chatter. Let's get back to work."

"You wanna try and lift some prints here, or should we take the board back with us?"

"We'd be here all day. I say we take it."

"Yeah, but then we gotta get it back," Troy put forth plainly. "We ain't got no fuckin' warrant. What say we just take a few packs? Prints are either on all or none of them, I'd wager."

"Fine."

While Peter collected numerous samples of dust, dirt, fibers and hair, and Ian searched for signs of blood, a thorough search of the cellar continued. Twenty minutes later, the group was about to call it quits.

"Well, I see no place else to conceal a video camera or cassettes down here," Eric announced. "I don't see why we can't have a quick peek upstairs. I mean, illegal is illegal. No one's gonna give us a lighter sentence if we get caught. Right?"

"Wait a second," Nick said, leaning forward of the workbench while carefully tipping the Methuselah back with both hands, exposing a scored narrow lip that separated from the base of the container. "Ain't no wine in this thing."

As Nick carefully lifted the bottle off its base, Marcus grabbed hold of a compact unit hidden within. "Easy does it."

"Camcorder," Eric said with utmost satisfaction.

"Well, it ain't Chris' 'cause I know he shoots a Sony, not a fucking Bell & Howell," Nick said in defense of the man.

"How many cameras *you* own and carry around, Nick? Just one? Huh?" Eric pressed, pointing to the man's video camera hanging from a shoulder—an SLR strapped around his neck, too.

"Listen to me, lamebrain. He didn't kill his own kid. All right? He loved Vivian. I may not know that he collected fine wine, but I do know the man. I worked with him for over a decade before I retired. Okay? And I'll tell you something else. The reason I'm back here today is because of Chris."

Marcus ignored the dueling duo, reaching for the larger bottle next to it.

"And guess what we're going to find in that jerry jar?" Troy nodded knowingly.

"Jeroboam," Marcus corrected.

"Whatever."

Marcus carefully tilted then lifted the large bottle. Wads of newspaper crammed in the bottom of the bottle secured the items within. Six videos were discovered. All were neatly labeled in capital letters: MR. W. WALKER. MS. G. BOWERS. N. ANDREWS. MRS. E. SCHROEDER. V. OSIP. MRS. R. REYNOLDS.

"I wonder where Denise Nathan's tape is," Ian commented.

"Matheson probably started his recording sessions *after* victim number one."

The others seemed to agree.

"I wish we could just go to Chris and Harriet instead of all this screwin' around," Eric complained.

"Well, we can't; so just quit wishing your life away and let's decide what we're going to do here."

"No fucking contest," Peter declared. "We take everything back to the lab. We've got this fucking guy," he swore.

"We hope. And if we don't lift a print off the camera or cassettes, what do we have then?" Ian challenged. "Circumstantial evidence that six of the seven murders were committed by whom? Some phantom who visited Osip's cellar and took videos of his victims, then probably typed out the labels on that relic over there."

"Maybe the videos will reveal something we need to nail his ass."

"Like what?"

"Matheson's voice, maybe. It's set for sound," Nick noted.

"Or like maybe he snuffed some of the victims next-door," Ian submitted. "I don't know why we don't have a look over there while Matheson's cooling off at headquarters. We're bound to find something."

Troy flashed a look at his partner but did not say a word, for Marcus' crew knew nothing of the earlier break-in next-door.

Nick picked up on the glance and smiled cagily, furtively running the tips of a forefinger and thumb across his lips like a zipper.

"Well, we could run the videos by Blockbusters for a quick previewing," Peter kidded. "They're right up the block. Fast forward one cassette, and we'd be back before Yolanda and Harriet broke a sweat."

As if on cue, Yolanda rang Troy's cell phone.

"Yeah."

"It's me."

"It's me, too, Yolanda," Troy expelled the words seductively against the mouthpiece.

"I got a problem."

"Let me guess. You're both outta shape and want to quit and come home?"

"She won't even go in! I had to pretend I had an engine problem to give you guys some time. Short of kidnapping Harriet or having a heart attack in front of her for my next performance, I'm afraid she's not going to buy anymore excuses. I'm pushing her too damn hard. I blew it, Troy. I'm sorry."

"You did no such thing. Where are you now?"

"Bathroom at the gym. She's waiting in the car and insists we head back. I told her I gotta poop. I'm good for five minutes, and then we gotta go. I'll try and push her to go shopping or something, but I don't think it's gonna fly. I might not have a chance to call again, so I'm letting you know now."

"Listen to me. Not a problem. Bring her back home. It's A-OK. We did good. But what we found has to be analyzed and evaluated and maybe brought back here. Maybe not. So try and set something up for tomorrow, just in case. Breakfast. Lunch. Dinner. Shopping. Soliciting. Anything. If you can't, you can't. We'll figure something out."

"Right. You got fifteen minutes to get the hell out of there."

"Like the wind. Oh, one more thing before you go."

"What?"

"Don't forget to flush." Troy smiled and holstered his cell phone. "Let's pack it up, boys."

"Okay by me," Nick said as he sneezed from all the dust. "At least we're not going away empty-handed."

"You know, we didn't find any heat gun, shrink-wrap, cord, tape or rope. Just these leaders and tippets. Find that strange?"

"Nope. Probably discarded those items. Buys what he needs when he needs it then shit-cans the stuff."

"Why not some of this stuff, like the leaders?"

"He's setting Chris up."

"Hey, Marcus," Nick called over. "Got a quick question."

"What?"

"You said a Methuselah wasn't the largest bottle they make. Curious. What is?"

"Nebuchadnezzar."

"Neb-a-what?"

"Neb·a·kad·nez·er," he answered phonetically.

"How much bigger?"

"Twenty quarts or eighteen point nine liters."

"Geez. Can you even lift it?"

"Comes with an over-the-shoulder sling."

"Sounds like it should come with a kidney belt."

"Wouldn't need one."

"How come?"

Marcus grinned. "People who pour and drink from them don't have any."

"Kidneys? Don't you mean the liver?"

"Both actually. Livers. Kidneys. Excessive alcohol can take its toll on the brain, lungs and heart, too."

"Christ, I'd wager if we found one of those down here, we'd find a body in it."

"I wouldn't take that bet," Marcus swore. "Not on your life."

Chapter 51

By late evening, both Brian and Gary marched into the tomb of doom, leaving the door to the crypt open wide behind them. Brian was the first to reach their prisoner, peeling Kalvin from a corner of the floor on which he slept. Gary grabbed hold of the killer by the back of the collar, and the two detectives led the startled man a step beyond the threshold, turning him about abruptly. Brian wrapped his fingers around the killer's face, a thumb locked firmly beneath the figure's jaw, forcing it upward.

"Read," Brian commanded.

Through bleary eyes, Kalvin peered at the sign above the doorway.

"I said, READ!" he repeated.

𝕿𝖍𝖔𝖚 𝕾𝖍𝖆𝖑𝖙 𝕹𝖔𝖙 𝕶𝖎𝖑𝖑 were the words engraved within the wooden tablet.

Kalvin looked from Archer to York, then back again and laughed. "Good cop. Bad cop. You guys forget your roles?" he questioned through a lazy yawn.

"Not awake yet?" Gary brought Kalvin quickly to his senses with a knee planted solidly against the serial killer's groin. "That better?" the detective obliged.

But Matheson screamed bloody murder as soon as he sucked in a column of air. "POLICE BRUTALITY!" the man raved like the madman he truly was. "THEY'RE TRYING TO KILL ME!" he cried out and bawled like a baby.

A detective coming down the hallway kept her eyes dead ahead, ignoring the trio standing beneath the caveat.

"Please help me—pl-please," Matheson whined and wailed

most mournfully. "They hurt me. Please. I did nothing wrong."

The female detective stopped abruptly and turned on her heels, walking up to the three of them.

"You've got to report them, lady." Matheson trembled before the black female. "Call Chris and Harriet Osip in Quogue. They're listed in the book. These guys are going to kill me," the frightened figure swore. "I'm innocent. I don't even know why I'm here. Please find someone. Please. Call Harriet Osip in Quogue," he repeated. "Osip. O-s-i-p. Just like it sounds. Hurry. I'm begging you. I'm their neighbor, Kalvin Matheson."

"Let go of him," the woman said succinctly.

The pair looked at her as though she had lost her mind.

"I said let him go," she ordered, ripping Brian's hand from Kalvin's shirt sleeve before either detective could protest, delivering a roundhouse kick squarely against the multiple murderer's temple that sent him back through the doorway and down to the floor. The petite brown belt immediately went in and stooped over the cowering form. "This *lady* is the one who found you, fuckface," Kim Archer whispered in Kalvin Matheson's ear. "This *lady* and her teammates are going to fuck you up real bad, mister. Just for the record, Matheson, Vivian Osip was my goddaughter."

Kalvin tried to pick himself up. "*Was?* Was, you said? Asshole, there, tried to tell me she's alive. You got nothing. Nothing, Aunt Jemima. You hear me?"

Kim could have and would have killed Kalvin Matheson where he lay if not for her husband and Gary who held her at bay.

Barely.

Matheson crawled and shielded himself back in a corner of the 8 x 8 foot interrogation room.

Four detectives moved forward quickly, leading Kim quietly away. Brian and Gary picked Kalvin up like a rag doll, dragging the figure into another corner of the confining space—over to a steel ring fastened to the floor.

Another man noisily removed a shackle from a wooden box just outside the doorway. "Strip," the bald six-foot-four burly figure commanded as he stepped across the threshold.

Kalvin shook his head.

Slashing the shiny chain maniacally against the steel deck, the imposing behemoth showed that he was tall of stature but very short on patience.

It did not take long for Kalvin to get down to a pair of socks and underwear—trousers encircling his right foot.

Gary and Brian secured their prisoner to the steel ring, took their leave, then slammed and locked the door to the room behind them.

"Skivvies, too," the big man demanded. "Know what they say about a fella with feet as long as mine?" the strange looking character put forth, grinning from ear to ear. "Oh, don't look at me like I'm bluffing, my man. I ain't the fucking fuzz," he lied. "I'm one of you. Rolled over on my cellmate in exchange for certain . . . considerations. I didn't believe them at first, but these guys *do* deliver. FUCK!" he declared, striking his forehead as if suddenly remembering something. "I forgot to ask them for some Vaseline." The giant of a man passed a hand across his bushy mustache, then down a rather long Vandyke. "Oh, well." Detective Enrique Valez spit into the palm of his hand.

Chapter 52

Kim, Brian, Gary, Justin, Enrique and Yolanda, filed into a large conference room down the hall and around the corner from where they were holding Matheson. The burly, mean actor, who had just spent the better part of an hour alone with the suspect, entered and disappointedly took a seat.

"He's scared out of his wits, but he's not going to give an inch," the cop began after everyone was settled. "He's screaming for a lawyer. Wants to be charged or set free. Wants his rights read if you're planning to keep him another night." The big man stretched his arms out wide before slipping into a chair at the head of the table. "Demands kosher food, now. Bottled water, too. Wants his clothing back. Especially the down coat he came in with because he's fucking freezing. A blanket and a pillow, too, can you believe the gall? Oh, and he has to go to the bathroom again. And I should tell you, Brian, that he swears he's going to murder you first chance he gets. Closest I could come to a full confession," Enrique stated and smiled easily. "I wouldn't dare repeat to a lady what he said he's going to do to you, Kim. I'd like another crack at him."

"Sorry, Enrique, but time's running out," Brian said decidedly. "But thanks for giving it a shot. Gotta tell you, I like Justin's idea a lot, and I believe it just might fly. That is, if the powers that be give us a green light to follow through from start to finish. Meanwhile, Gary's going to go back in there and lay it out for Mr. Matheson. Show our boy the videos so he'll know for certain we found them . . . particularly the one we altered."

"That's a mistake, Brian," Enrique said emphatically. "A bad mistake."

But Brian shook his head. "Kim's so-called slip of the tongue back there—her little ruse—is what's going to give the next one the wings of credibility."

"Was that a slip of your foot, too, back there, Kim?" Enrique questioned wryly.

"Actually, it was," she admitted freely. "I was aiming to break his fucking nose."

"I see. Inches away from a lawsuit, lady. Wanna give this department a black eye in the bargain?" he added playfully.

"What this department needs is a good swift kick in the ass from time to time."

"And you're just the one to do it. Right?"

"Me and Team Three."

"We're all team players here, Kim," Enrique reminded her politely.

"Not this time out. If anything goes wrong, Teams One and Two are out of it. They heard no evil, saw no evil, spoke no evil. We bear the brunt."

"And I assume you speak for everyone present."

"I do."

Brian, Gary, Justin and Yolanda nodded in the affirmative.

"Guess I've been out of the loop too long."

"The flu can do that to you, fella," Yolanda said to her partner. "You still look like shit."

"Thanks. I heard you did all right in my absence, though."

"She did great," Brian said sincerely. "We got in there and got the goods while she babysat Harriet, which was no easy task."

"I heard. I also heard that the lieutenant has no knowledge of this matter," Enrique tabled.

"Like he was on some other planet," Brian swore.

"And if you *were* to secure a confession and be given a green light—?" Enrique questioned carefully.

"Neither the lieutenant nor the inspector would ever be implicated."

Detective Enrique Valez nodded but remained silent.

Gary and Justin exchanged glances.

"For openers, they'll, of course, want to hear Matheson's confession for themselves before Justin's ever given the go-ahead,"

Brian stated categorically. "Gary's to wear a wire. They won't take us at our word because all of us sitting here know that the end justifies the means. If Matheson confesses to any or all of the seven, maybe eight, murders, they'll send Justin in for a final interview. If Matheson doesn't confess, I'm afraid it's over. We'll have to release him in the morning."

"But we have six—"

"We have six videos with victims clearly pleading for their lives, Enrique. We have no voice behind the camera because our serial killer remained mute on the matter. We haven't a shred of physical evidence that points to Matheson. Not a print. Not a hair. Not a thread. Not one fiber connecting *him* to any of the victims. The D.A.'s not going into open court with circumstantial evidence and his neck sticking out on something as thin as this. Want to know why? Because Matheson's defense attorneys would point an accusatory finger at Chris Osip, creating a reasonable doubt in the jury's mind. Does any reasonable soul sitting here doubt that for a single second? Think about it. Three of the murders were committed in the wine cellar in Osip's own home. The camcorder and tapes were concealed in two of Chris' prize display bottles, void of any wine—but with *his* prints and *his* hair, along with incriminating threads and fibers galore found floating all through *his* basement."

"Yeah, but not a single print of Chris' was found on any of those cellophane packets stapled to the board."

"Wake up, Enrique! It doesn't matter. They weren't on the camcorder or the tapes either. The defense will say that Chris or our Team wiped them clean, claiming that *we're* protecting Osip because he's one of ours."

"All right. You're right. I get the picture."

"But not the big picture. From what I'm hearing, Harriet Osip is going to pieces. With not too many good things to say about her husband. Can you picture either side calling her to the stand as a witness? Do you see where this is going?"

Enrique nodded his frustration.

"Good. I'm glad I'm getting through. I know Matheson's guilty. You know he's guilty. Proving it is quite another matter. That's why we need that confession, or he walks. If Gary succeeds in there, it'll be a go."

"I understand perfectly. But let me ask you this." He turned to Gary. "Do you know exactly how you're going to handle this guy in there? Precisely what you're going to say? Because there's no winging it with this creep. He's bright. Tired, but alert."

"Yes, to both your questions."

"Then go get 'im, tiger. And good luck."

Chapter 53

Detective Gary York put a tape in the VCR and switched off the overhead lights. The tiny room immediately took on a tomb-like appearance. Surreal. Kalvin cringed in the corner. Naked. Shivering. The killer's right foot was still chained to a ring in the floor. His underpants were down around an ankle. A partly filled bucket of urine, feces, water and some toilet tissue stood in the opposite corner next to a small pile of the prisoner's clothing.

"Pull up your draws and sit down," Detective Gary York ordered, propelling a chair forward with his foot. "Being that we found no video of Denise Nathan, probably because you never made one, we'll start with tape number one—victim two." Gary pressed PLAY and began the interrogation, taking a seat at the small table several feet from Kalvin.

"You actually ran up to him with your camcorder going. He certainly looks startled here, but not afraid at this point. What did you tell him? That you're doing a documentary? 'This is your life, William Walker.' Is that what you said? Look at the happy expression on his face. And then it all gradually changes. We go from startled, to happy, to suddenly confused. That's when you put the camera down in order to club but not kill him. Not yet, anyhow. Just enough to incapacitate him so as to record his final moments for your enjoyment," Gary narrated. "Feel free to jump in any time, Kal, and correct me if I fail to hit the mark."

Kalvin remained as silent as the film.

Gary leaned forward. "We tried picking up a reflection before his glasses fell off. Then we'd have had you right off the bat, ol' bean. But I'm sad to say we had no such luck. Lucky for you. But you missed something that we didn't, which we'll come to in another tape. Let's just watch this one for now. Shall we?

"Look at that helpless, pleading, screaming, bleeding face. Why aren't you watching, Kal? Please pay attention. You may never get to see this again, although I'm sure it's etched in your fucking memory forever. Forever, Kal. That's a long, long time. Think you'll be around? Remains to be seen, huh?"

Kalvin Matheson seemed upset but not devastated by the turn of events, believing that he was still in the catbird seat—not necessarily the hot seat. Not yet, anyway.

"Here's where you turned on the sound. So at least listen, Kal." Gary turned up the volume as the helpless figure wept and writhed upon the ground before the killer garroted the last bit of breath out of him. "Neat the way you just laid the camcorder on the ground. No need for a tripod. You know, this is better than any horror flick I've ever seen. Know why? Not so much because it's real, but because you caught the essence of dread. William Walker is still alive at this point. Look at those eyes filled with hate. Now, fear. Where did they suddenly go? Rolling back into his head. Yep. The quintessential be-all and end-all of the act. Brilliant. You certainly captured it there. Short but sweet."

Kalvin was watching and listening. A slick, sick smile suddenly curled upward at the corners of his mouth.

"Give me a moment here, Kal, and we'll go to video number two—victim three. Gretchen Bowers. Never saw anything like it in my life; that is, until I viewed tape number three. But I'm getting ahead of myself." Gary ejected the Walker cassette and put in the second tape. "Here we go." The lens of the killer's camcorder moved in for a close-up of Gretchen Bowers' duct-taped mouth and frightened eyes.

A shrieking woman's plea—not from any sound system, but playing solely in Kalvin's head—surreally filled the killer's brain.

"We tried to determine the room in which you killed her, Kalvin. At first, we thought it might have been in her home or yours. But this video clearly indicates you murdered her elsewhere." Detective Gary York continued speaking through a series of muffled screams and music still playing in the madman's mind. "It certainly wasn't in Osip's cellar, where you poisoned the Andrews boy before moving his body to that abandoned building across from the train station in Riverhead. Did you kill Salvatori Passaro, too? Hum? If you did, we *will* find his body, Kal. However, we won't need it to nail you to the wall. Vivian did that for us."

"Yeah. First she's dead, Detective York. Then you tell me she's very much alive. Next, that angry cop bitch has a slip of the lip and makes it very clear that Vivian's dead. What do you have to say on that subject now, pal? Or is the jury still out?" Kalvin giggled.

"Vivian speaks to us from the grave, as you'll soon see for yourself. Yes, I tried to trick you at first; however, you were too smart for me, Kal. But then we found the tapes. So the games are now over and done with. Anyhow, let's see what Gretchen is trying to tell us." Gary directed Kalvin's attention back to the action. "Watch her lips after you rip the tape from her mouth . . . right here. See? 'I have a bad heart,' is what our lip reader tells us Gretchen's telling you. Remember? She's desperately forming those words, telling you over and over again. I imagine she can barely breathe with that Constrictor Knot around her neck, digging into her throat. See how you stop the camera when she suddenly tries to scream, which tells us that she's probably within earshot of other unsuspecting folks. Perhaps a cheap hotel or motel room, Kalvin? Now we see her with a pair of headphones on, a rag jammed into her mouth and secured in place with duct tape. All we're left with is the language of her eyes and silent screaming as you blasted her eardrums until she died of fright. Her weak heart finally giving out."

Kalvin Matheson sneered. "Only a monster would do something like that. I'm a nice person."

"Maybe when you're sleeping, which I can assure you you're going to be in due time. Permanently."

"Is that another threat, Detective?"

"Unveiled. You'll see. Now, let's go to tape number three— victim four. Nolan Andrews. What kind of sick mind could do this to a little boy? Just look at that web. Its intricate pattern and design. Tell me that's not the work of a madman."

"That's why you should know perfectly well that you've got the wrong guy, York. I'm as sane as sane can be."

"That would have been for the shrinks to decide. But we're well beyond that point, Kalvin. As you well know, this is a very long tape, so we'll just speed things up a bit." Gary hit FAST FORWARD.

Stopped the action. Rewound. Then hit PLAY. "There! You almost put your foot into it that time, literally speaking. Pushing the boy back into the storage closet in your neighbor's cellar while you kept the action going."

Gary studied Kalvin there in the dim light as the serial killer watched his own home movie with fascination. Spellbound.

"It was very clever of you to maintain presence of mind and turn off the audio so as not to record your own voice when speaking directly to your victims. We thought for a moment that you might trip yourself up. But I'm sure you previewed the cassettes to be sure you hadn't. And in case they *were* discovered in the wine bottle, blame would undoubtedly point to your good neighbor, Chris.

"You know, what absolutely amazes me is how you kept all those tapered leaders from becoming tangled as you transported Nolan Andrews' body to that abandoned building in Riverhead. That was quite a feat. Hair. Fingers. Toes. Even his tongue, penis and testicles were tied beforehand. How? Why? What kind of a twisted mind would do that, Kal? I just love all those elaborate clues you left behind, keeping score with a series of loops and knots so that we'd think it had to be someone else when you supposedly can't even tie your own tie. Very clever, indeed, Kalvin. Or so you thought. Look. Just look at Nolan's expression right there. Thank God no jury has to witness something like this. I think we'll stop the tape here and move on."

Kalvin's stomach was starting to knot.

"Ready for Emily Schroeder?" Gary ejected the Nolan video and put in tape number four. "'Moving on to bigger and better things,' I guess is what you were saying to yourself. No?" A noose hung loose like a necklace from around the large woman's neck. "Zapped her with a stun gun to incapacitate her first. Yes?"

The two of them watched Emily Schroeder swing back and forth in an eerie, dim, shadowy light before the cord and body began untwisting simultaneously . . . faster and faster.

"That was before you changed the light bulbs, buddy. Leaving her in the limelight was for our benefit, I suppose." With his thumb, Gary tapped the SLOW button, then the adjacent PAUSE control. "This your idea of a Kodak moment, Kal?"

Matheson looked up from the wall projection back to York.

"You know what I think we'll do here, K. M.? We'll skip tape number five—victim six; that is, Vivian Osip. Instead, we'll concentrate on tape number six—victim seven. Rebecca Reynolds. Know why? Always save your best for last, I say. What do you say? Not much, huh? Oh, but you will. You'll see soon enough. Mark my words. You're gonna flip when you realize your mistake." Gary smiled brightly, holding back the alleged key to the serial killer's true identity.

The VCR regurgitated Schroeder's tape then swallowed up Reynolds'. The camera lens scanned a walk-in freezer then immediately moved in for a close-up of an exhausted figure lying still upon the floor. Breathing. Sleeping. Shivering.

"Funny. That's exactly how you looked when Detective Archer and I found you curled up in the corner earlier. You still cold, Kalvin? Let's watch. Watch her move toward the heavy door before she collapses. There. And here you stopped the camera. Started it back up. Stopped the action. Started it again. You waited until you knew she couldn't move a muscle. Did you touch her to see for sure? Did you compare the firmness of her flesh to that of a frozen side of beef like the one hanging there behind her? Bet you did. You had to be certain. But the lock was as faulty as your plan because she did manage to mark the floor of her coffin with saliva, leaving three initials, K. F. M.," Gary fibbed. "You can't see it here, but it's there. Of course, in her delirium, it could be argued that her last request was for a prime Kansas Filet Mignon." Gary grinned. "What do you think, Kalvin Frederick Matheson?"

Kalvin did not want to have to think. Besides, he knew the man was lying.

"It doesn't really much matter, Kal, because we've got the *pièce de résistance* in tape number five—victim six. Vivian Osip. With me so far? So, let's go to *the* videotape, shall we? Alive with five."

Gary ejected Rebecca Reynolds' tape and put it on the table next to the others before inserting the final video.

Kalvin's heart started racing as Vivian turned around and waved happily before the enigmatic cameraman.

"Seems she's really enjoying herself there, Kalvin—tying the last of the leaders onto Nolan Andrews' toes. You teach her those knots? Were you her Svengali? Or is it Chris who's behind the camera that you'd like us to believe did this to the Andrews boy in concert with his own daughter? Your *good* friend and neighbor. As soon as we finish up here, I'm going to have this tape cut and spliced for obvious reasons. The Osip family must never ever see this video in its entirety —of Vivian assisting in torturing that boy. Just the parts where she's obviously being badgered by you and finally gives you away as you will see in a moment. You poisoned that young girl's mind just as surely as you poisoned Nolan Andrews with ricin."

Oh, how Kalvin wanted to tell him that it was Vivian who had given Nolan his *medicine* mixed with tapioca. But of course, he could not.

"You're shaking your head, Kalvin. And shivering, too. Please don't come apart at the seams on me before the grand finale. Let's speed this up some. Oops! Back a bit. Bit more. There we go. Right here. Now, look. Note Vivian's face when Nolan drops his chin to his chest. Suddenly, she's not smiling anymore. As a matter of fact, she looks quite scared. But she's trying to put up a very brave front. Now, why do you suppose she's shaking her head? Huh? Could it be because you're telling her that she's now, or soon will be, an accomplice to murder and that she'd better keep her trap shut? I wonder. I mean, how many kids besides Vivian know the score? Know how things really worked in a court of law? Know that she'd be marked for life? Not too many were as savvy as she. When did you decide to kill her, Kalvin? I guess it really doesn't matter. What matters is that you did."

Kalvin was shivering. "I loved that little girl. I would never ever hurt her."

"Maybe not the Kalvin who Vivian came to trust and even love. But the other Kalvin deep inside you. The evil one."

Kalvin Matheson was shaking his head. "Only a monster . . . ."

"Yes. A monster, Kalvin. Now, watch closely. Watch her lips. Two syllables. See? '*Kal·vin*,' she's saying. It's unmistakably you— confirmed by linguistic experts and matched against an earlier audiovisual of her calling out your name several times at her last birthday party. Recall? But you were so angry here that you missed it. And now she's crying. You must have said something that made her stop immediately. Look at her expression. And then you stopped the action for a moment—probably to lecture and threaten her with her life. Vivian is very frightened as you begin again, Kalvin. Yet, she regains her composure and remains cool as a cucumber. All you did was piss her off. Watch what she does next. So subtle. You'll flip.

Note. She turns and faces away from the camera. Inserts her thumbs and pinky fingers in the rear pockets of her designer jeans. And with her forefinger, starts tapping the sewn-in leather label to the right." Gary hit the ZOOM button. "See the logo? **C K**.

"Kalvin, but with a C standing for a **K**, of course. **Kalvin**. **Kalvin**. **Kalvin**. **Kalvin**, she's signaling, probably now realizing that you would kill her." Gary alternated between the SLOW and PAUSE buttons. "Now, note—here—how she suddenly points three fingers downward to form the letter **M**. Slick? Could anything be clearer than that, Kalvin Matheson? And what's the great irony in all of this? Huh? Do you remember what you gave Vivian for her last birthday? Of course, you do. Those very same Calvin Klein designer jeans that she wanted so badly. Remarkable," Gary concluded, stopping the tape, ejecting it and cutting the power.

Kalvin continued shivering as he watched the projector lamp go dim, oblivious to his surroundings.

Gary stood, switched on the overhead lights, unlocked the shackle fettered at the prisoner's foot, then gathered up all six videos. He went over and picked up Kalvin's pile of clothing. "Get dressed; then you and I will have a quiet little chat."

Slowly, Kalvin came out of his trance and grinned broadly.

"I want you to know, Detective York, that you have nothing but a bunch of finger-pointing. Hear me?"

Chapter 54

Detective Lieutenant Ethan Powell's absence that morning was as obvious as the World Trade Center missing from the skyline of lower Manhattan. Deputy Inspector Sean O'Leary was shaking his head insistently while Brian was bitterly pacing the lieutenant's borrowed office. Justin Barnes was waiting in the wings at the other end of the hall. Yolanda and her partner, Enrique, had just returned from the airport with Bishop John. Gary and Kim were seated at a desk across the hallway from the glass partitioned office, listening to the commotion within, watching with furtive glances at the angry posturing and gesturing between two determined men. O'Leary placed his hands firmly on his hips and once again sternly shook his head. He went over to the glass wall and peered out at the two pretenders, their heads now buried between piles of paperwork, supposedly studying police reports. O'Leary drew the vertical blinds and returned to the heat of battle.

"You knew what the deal was, Brian. No confession, no Justin Barnes."

"I understand. But just give Justin the opportunity to *talk* to him. That's all I'm asking. He's not going to walk in there and kill him, for God's sake."

"You were told to secure a confession. But Matheson didn't buy York's picture story. Did he? So what makes you think he's going to swallow Barnes' fiction, goddamn it? I told Powell like I told you— and now I'm telling you again. Justin doesn't step foot inside that room without Matheson's confession."

"And I'm telling you there's a damn good chance he can get it."

"And I'm tellin' you for the last time he'll never get the chance. He's not trained in interrogation. God knows what he'll say in there. Look at the damage that's already been done—what's been revealed to that sick fuck, Matheson. I must have been crazy to go along with this charade. To allow you to tamper with those tapes."

"It's a copy of a copy for cryin' out loud, Inspector. Listen to me. Please. Matheson's on the ropes. Justin can topple him. If he can't shake him, that'll be it. But if he gets Matheson's confession, we take it to the next level. What do we have to lose? Nothing."

"Nothing? What about time? Look. I'll tell you what. Gary's your closer. He's your partner. Give him another shot."

"Gary's not prepared to handle this like Justin is. He's spent time with Bishop John. Gary hasn't. I'm the case detective. I make the call."

"Oh, you're so wrong, Brian. *I* make that call. And I'm telling you that if you don't have Kalvin Matheson's confession by morning, he walks. As a matter of fact, it is morning."

"You're just going to let a serial killer walk?"

"We can't prove it, Brian, and Matheson knows it. Otherwise, he'd be looking to strike a deal. All I'm hearing," O'Leary shouted, bringing the tape recording to his ear, which Gary had secreted on his person earlier, "is the sound of both you guys pissing in the wind."

"You'd really let him walk."

"You're not hearing me."

"All too well."

Brian withdrew his badge and revolver and set them down upon the desk matter-of-factly before walking over to the vertical slats and opening them wide. Directly across the corridor stood Kim and Gary; Yolanda and Enrique. The four withdrew their badges and weapons and placed them in the center of Yolanda's desk.

"I guess Justin's in the other room with Bishop John, Inspector, awaiting your answer." Brian said it without vindictiveness—void of any emotion.

"You'd throw your careers away for a piece of shit like Matheson?" the man questioned in sheer astonishment and disgust. "All of you?"

"You're not hearing *me*, Inspector," Brian Archer stated firmly, opening the door and stepping into the hallway, closing the portal behind him.

The inspector went over and sat down at Detective Lieutenant Theodore Groche's old desk, taking in Ethan Powell's inherited space. He watched as the four insubordinates walked away.

"Fuck!"

Chapter 55

Standing apprehensively at the threshold of the interrogation room, Clonite's Pennsylvania based representative, Bishop John, set a small crate down upon a long rectangular wooden box in which the homicide squad stored its manacles and leg irons. The plaque above the doorway to the 8 x 8-foot space caught the man's eye.

"Are you sure I won't have to go in there or say anything?" The bishop's slender fingers fidgeted with a loose piece of yarn at the sleeve of his sweater.

"Not one step. Not one word," Justin promised. "You just stand here by the door and hand me that crate when I ask for it. Make damn sure Matheson sees you. That's it. Detectives will escort you back to the airport in a little while."

"The same two who picked me up?" the bishop asked anxiously. "They were both very nice to me."

"What did you do? Promise them eternity?" Justin jawed.

"Oh, good heavens, no. But will Detectives Ivers and Valez still be taking me? I'd really feel more comfortable."

"To tell you the truth, which I hardly ever do, except in this case—" Justin swore, exposing his pearly whites for all they were worth—"I don't rightly know, nor do I really give a shit. What I do know is that you're almost off the hook and outta here. So, you ready?"

"Yes, sir."

"Then pick up the crate, asshole."

"Yes, sir."

"Here we go." Justin opened the door and stepped into the claustrophobic space.

Kalvin Matheson was fully clothed, showered, clean shaven and seated in handcuffs beside the small table. The room was spotless and smelled of disinfectant.

Bishop John stood just outside the doorway.

"Hey, chump," Justin greeted Kalvin. "You look like you're goin' somewhere with that coat on. How you been, buddy? Ain't seen you since the arrest."

"I haven't been arrested. I haven't even been charged. Nor have I been allowed to call my attor—" Kalvin cut his sentence short and stared past Justin to the figure holding a crate at the doorway.

Justin turned to Bishop John. "May I have that, please?"

The man handed over the case and was gone in the blink of an eye.

"WAIT!" Kalvin screamed. "Wait. Come back here, Bishop John." The prisoner began to seethe. "They've got nothing . . . just a lot of ac-accu—" the serial killer stammered "—accusations, is all," his voice trailed. Suddenly, the man began to tear.

"Get a grip, fella," Justin implored, setting the crate down upon the table very carefully. "Dude's got a plane to catch and some papers to sign before he leaves. Something to do with immunity from prosecution. And you and I got some business to discuss."

The door to the 8 x 8 foot room closed abruptly and suddenly locked from the outside.

Justin pulled a chair up to the table. "So. Here's the deal. Oh, before I forget. You told someone earlier that you wanted your coat back. Well, you can thank me for that. That's one hundred percent goose down you got there. Right? Filled with all them fancy, fluffy feathers. It'll keep you nice and warm while you make your final decision. And I do mean final, 'cause either way, you're goin' down for the count.

"Now, let me tell you what we've got in this box." Justin rapped the case with his knuckles, and Kalvin flinched. "Want to take a guess first? Huh? Guess not. It's a box of tissues, Kalvin. Not the kind you wipe your nose with, but the kind Clonite's doctors cut from your body and sent off to some secret laboratory for storage and preservation. Got Alvin's in here, too—obtained sometime after Pilgrim State buried him—where you later dug 'im up, cut out a section of his flesh, then replanted your twin brother. Got Clonite's receipt right here with your signature on it. See? Three hundred dollars a year for safekeeping. The least of your expenses. Bishop John and others went through a whole lot of trouble to get this box back from the lab."

Kalvin had not taken his eyes off the crate.

"They got it all packed up in somethin' like Dry Ice. Good for up to twelve hours, I'm told. After that, the tissues begin to deteriorate. The culture *must* maintain a temperature below zero degrees Fahrenheit, or minus seventeen point something Celsius, Bishop John explained to me. Has to do with cryonics or some kind of crap like that. Actually, a human body or a pet, say like Poochie, requires extremely low temperatures below two hundred degrees Fahrenheit, or minus one hundred thirty Celsius. But with these tissue cultures here, you're at minus twenty degrees Fahrenheit right now, which is fine for the moment. See the temperature gauge? This box has been in transit for four hours since the moment it left the lab. Bishop John's plane doesn't leave for another two hours. It's only twenty minutes to the airport. But then they want you there an hour early. Don't want to cut it too close, I'd imagine. What do you think? You can do the math, Matheson."

"To do what?"

"To make *theee* biggest decision of your life, buddy."

"Just confess. Right?" Kalvin laughed ridiculously.

Justin shook his head. "No, Kalvin. Not *just* confess, but also to end everything—once and for all."

"What do you mean, end everything?"

"The answer to that question can be found in the lining of the coat you're wearing."

"What are you talking about?"

"When you leave here, you're going to be taken upstairs to a cell a little bit bigger than this one. More room—less time to reflect on matters. Along the bottom edge of your coat, behind the lining, you'll find what you need. But first, I need that confession along with some particulars you know the police couldn't possibly have."

"Who are you?" Kalvin asked with malice.

"Official title? Consultant. But actually I'm a high-priced janitor. They bring me in to do their dirty work, Kal. This is one of my clean-up operations," he added quite candidly.

"And I'm supposed to believe that's actually Alvin's and my cultures in that crate," he stated with a hint of disbelief. "I have a binding contract with Clonite. I don't believe a word you're saying."

"Now, that's exactly what Detectives Archer and York said you'd say. So I had the bishop instruct the lab to pack this in such a way that would erase any and all doubt. Watch very carefully, Kalvin." Justin inverted the crate and pointed to two perfectly round porthole-like windows. "Those are the Petri dishes that contain both Alvin's cells and yours. Sealed, signed and delivered. See the row of microchips above the first culture? That's your genetic code in those teeny-weeny squares. The second dish and set of chips is Alvin's complete DNA profile, too. Six million letters separate all but identical twins, I'm told. And that last chip up there in the corner, consisting of a measly four letters, is your own encoded inscription that no one else in the whole wide word knew—up until now, Kalvin: A_T_ G_C_. Your secret PIN, pal."

Kalvin was visibly shaken. And not from the prolonged exposure to the cold air he had suffered, but rather with air conditioning pumped in purposely and purely for his discomfort and displeasure. The serial killer was sweating profusely now.

"Those four letters alone can cancel your contract with Clonite at any time, Kal. And for whatever reason. Now, or in the future. I know you're just dying to know how we broke the code. And believe me, I'm dying to tell you. But all I'm permitted to say is that we have a wizard in our midst. One who practices a brand of black magic all her own—against evildoers like yourself. She wanted the satisfaction of my telling you that. I told her I'd be honored, and I am."

Justin turned the container back over.

"See what the box says, here? See the arrows? THIS SIDE UP because cold stays down. So, we better adhere to these instructions. If you don't follow mine to a T in the next sixty seconds, I'm going to stick this box in the fucking furnace downstairs. That's a promise. It's ready and roaring. Are you?"

Kalvin was nodding dully, his eyes fixed on the crate as if he were in a trance.

"Good. Now, you're going to cleanse your soul and ease your conscience. Did you kill Denise Nathan?"

"Does this box go back to where it came from?" Kalvin asked

with pleading eyes. "Immediately to the lab where it belongs?"

"I swear on my mother. And please don't ask me, 'Why should I believe you?' because we both know you have no fucking choice."

Kalvin nodded. "All right, then. Yes."

"Yes, what?"

"Yes, I killed Denise Nathan."

"Why?"

"For confidence building and power. You wouldn't understand."

"Oh, wouldn't I." It wasn't a question. "And . . .?"

"And to send authorities down that money trail."

"On a wild-goose chase."

"Yes."

"Of which you wouldn't receive a dime because . . .?"

"Because I wasn't connected with her or her family in any way."

"A seemingly random killing."

Kalvin took his eyes off the box for an instant. "Yes."

"Unlike Gretchen Bowers, who you killed along with Salvatori Passaro for his share of the one million dollars he collected on her life insurance policy."

"Yes."

"Where's Passaro's body?"

"In an old mine shaft in Pennsylvania. Right outside Lancaster. I could take you there."

Justin laughed and broke out a pen and pad. "Just draw me a map of the outlying area leading in. Town. Woods. Quarry. Streambed. Whatever and wherever. Pretend it's a treasure map. X marks the spot. Precisely where you dumped the body. And while you're doing that, because the clock's-a-tickin', tell me more about Denise Nathan."

"Beautiful little rich bitch who never did anything for her family or herself. Just one waitressing job after another. Go figure that. Not like Gretchen Bowers who had no family except for her Uncle Sal who she'd visit every week at Pilgrim State without fail. Rain or shine. Snowstorms or major flooding, she'd be there like clockwork. Always with a present in hand."

"Backing up to William Walker. You kill him?"

"Yes."

"Did 'im how?"

"Clubbed him. And then I strangled him with a garrote."

"Why Walker?"

"Random. He had nothing to do with any insurance money or inheritance. He had nothing."

"You're doin' good, guy. How you comin' with the geography? I ain't gonna need no GPS, am I?"

"No. He's going to be pretty easy to find. But it won't be a shallow grave is all." Kalvin cracked a grin.

"Nolan Andrews."

"I lured him as a favor to Vivian. Nasty little boy."

"Method?"

"Ricin."

"Administered how."

"Tapioca pudding."

"You lured him, and then you poisoned him."

"No. Vivian did that. As a matter of fact, she insisted."

"You didn't assist her?"

"No. It was her show. He was already dead when I put him in that crawlspace in Riverhead. But I did most of the knots," Kalvin boasted.

"Next. Why Emily Schroeder?"

"Her connection to Pilgrim State and the fact that there was no insurance money either. The house was all she had and would be part of the estate. Nothing to do with me. I thought perhaps it would keep the police from pursuing a 'money as motive' trail exclusively and maybe send them looking for nut jobs recently released from the institution, like Salvatori Passaro, so that when I made another score, it would just seem a matter of course that I would be named beneficiary."

"Meaning the Reynolds."

"Yes. After all, the money wouldn't be coming directly from Rebecca, now would it?"

"So, you planned on murdering her husband."

"After I was sure Phillip would write out a will making me sole beneficiary. A will, Mister Consultant—not his piddling life insurance policy monies amounting to mere peanuts. I'd be above suspicion." Kalvin started giggling.

"What's so funny?"

"The title I picked for the Rebecca Reynolds operation."

"Title?"

"Yes. Frozen Assets."

"Catchy. So, you killed Rebecca."

"I'd have to say the cold did that."

"But you're the one who put her in that walk-in freezer in Mattituck. True?"

"Carried her in all by my lonesome." Kalvin smiled spookily.

"And Vivian Osip?"

"I really loved that girl."

"So what happened?"

"She turned on me."

"How?"

"How? She wouldn't listen. That's how."

"Listen to what, exactly?"

"To the fact that she, not I, killed Nolan Andrews. That she enjoyed it. Little things like that."

"Why did you seal her up in shrink-wrap? Kinda weird. No?"

Kalvin was shaking his head. "I gave her every opportunity— right up to her very last breath, which I sucked from her body as I sealed both her fate and the plastic sheet with a heat gun."

"Opportunity for what?"

"Opportunity to live forever. With Alvin and me."

"Aha. And she said no, I suppose."

"She said that one Matheson in her life was enough. Thought the whole thing was one big joke. That's when we took a little ride together to Indian Island in Riverhead. I told her that I was going to teach her how to fly-cast at the golf course over there. Lots of open space to practice. I gave her a hug from behind and put her in a sleeper hold. She was still breathing when I set her upon the plastic sheet, tucking and securing the edges with special shrink-wrap tape."

"You ever touch her, Kalvin?" Justin asked out of a morbid sense of curiosity. "You know; have her in the biblical way? Any way, for that matter?"

Kalvin looked hurt. "Number one, I don't believe in the Bible; I believe in science. Number two, I'm not that way."

"Oh, and what way is that?"

"Sexual. I'm what you would call asexual. A neuter. Our relationship was purely platonic. I was like a father to that girl."

"A father?"

"Yes."

"Yet, you killed her."

"Yes. But I left her in a state of bliss. That wasn't just a plain white sheet of plastic that I wrapped her in."

"No?"

"No. It was a metaphor that was lost on all of you, I suppose."

"Metaphor?"

"Sure. I set her down on cloud nine so that Chris and the others might catch my drift."

"Cloud nine?"

"Yes. The sixth hole; a nine turned upside down."

Justin shook his head sadly. "Sorry we didn't catch that one, Kalvin. It went right over our heads. But I'll be sure to pass along its significance so that you receive full credit. How's that?"

"You can tell Chris for me that I didn't kill his darling daughter for any sort of revenge."

"Revenge?"

"Yes, for working the evidence surrounding Malcolm Columba and Clarence Emery—my two heroes. Chris worked night and day on those two cases. You have to understand that I exacted my pound of flesh by driving a wedge between him and Harriet years ago . . . between father and daughter, too. I'm only sorry that I didn't have more time to frame him for those murders. I was formulating a plan when things got hectic. You see, I know lots of little secrets because I would visit Chris' study from time to time—when everyone but Vivian was out of the house. I learned many things needed to tie you all into knots. It's really such a shame how things turned out."

"How you comin' with that diagram?"

Kalvin pushed the pad and pen toward Justin. "You won't have any problem finding Sal."

"I got one more question for you, Kal," the interrogator stated, putting the items away. "Please don't fuck it up."

"I won't."

"Where did you kill Gretchen Bowers? Because we know from the video that Passaro's niece wasn't killed in Chris Osip's home or yours."

Kalvin was smiling.

"Not gonna tell me where you wasted her?"

"Not going to send that box back with Bishop John unless I do?"

"No, a deal's a deal. You confessed to the murders. I didn't say you had to say where," he said quite frankly.

"But you'd like to know."

"They'd like to know," Justin pointed toward the door. "Personally, I couldn't give a crap."

"Yet, you wanted to know Passaro's whereabouts."

"It lends credibility to your story."

"I see."

"You know what I think, Kal? I think you want to tell me where you murdered Gretchen. I think you're busting at the seams for me to know."

Kalvin was nodding excitedly in the affirmative. "The only problem being is that you won't believe me."

"Try me."

"I murdered them right under their goddamn noses."

"All right. I'll bite. Under whose noses?"

"Pilgrim State's." Kalvin was ecstatic.

"You're telling me that you killed Gretchen Bowers at Pilgrim State Hospital?"

Kalvin was shaking his head. "Not *at* Pilgrim State; *in* Pilgrim State. In Alvin's old room. I took her there for a visit. A last look around, you might say. Lots of new nurses. Lots of old faces. Mostly patients, of course. Several of them were actually running around screaming, 'Alvin's back. Alvin's back.' But nobody would believe them."

Justin studied the man seated before him for a good minute before he said another word. "Did anyone downstairs take your fingerprints after they brought you in?"

Matheson was laughing so hard that he could barely contain himself. "No," he finally answered after calming down somewhat. "All they did was bring me immediately to this room. 'For questioning,' they said. As I've been telling everyone—and I *do* mean *everyone*—I have not been arrested or charged with any crime. Just *accused* of horrible, horrible things. I have not been allowed to call a lawyer, or Harriet, or anyone. They make these terrible accusations, but then refuse to read me my rights. I've been taken to the bathroom once and afterwards handed a bucket and some toilet paper. I haven't had a thing to eat except for two slices of buttered bread in what I would estimate to be more than thirty or forty hours. One quick sip of water from a fountain outside. And a gulp from the bucket before I pissed and shit my brains out."

"You're not Kalvin Matheson, are you?"

The figure before him took a deep breath. "You know something? You're the first to ask."

"What happened to Kalvin, Alvin?"

"Kalvin, Alvin. Alvin, Kalvin. Who cares?"

"I care."

"Why?"

"I'm the one who's asking the questions here."

"Sorry."

"Tell me what became of Kalvin?"

"He went mad." The man began rocking.

"How?"

"How? How does anyone go mad? When people around you don't listen or care. That's how. I told him over and over again how we could live on forever. Just like Vivian, he thought it was a big joke. He said that *I* was the one who was crazy. Well, I fixed his wagon but good." Matheson moved closer to the precious box and stroked it. "When he came to visit me at the hospital one stormy evening, I pulled the old switcheroo. But first I told him what he didn't think I saw one evening in our parents' bedroom when we were kids growing up. I told him I was going to tell *everyone*: his employer, his friends and acquaintances—which you could count on one hand had you been a thief and caught stealing in India." The lunatic giggled, holding up a pinky and a thumb before tucking down the other three. "When I walked out of there that night, there was no question as to who was the madder of the two. For years afterward, the doctors all believed he was curable. *Redeemable*, I tried to tell them. You know how *they* listen. Before he died, however, I made him and myself a promise that I'd handle what he refused to do."

"Obtain immortality for the two of you."

The prisoner nodded.

Justin turned the box back over, pointing to the Plexiglas windows, digesting Matheson's story. "So, then this is actually Kalvin's dish, and this one's yours," Justin tested.

"Please be careful with that." The man was trembling. "Please."

Justin righted the crate.

"I trust you'll keep your word and return this to its rightful place."

"Absolutely," Justin promised.

"Thank you."

Justin lifted the box with both hands and walked over to the door. Immediately, someone opened it from the outside.

"Along the hem of the coat, you said. Yes?"

"*You* said hem. *I* said along the bottom behind the lining." Justin paused and smiled. "Although one could say *you're* hemmed in. Just remember—as soon as we move you to a temporary cell upstairs. Not before. It would be impossible to pull it off down here. They're watching."

"I understand."

"I'm sure you do."

Chapter 56

Within minutes, Yaphank's infamous prisoner was taken from the interrogation room and booked. The serial killer's prints were processed and immediately sent through AFIS: Automated Fingerprint Identification Systems.

Deputy Inspector Sean O'Leary, along with Detectives Brian and Kim Archer, Gary York, Yolanda Ivers and Enrique Valez, had listened in astonishment to Matheson's taped confession. It was evident that the six individuals had been arguing. Heatedly. As to which Matheson, Kalvin or Alvin, the police retained, remained a mystery for the moment.

Justin knocked upon and immediately opened the door to Detective Lieutenant Powell's office. The maverick stood in the doorway, taking in the brood of sullen faces. "I just faxed a report along with a copy of Matheson's diagram off to Lancaster P.D. They're on it," he announced, stepping inside and off to a corner.

"You live in a barn, Barnes?" the deputy inspector snapped.

"Used to. A few of them, in fact." Justin reached over and closed the door. "But now that I'm so high and mighty—zoom!—el-e-va-tor right to my new penthouse apartment in a mostly integrated neighborhood. Black, white, and yellow. Mastic/Shirley." The consultant grinned. "Doors open and close au-to-mat-i-cal-ly for *moi*, via an electric eye—pho-to-cell. So so*ll*y, I have this tendency to forget."

"How you spend your money is your business, Barnes."

"Down in the lobby, we tenants got us a white knight," Justin jawed away. "Doorman sportin' a blue cap and matching coat with brass buttons. I couldn't help but notice that you got yourself one o' dem ceramic ceremonial sambos standin' 'longside your driveway— holdin' up one of 'dose 'lectric lanterns, Inspector. But I never, ever see it lit on those evenings when you come home late. You should, though. Just can't be too careful nowadays, you know. Cop or no cop."

O'Leary stood up from behind Powell's desk and walked brashly up to Justin. "Are you threatening me?"

"A Suffolk County deputy inspector? You think I'm crazy?"

"I catch you *anywhere* near my house, day or night, I'll thrash you. Got that?"

"Catch me doin' what?"

"You stay out of my neighborhood. Hear?"

"Well, you're welcome in mine any ol' time, Inspector. Course you might not make it out in one pi—"

Kim had stepped forward, placing a hand over Justin's mouth. "Save it, J."

"No, let him say what he has to say," O'Leary challenged. "Hey! Tough guy. Just remember. I know firsthand how you made your money before you ever came aboard here."

"Really?"

"Drugs, gun running, and prostitution," the inspector stewed. "Think I don't know about your past?"

"Think I don't know about *your* escapades? Like Flora, one o' my *fine* lady friends who entertained you for an evening every now and again. Initially, I thought I knew *all* her johns. You're the guy she talks about who removes that rug you wear atop your scalp and sticks it between your legs for laughs, asking her to rub your pussy. Yeah. You're the one my Asian girls called F*r*uzzy?"

O'Leary's face was beet red. "You're only here because of Theo Groche, Barnes," the inspector blew, pointing to a picture on the wall of Homicide's recently retired commanding officer. "But that's drawing to a close—and soon. Powell's got his eye on you, I want you to know."

"And my baby browns on him as well," Justin mocked in an affected, effeminate manner and tone, standing toe-to-toe before the man. "Nice cheeks on that boy, too. Rather big, but *ni·ice*, nevertheless," he babbled away gaily as Brian moved him back a step.

"You're fuckin' sick, Barnes. Know that?"

"Or maybe you'd like to inspect this, Inspector," Justin jawed, grabbing his crotch and blowing the man a kiss. The covert operative addressed the others. "I think that's truly his pre-di-lec-tion. I say that because Fruzzy, here, never really got it on with the ladies. Word on the street is that you get your kicks drinking warm sake while jerking off into your hairpiece."

"You're on report!" the inspector flared.

"Sorry, deputy, but I don't exist. So take your tin and shove it where the sun don't shine." Justin turned to Gary. "Line from some western long forgotten," he whispered, bringing a limp wrist to his brow in contemplation. "I'm trying to think who was in it, but I can't because they were all white."

Brian had had it and interceded. "Enough, J! We've all got work to do."

"And I said we're not moving on this till we match his prints," the inspector affirmed.

"I thought they can determine ID in a matter of minutes," Yolanda said in exasperation.

"Normally, they can," Kim explained. "But someone please tell me what's normal about this case? Even AFIS has its limitations. We're dealing with identical twins that have similar arch patterns, loops and whorls. A trained examiner, not a computer, will have the last word, Yolanda. Hence, the delay."

"Well, I don't think it makes a good goddamn bit of difference if that's Kalvin, Alvin, or Attila the Hun in there," Yolanda's partner, Enrique, fumed. "We got the guy who did the deed; or in this case, at least eight victims that we now know about. We got his confession on tape, thanks to J. We got a detailed drawing, in Matheson's own hand, of where he put Passaro's body. What happened to our agreement? Huh, Inspector?"

O'Leary ran his eyes over everyone. "The problem, my insubordinate renegades, is a tricky legal one that's plagued our judicial system since the dawn of modern madness. Insanity versus sanity. To which warehouse do the courts send these people? The nuthouse or the jailhouse? And now with the death penalty back on the books, we further complicate and compound matters. If that's truly Alvin and not Kalvin in there, do we execute a deranged man who the doctors as well as the courts deemed certifiable more than a decade ago? A lunatic who spent a good part of his life in a mental hospital."

"We're not executing anyone. We're just giving him the means to expedite matters for himself."

"Do you hear yourself, Kim Archer?" O'Leary snapped. "That's not an unbiased professional talking. You're taking this very personally because one of the victims happened to be your goddaughter."

"For openers, if that's Alvin we have back there, which I believe it is, he spent the better part of his life as a *free* animal. Free to torture, torment and murder men, women and children. We really don't know how many people he's actually killed, while his innocent brother rotted away inside Pilgrim State."

"Remind the inspector why you think that it's Alvin we're holding back there, Kim," Yolanda proposed.

"Because Alvin Matheson was an electrician's helper whenever he did work, which accounts for how he knew to rig the golf cart with an electric heat gun applicator to seal Vivian's fate. Also, the way he strung Emily Schroeder's body from the ceiling fixture with electrical cord. Recall how neatly the connections were spliced? Not to mention the fact that he ran the electric that lights the steps leading up and down Chris and Harriet's spiral staircase."

"And what difference does it make if it is Alvin Matheson? Why can't we move this ahead as planned?" Gary pressed. "So what if we're dealing with a split personality or a multiple personality or whatever. What's the goddamn point? Maybe Alvin's a very good actor. Or maybe Kalvin's really the actor. Who cares? I say we move this along now. Let him end it himself. Whoever it is in there, Alvin or Kalvin, he's not going to wait around for a decade to receive a lethal injection, sitting on death row while his lawyers file for appeals. Nor will he hang his hat on the hook of hope for even a year, awaiting a more preferable outcome than prison life, like landing on his feet in some loony bin. This guy sees the proverbial bright light at the end of a very short tunnel. Justin knows Matheson wants to commit suicide. The guy is primed. But will he have the means once he's out of our hands. The answer is probably no. But more importantly, we'd be giving Chris and Harriet closure today rather than some future date. We owe them that much. We'd be doing them, ourselves, and the public a favor now rather than enduring hearing after hearing followed by a lengthy and expensive trial. We're simply the ways and means committee, Inspector."

"Oh, you're good, Gary. I give you that. I see why they call you The Closer. But I want all of you to think about this. If we allow ourselves to let him commit suicide—this sick-minded man—we have to live with our conscience till the end of our own days."

Brian laughed. "Our conscience?"

"Yes, our conscience, damn it."

"Define that."

"Define what?"

"Conscience, Inspector. If I'm going to live with something for the rest of my days, I want to know exactly what it is I'm dealing with."

"Come on, Brian. The awareness of what is simply *right* and *wrong*. The *awareness*," he repeated. "Otherwise, we're no better than any of them that pass through our doors."

"Why don't we take a vote and see exactly where we all stand on this matter?" Enrique suggested.

"You see, Detective," the inspector said while exhibiting a good degree of condescension and body language, "you're still young yet. You just can't stand there and view this whole business as a single picture. You have to examine each piece of the mosaic. Alvin as an escapee from a mental hospital, if that be the case. Kalvin as a split personality. Actor, or genuinely disturbed. Slick or sick. You simply do not harm, or cause to bring about harm to a sick-minded individual, Detective Enrique Valez."

Justin had to laugh. "Just a moment ago you said that *I* was sick. And what did you want to do to me? Thrash me, were your words, or worse. So, with all *un*due respect, I got you figured like this, Inspector. You're prejudiced, you're jealous, and you're afraid of the fallout from a full-blown investigation if either Alvin or Kalvin takes his life on your watch because no one will be watching the prisoner as he takes the E-ZPass. Well, I'm not going to stand around here and placate anyone by picking apart this and that. I refuse to suffer the paralysis of analysis. No, sir. Not me. I choose to lump all this shit together because it all *belongs* on a single plate. It doesn't really matter to me at all whether it's Kalvin or Alvin in there, whether he's sick or slick or deserves an Academy Award. That man in there, whoever the fuck he is, admitted to killing eight human beings with malice aforethought. He's not some babbling idiot who picked up a hatchet thinking it was a compress to help relieve his mother's migraine. He calculated and planned those murders to a T. That's *my* mosaic. I choose to see the complete picture, Inspector. Not all the little squares."

Kim, Brian, Yolanda, Enrique and Gary gave Justin a standing round of applause.

"You're a fine one to talk, Barnes," O'Leary snapped. "A stone-cold killer in your own right. I know your record. The one that doesn't exist. You're actually a disgrace to this department and its teams of fine detectives, this county, this state—the entire country, in fact!"

"Huh. Now, that's what I call coverage!" Justin remarked.

"Great men like Theodore Groche and Ethan Powell have been blindsided by your results, Barnes. But results without conscience make for a shallow, hollow shell of a man. And like a cancer, you've corrupted several good men and women like Brian and Kim, Gary, Enrique and Yolanda. Corrupted them with your evil ways."

"My God, man! And where do you fit in along the line, Inspector?" Kim asked in amazement. "Part of your problem is that you sit behind that desk of yours and wield power from another world while we're down here in the trenches. You've earned that right, God knows. See, I know *your* record. But to come down here with your platitudes and attitudes and pass judgment, when you don't even know this man, is unfair."

"Unfair? I know all I need to know. I've dealt with a thousand smart-ass punks like Barnes, up through the ranks and down through the years. He's no different than any of them. The only reason I went along with this business, up to a point, was because of circumstances. But the circumstances have changed. Haven't they, Kim? You don't take the law into your own hands. Period."

"Oh, but *you* and the higher-ups can and do exactly that. You play God when it's convenient. That's why Justin was sanctioned and brought on board in the first place. It wasn't Theo deciding alone."

"There are certain circumstances. Yes."

"And this is one of them."

"It is, if and when I say it is. And I say we wait and see exactly what we're dealing with."

"By then it may be too late."

"Dem's the breaks, kid." The inspector smirked.

"Once the county jail gets ahold of Matheson, we're dead in the water. I want this fucker stopped. Now!"

"Now, you just stop it, Kim. All of you! I didn't want to get into a rather sensitive area, but I see that I have no choice. It starts with you and Brian. It ends with Barnes, as it always does. Gary, Yolanda and Enrique are stuck in the middle of this mess. I'm trying to stop all of you from making a terrible mistake here. I'm trying to save your careers. Take your fucking blinders off, folks. Take the wax out of your ears. Look, listen, and learn. Osip fucked up. All right? He fucked up with those pics and reports, and he fucked up with his daughter. You were godmother to Vivian, Kim. Vivian's dead. Brian. You are Chris' friend. Right away we got a bad batch brewing. Friends of the family, and a conflict of interest." Sean O'Leary shook his head sadly. "Gary. You're Brian's partner. Yolanda and Enrique. You two worked this case closely with those in this room. You're all too personally involved. See the big picture as Barnes puts it? And because I sit behind a desk at a distance from all of you, I have a much clearer perspective. If you take away these elements, this intimacy if you will, this Alvin/Kalvin killer is a boy scout compared to Malcolm Columba and Clarence Emery. Matheson is just your garden variety serial killer. Like it or not."

"In case you haven't noticed, Inspector, this garden variety psychopath is a Columba/Emery emulator who started collecting all their merit badges," Kim hammered away.

"I suppose so, Kim."

"So, we're supposed to sit on our hands and wait? I know what's going to happen. We all know what's going to happen. We'll wait for the print match. Then we'll wait for a psychiatric evaluation. And then we'll wait to see if this goes to trial or if he's shipped off to a mental hospital."

"Three death penalty cases in this county back in 1999," Gary reminded the group. "Three at the same time for one good shot in the arm. Howard Mills alone cost this county beaucoup bucks. An unprecedented fifteen-month trial. Can Suffolk County even afford another one, Inspector? It would be cheaper in the long run if we recruited more covert operatives like Justin. Believe-you-me."

"Consultant, if you please," Justin underscored with a grin.

"Consultant. Covert operative, my ass," O'Leary rejoined. "Suffolk County's stone-cold killing machine would be calling a spade a spade. One of you, Barnes, is too many if you ask me. If I had my say, you'd be long gone."

"You know, it's not like J's going in and blowing the guy's head off," Yolanda contended. "He's simply handing the man his coat and saying *adiós*."

"*Hasta la vista*," Enrique added.

"*Hasta luego*," Yolanda concluded, waving her fingers as a final farewell gesture.

"It's like I started telling the inspector a moment ago," Justin interjected. "In my new digs and upscale neighborhood, the lingo is 'sayonara, muthafucker.' Don't really matter what your creed or code. You know, I even got me a samurai sword hanging over the couch. I'm telling you, culture-wise, I'm really getting into the swing of things. Not with the Mau Mau mentality I used to muster, brothers and sisters. No, siree."

The inspector stared at Justin for what seemed like an eternity. Finally, O'Leary spoke. "You've heard nothing of what I've said here, Barnes. But I want you to hear what I'm saying now. And that is, I don't like you at all."

"Oh, now *that's* a fucking surprise!" Justin turned to Brian and whispered. "That's a line from *My Cousin Vinny*. You know. After Fred Gwynne as the judge turns to Joe Pesci playing Vinny, and tells him he's going to find him in contempt and that—"

The phone rang. The inspector snapped it up. "Yeah . . . Uh-huh . . . Right . . . No, I understand perfectly . . . All right . . . Thank you." He set the receiver down carefully upon its cradle as if he were putting a wee infant to bed.

The five detectives were at a loss to read the deputy inspector's poker face.

Justin just scratched his nose. "Well, was I right as usual?"

"It's Alvin Matheson," O'Leary finally said. "Fingerprints confirm we're holding Alvin Matheson. "Also, Kalvin's sign-in signature of his last visit to his brother at Pilgrim State was forged and matches Alvin's handwriting. Kalvin Matheson apparently died in his sleep in that institution five years later—buried as Alvin Frederick

Matheson."

"They even shared the same middle name," Yolanda said through a sigh.

"And all Alvin had to do was add a K to his given name and assume his brother's identity," Kim added, shaking her head in wonder. "A role which he played brilliantly."

"K for killer," Gary affirmed.

"So, how do we stand, Inspector?" Enrique asked. "Or you just wanna stand around here and beat up on us some more?"

O'Leary turned about like a turret and took aim at the detective's questions. "You're right, Enrique. The moment of truth is at hand. The time has come for me to make a final decision. The truth of the matter is . . . I can't. Not without losing a part of my soul versus losing five good detectives who threatened to mutiny or walk or whatever." He paused and sighed so sorrowfully. "So, here's what I propose," he continued, dipping a hand deep into a pant pocket. "No matter how silly it may sound." O'Leary produced a silver coin. A quarter. "If I'm forced to make a definitive and final decision, it's going to be that we hand Alvin Matheson over to the courts. You can count on it. But first, I'd order you to remove the item from the lining of his coat, Barnes. If, however, I flip this coin and lose the toss, you may proceed, realizing, of course, that Alvin Matheson may not comply with your wishes anyway. In which case, it'll be the same as my having won the toss. Then, if he takes his life at some later point in time, without anyone here helping him along the way, you'll all have a clear conscience, or so you'll convince yourselves. The flip of this coin decides his fate. Not us, exactly. What do you say?"

The six knew they had but little choice. Left to the discretion of O'Leary, the matter would be completely out of their control. On the other hand, there was a fifty-fifty chance they might have their way.

The five detectives formed a huddle.

Justin Barnes and the inspector exchanged formidable stares.

Fifteen seconds later, the team's quarterback spoke up. "I want to see that coin; and *I* make the toss," Brian said.

But the inspector smiled and shook his head. "Barnes has the honors." He handed over the coin for examination. "High in the air and you let it fall to the carpet. Heads, Alvin Matheson heads for arraignment. Tails, it's a question of destiny. Fair?"

Justin took and examined both sides of the coin then nodded. "Funny. We be *The Magnificent Seven*. You, Sean, be da man. But good ol' George, here, gets the deciding vote. If that don't beat all." Suddenly, a thumbnail shot the quarter upward from beneath a cocked forefinger, sending the silvery item end over end, missing the ceiling by a fraction before falling to the blue-green carpeting.

Chapter 57

Returning to the interview room, Justin took a seat opposite Alvin Frederick Matheson.

"You're going to be taken upstairs to a holding cell in this building in the next few minutes, Alvin. These days, it's used mostly for storage. Across the top of the cage is a set of horizontal bars. Nice and high. Not as high as the ceiling in Emily Schroeder's home, but it'll serve to do the job. I told you earlier that you have exactly what you need."

The tips of Alvin's anxious fingers toyed with the hem of his down coat—the seemingly tenuous but deadly item buried within the bulky, fluffy feathers that filled the lining.

Justin nodded solemnly. "It's there. Believe me."

"I'm sure. Do I still have your word that Bishop John will take the box back with him? Return it to the lab? Kalvin's passport to immortality as well as mine?"

Justin nodded. "That you do, Alvin. There's no need for us to hold onto you or your brother's DNA. We have your confession. The Pennsylvania police found Salvatori Passaro's body exactly where you said it was. Just as soon as we remove your body from the holding cell, we'll send the bishop back. Not a second before."

"All right then. Let's get this over with."

"I'm throwing you a lifeline, Alvin, so that you won't have to rot away for years in a prison cell or a psychiatric hospital. As soon as you get upstairs and the guards leave, not a second later, I want you to rip open up the lining. Time is of the essence, as I'm sure you realize. We wouldn't want a meltdown, now would we? You'll remove the section of piano wire threaded along the border of your coat. It's sort of like concertina wire that they use around prison walls. Only yours is thinner and special order. Five hundred fifty pound tensile strength— looped at one end through itself. No knots, which I'm sure you realize could reduce its pound-test rating by as much as half. What you've got there is one hundred percent break strength. We experimented with different materials and techniques. What we came up with is one end of the wire passing through a core to form the noose. State of the art, fella. Follow?"

"But how do you know it will hold . . . when I let go?"

"I tested it, and it held securely. You're a hundred seventy-five pounds soaking wet. When I dropped a two hundred fifty pound sandbag six feet off the floor, it held like no tomorrow." Justin winked and nodded. "It's fail-safe. The noose section is razor-sharp and will slice through human flesh like butter. The loop will easily fit over your head and around your neck. You'll tighten it like you would a tie, although it doesn't have to be as tight. The other end you'll securely wrap seven times around the center horizontal bar across the top of the cage by stepping up and onto the boxes that I've arranged. Kind of like a staircase to heaven, or wherever the hell it is you're going. No need to even tie it off, but you can use a simple overhand knot if you prefer. So, are we clear on everything?"

Alvin swallowed and nodded gravely.

"Good man. This way, everybody gets what they want. It's a win-win situation."

Chapter 58

Two uniformed police officers escorted Alvin Matheson off an elevator and down a long corridor to a storage area cluttered with dusty cartons, crates and file cabinets; buckets, mops and brooms. The younger cop yanked open a squeaky cell door and put the prisoner inside. The elder officer stepped forward, unlocked and removed the killer's handcuffs. Seconds later, the sergeant closed and locked the cage. The pair walked away without a word.

Alvin removed his coat, tearing open the lining along the re-sewn hem. He dug through the down feathers and carefully withdrew the length of silver wire.

Fluffy tiny white feathers lifted and drifted off in a light draft, floating through the space as Alvin put his coat back on, then awkwardly climbed the makeshift stairs situated center stage.

"Careful, now. Wouldn't want to slip and break my neck before I reach the gallows. Now would I, Kalvin? You don't know the lengths I go through to protect you. Do you? If only you had listened to me from the very beginning. Still, things have a way of working themselves out. Don't they?

"Tell you a bedtime story before we meet face-to-face once again, my dear brother. Mom and Dad never meant to hurt you. You see, they thought it was me when they came into our room and carried you off. It was really very dark. Black as pitch with the blinds and curtains drawn, in fact. A few minutes later, I got dressed, and went outside. It started to snow like it's doing now." Down feathers as large as any snowflakes Alvin had ever seen came to settle upon the floor. "They wouldn't have done what they did had they known it was you. Believe me. At least that's what they told each other in the morning.

But I was tired of being gagged, tied up, poked and prodded—their fat, sweaty bodies pushing and pressing against mine. It was the first time I decided to switch identities with you—that one cold wintry night before you gave up looking for your long underwear and came to bed. *You*, always in those stupid long johns. Even in late spring. *Me*, in my birthday suit or briefs. I had to think of something so they'd think that you were me. Just once. Just for you to see what it was like. So I hid that silly union suit of yours till you grew tired of searching and finally fell fast asleep. Then I climbed into your itchy, scratchy garment and gently rolled you over to my side of the bed. Like clockwork, Mom and Dad came in and passed right over me like a hot potato, carrying you back to their bed. A few minutes later, I went outside and watched from the window . . . standing on some old wooden boxes exactly as I'm doing now." Alvin stood at the top of the cage. "I'm telling you, Kalvin, I'm glad I had those long johns on that evening because it was pretty damn cold out there in the snow. But the action inside was as hot as hell. Not that I needed the moonlight to know exactly what was going on.

"Always on Sundays and Wednesdays, Kalvin. The first and fourth days of the week. We were only five."

Alvin reached for the center overhead bar and carefully began wrapping one end of the flexible wire around and around—five times —tying it off securely before putting his head through the noose, easily tightening the loop firmly around his neck while staring down blankly at the floor as he began singing the refrain from *Fame*:

"I'm gonna live forever.
I'm gonna learn how to fly
High."
Alvin was crying.
"I feel it coming together.
People will see me and cry
FAME!"

Alvin simultaneously stepped off and kicked back the dusty top black box upon which he was precariously perched, his body dropping downward to a five-foot Hellish sudden stop as the razor-sharp wire caught, scored and cut deeply into his throat. Frantically, the killer's legs flung out in all directions as he grabbed for but fought in vain to grip and hold onto the single spidery strand in order to pull himself upward . . . the sheer smoothness and sharpness of the wire slipping and ripping through his fingers . . . the pair of bloody, sweaty palms dripping steadily as he desperately gasped for air.

"*Re-mem-ber me*," seemed to be the last words Alvin choked on as he twisted and bled there for a time . . . until a stark stillness followed a perfect silence, filling the eerie space entirely.

Chapter 59

Detective Lieutenant Ethan Powell returned midweek after a purported bout with the flu, which he jokingly blamed Enrique for passing on to him. A file folder was sitting on the commanding officer's desk. Brian, Kim, Gary, Yolanda, Enrique and Justin were clustered around the man.

"I trust everyone here got on with the deputy inspector in my absence," the lieutenant put forth righteously.

"Yes, sir," Brian answered up smartly. "Famously, in fact."

"That's good to hear because I know he can be one tough son of a gun to get along with. By the way, his secretary called on his behalf and told me that he had nothing but the highest regard for all of you." The lieutenant took a sip of coffee. "It's a shame what happened here while I was out . . . for Matheson to pull a stunt like that."

"Yes, sir."

"Very clever of him, though, to conceal that wire in his coat beforehand, figuring he might get caught."

"Yes it was, Lieutenant. Saves us all a headache."

Powell nodded. "I don't think we can be faulted."

"No, sir. Not since it was hidden in his lining."

Everyone, including the lieutenant, nodded in agreement.

"Of course, those two officers who brought him upstairs will probably take a little heat," Lieutenant Powell went on.

"Could happen to anyone. They weren't gone but five minutes, sir. I was on the phone with Central Islip making arrangements for the prisoner's transfer. Gary brought the car around, logged out to C.I. for arraignment."

"Well, we'll make it up to those two boys somewhere down the road."

"That will certainly be appreciated, Lieutenant."

"So, before I try and catch up on all this paperwork the inspector left me, does anyone here have anything they'd like to say?"

"No, sir," Brian Archer answered for everyone.

"Good. Then I guess we all have work to do."

"Hope you're feeling better, Lieutenant," Kim offered politely.

"Never felt better," their commanding officer stated sincerely. "Fine job. Everyone. Oh, by the way, J. That box. The crate with those porthole-like windows in it. Why two tissue samples if identical twins share the same DNA?"

"That's not necessarily so, Lieutenant. Kim can fill you in," Justin deferred.

"Kim?" Ethan Powell prompted.

"Well, I learned from my buddy Quentin at the lab, that with true identical twins, one offspring's DNA *may* differ infinitesimally from the other, either through gene mutation or several other factors, but differ nevertheless, which in Alvin's and Kalvin's case it did. That's the short answer. If you like, I could expand upon other environmental effects: mother's womb, placenta, uterus—et cetera, et cetera."

The lieutenant made a face. "That won't be necessary, Kim. I get the picture."

"Thank you for that, Lieutenant," Gary tendered.

Yolanda giggled.

"Was the crate and their DNA actually from Clonite, J?" Powell continued.

Justin shook his head. "No, sir. Marcus and his techies threw something together out of some scrap wood, old computer chips and Plexiglas."

"And the culture dishes? What was in them if not cell tissue?"

Justin grinned. "Knox gelatin."

Their lieutenant laughed until his sides hurt. "Love it. I absolutely love it, guys and dolls."

Robert Banfelder is an award-winning novelist and outdoors writer. He has written five psychological thrillers: *No Stranger Than I*, *The Author*, *The Teacher*, *Knots* and *Trace Evidence*. *The Author and The Teacher*, the first and second books in the Justin Barnes series, both received "Best Suspense Book" accolades from NewBookReviews. *Knots* is the third thriller in the Justin Barnes series. *The Good Samaritans*, the final in the series, is scheduled for publication in 2014. Robert weaves his knowledge and love of the outdoors through his novels.

In addition to his novels, Robert writes outdoors articles which have appeared in numerous publications: *Nor'east Saltwater*, *The Fisherman*, *On The Water*, *Big Game Fishing Journal*, *Hana Hou! The Magazine for Hawaiian Airlines*, *Deer & Deer Hunting*, *New York Game & Fish*. He presently maintains a monthly online report titled North Fork Bays for *Nor'east Saltwater*. He is a member of the Long Island Outdoor Communicators Network and the New York State Outdoor Writer's Association.

Robert also co-hosts (with Donna Derasmo) Cablevision TV's *Special Interests with Bob & Donna*. They have interviewed a number of outdoors enthusiasts, artists and writers such as Bob Bourguignon, Eileen Gerle, Pat Mundus, Christopher Paparo, Tony Salerno and Mary Van Deusen.

www.RobertBanfelder.com
Facebook @Robert Banfelder
Twitter @RBanfelder